Tony Birch is the author of *Blood* (UQP, 2011), which was shortlisted for the Miles Franklin Award. He is also the author of *Shadowboxing* (2006), and two short story collections, *Father's Day* (2009) and *The Promise* (UQP, 2014). Tony is a frequent contributor to ABC local and national radio and a regular guest at writers' festivals. He lives in Melbourne and is a Senior Research Fellow at Victoria University.

Bookclub notes for *Ghost River* are available at www.uqp.com.au

TONY BIRCH

GHOST RIVER

UQP

First published 2015 by University of Queensland Press
PO Box 6042, St Lucia, Queensland 4067 Australia

www.uqp.com.au
uqp@uqp.uq.edu.au

Cover design and photograph by Josh Durham (Design by Committee)
Typeset in 12/17 pt Bembo by Post Pre-press Group, Brisbane
Printed in Australia by McPherson's Printing Group, Melbourne

National Library of Australia cataloguing-in-publication data is available
at http://catalogue.nla.gov.au

ISBN
978 0 7022 5377 5 (pbk)
978 0 7022 5569 4 (epdf)
978 0 7022 5570 0 (epub)
978 0 7022 5571 7 (Kindle)

University of Queensland Press uses papers that are natural, renewable
and recyclable products made from wood grown in sustainable forests.
The logging and manufacturing processes conform to the environmental
regulations of the country of origin.

For our dear friend and brother,
Stephen John Ward (1958–1979) –
we love you always.

And for the river boys – Danny, Peter,
Colin, Lawrie, Russell, Sparrow, and Garry Arnold (1955–2011);
and the beautiful river girls – Debbie and Irene.

CHAPTER 1

The afternoon Sonny Brewer moved into the street Archie Kemp was resting his tired body on the front verandah in a beaten wicker chair he'd retrieved from the side of the road. When he wasn't driving trucks for a living Archie parked himself in the chair and kept company with a book. Distracted from his dog-eared paperback, he lifted his eyes and saw Sonny dribbling a tin can along the footpath. Archie's look of contempt was met in equal measure by the boy's. While he couldn't have been more than thirteen years old at the time, Sonny wore a *fuck you* attitude and liked to show it off.

Archie was unhappy to see the boy go into the house next door. He stood up, dropped the book on the chair, walked into his own house and announced *trouble's moving in next to us*. Loretta Renwick, his wife in every way but marriage, was standing with her back to him at the kitchen sink. She went on peeling potatoes as if she hadn't heard him. Experience had taught her there wasn't a lot that came out of Archie's mouth in need of her attention. While she barely tolerated his occasional outbursts, Loretta did love Archie. They'd met in hospital, eight years earlier, when Archie was laid up with a badly broken leg after a truck accident. Loretta worked in the hospital kitchen on the meals trolley and came to enjoy Archie's bedside cheekiness.

Loretta was a hardheaded woman who fell for his rare qualities. Archie never drank or raised a hand in anger, and he was a hard worker. If there was more she would have hoped from a man, she never let it be known. Loretta had a twelve-year-old son, Charlie, who went by the name of Ren outside the house. His *natural* father, a man he'd never met, had got Loretta pregnant in the darkness of the back stalls of the local picture theatre and hadn't been seen since.

When Archie ambled into the kitchen that afternoon Ren was sitting at the table, with pencil in hand, drawing a picture of a blackbird he'd seen preening itself on the back roof that morning. Ren had been sketching from the day he could hold a pencil. The mantel above the open fireplace in his bedroom was lined with exercise books full of his drawings, mostly of birds. He looked up from his book to Archie, with no idea who his stepfather was complaining about. Nor did he know that the boy Archie was referring to would soon become his closest friend, and that the two boys would discover more trouble and adventure than even Ren's vivid imagination could wish for.

As it turned out, Archie wasn't far off the mark on his prediction about Sonny. It took only a week for the boy to announce his arrival on the street. He was exploring the railyards that cut off the rundown neighbourhood from the city's growing urban centre of prosperous high-rise buildings and expensive shops. The railyards housed the suburban trains that returned late each night, along with freight trains, diesel engines and row after row of broken-down carriages left to rot and provide shelter for bands of stray cats and the occasional runaway teenager.

Sonny picked up a sleeper spike he found laying between the tracks and stuck it in his back pocket. He was later seen hurling the missile through the milk bar window at the end of the street and running away to the sound of breaking glass. The police knocked on his door the same night. When he refused to let them into the house they asked after his parents. Sonny had no mother, and at the time his father was asleep on the couch after a solid day on the drink. While the police thought it a good idea for the boy to take a ride with them in the divisional van, he declined the offer. Street-smart beyond his years, he knew better than to give up the safety of the front doorstep. The police could have dragged him into the street and thrown him into the back of the van, and they would have, except the neighbours, after noticing a flashing blue light in the night, had gathered on the footpath outside the house. As notorious as local police were, they knew it was a poor look, hauling a kid from his own home. Such a scene could turn a crowd and earn a copper a house brick in the back of the head.

During the doorstep interview the officers asked Sonny for his explanation about the broken window. He told them he'd been aiming for a bird perched in the branch of a tree out front of the shop.

'I weren't meaning to kill it or nothing. Just wing it. Maybe frighten it.'

'You're full of shit, son,' one of the officers said. 'We just come from the milk bar and there's not a blade of grass on that street, let alone a fucken tree.'

Sonny was ordered to present himself at the police station the next morning, along with his father. He was interviewed, fingerprinted, photographed and charged with vandalism. The conviction, handed down six weeks later, earned him a criminal bond. Worse was the belting he received at the hands of his father, who was found liable for the expensive bill for the broken plate-glass window. Having come to their attention, the police kept an eye on Sonny from that day on, sweating on him to step out of line.

As Sonny walked out of the police station into the sunlight that afternoon, one of the detectives on duty, Sergeant Foy, turned to the desk officer and said, 'You see that kid who just walked out, Ollie? He's got fucken bad blood pumping through his veins.'

'How do you know? He's just a kid. No different to any other young troublemaker around here. He's no gunnie, Roger. He only smashed a window.'

Foy's seniority rarely brought him into contact with petty vandals. Most of his work was spent dealing with gunnies and career criminals. With the slow demise in local bookies and the opening of TABs near of ten years earlier, armed robbery was the growth industry of the 1960s. As the crims got more dangerous, so did the police. And Foy was one of the most dangerous of all. 'Nah. There's something more in this kid. He'll take some beating down soon enough.'

★

Sonny Brewer was an oddly built boy. He stood long and pale with dark ragged hair and a bird-shaped chest. From a distance he resembled a scarecrow standing in a field. Up close there was something of a scraggly pigeon about him. He kept his left eye to himself, the lid lazily resting on his cheek, and fixed his sight with his right eye, a marble that appeared to have exploded and shattered to pieces. He liked to claim the eye possessed powers and brought him luck, which could only make sense if he was referring to bad luck, of which he'd had much experience. When Ren first ran with Sonny, the eye spooked him so badly he was unable to look at it for more than a second or two before turning away.

Given the choice of the right or wrong way to do something, Sonny mostly steered the wrong way. After the night of the broken shop window, any time the police grabbed him in the street or came knocking at his door, Sonny wasn't surprised to see them. And when his drunken father bowled into his room of a night, drunk and swinging his trouser belt, Sonny wouldn't bother asking what it was he'd done wrong. He'd simply drop his pants, eager to get the whipping over and done with. He never felt sorry for himself, and took every knock like he deserved nothing better.

While it wasn't unexpected that the police would hold local boys in poor regard, they fared little better with their own schoolteachers. Only weeks before Sonny's arrival, the headmaster, Dogger Dean, told Ren, after giving him the strap when he was caught spitting on the ground, that *your kind live at the arse-end of the world*. Ren wasn't offended by the comment, seeing as he didn't have much respect for the headmaster either. Dogger wore the same wine-stained jacket to work each day

5

and smelled little different from a drunk on the street, but was held in less regard, as he had money in his pocket and a home address that wasn't automatically looked down on.

Ren lived on a row of terraces opposite the towering red-brick wall of the old cotton mill. At one time the mill had employed hundreds of workers from across the suburb, until the day the gates were shut and it was abandoned. At the bottom of a steep bank below the mill a wide river ran from the hills in the distance and wound its way through the suburbs and inner city, to its mouth at the bay. The water was the colour of strong black tea and didn't smell all that different, except on hot summer days when a stink rose from its surface.

Its banks were often used by people ridding themselves of possessions they no longer wanted – old machinery, cars and broken furniture. Even dead animals. On one of his many walks along the riverbank Ren had once come across a maggoty draught horse laying on its side. No one could work out how the horse got there. The bloated corpse was left out in the sun for days and picked over by birds and rats until a council worker eventually turned up, scooped the animal into a front-end loader and drove it to an offal yard, where it was sliced apart with a bandsaw and boiled down for glue.

The river had long accepted human refuse as well. It was the favoured dumping ground for dead bodies whenever a gang war kicked off, which occurred like clockwork every decade or so. Those disposed of were rarely weighted down to ensure their bodies would not be found. Instead, the dead were put on display, their beaten corpses floating downstream with shotgun blasts to the face, slashed throats or missing fingers and toes. And then there were the jumpers, suicides who leaped from the river's highest bridge, the Phoenix, some filling their pockets with stones before leaving the bridge behind. Many of the jumpers were female, handsome and well-dressed women, who for reasons unknown left the comfort of their homes on the high side of the river for the murky water below, where, with good fortune, they found peace and salvation.

Although Sonny was a year older than Ren, when he enrolled at the local school he found himself in the same class. His looks, particularly the demented eye, didn't invite friendship. A loner at school, he could never focus on study and spent most of his time fashioning darts out of matchsticks, string, cardboard and the dress pins he stole from the art room. Like everything he produced with his own hands the darts were beautifully constructed and flew like miniature space rockets. If the work had been graded, Sonny would have picked up an A-plus. He launched the darts into the back of the heads of boys he didn't like, which accounted for most kids in the classroom.

His unlikely friendship with Ren began when the younger boy was taking a pounding in the schoolyard one lunchtime from a mound of a kid, *Milton the Monster*. The overweight Milton was being teased from the far side of the school handball court. Mistaking Ren for the offender, Milton took off after him, knocking over other boys in the process and spreading them like bowling pins. Ren, who was built like a whippet and just as fast, should have been too quick for the bigger boy. Unfortunately, he took a wrong turn around a game of marbles and was soon cornered, wrapped in a bear-hug by Milton and thrown to the ground and sat on.

'Say my proper name!' Milton screamed at Ren, his hands at his throat.

In that moment Ren would have been happy to call Milton by whatever name he wanted, but it wasn't possible. Every kid in the school had been calling Milton by that name for so long Ren couldn't remember his true name. Other boys, sensing a murder, circled the writhing bodies, chanting *Kill! Kill! Kill!* Until Sonny appeared from nowhere, bulldogging through the crowd, and tore Milton off Ren. Although Sonny stood no taller than Milton and was at best half his fighting weight, he gave Milton a brutal lesson that day.

Sonny stood by the gate after the school bell rang, keeping his good eye focused, in case Milton decided to come after Ren a second time. They walked home together, not saying a great deal, except for Ren's mumbling attempt at a conversation he couldn't stitch together.

'You live next door to me,' was the best he could offer.

'Yeah, I know,' Sonny answered.

They stopped outside Ren's front gate.

'That Milton, he would have crushed me to death if you hadn't saved me. Why'd you jump in?' Ren asked. 'I suppose it's because we're neighbours.'

'Nah. Weren't that.'

'Was it because he's a ton heavier than me and it was no fair fight?'

Sonny shrugged, indicating he hadn't entertained the concept of fairness.

'Couldn't care less how big he is. Could have punched a hole straight through you for all I care.'

'Really? Why'd you do it then?'

'I was after a fight and he stuck his head up. No reason more than that.'

Ren looked disappointed. He'd walked home with Sonny feeling he'd found a friend, one who'd look out for him on the street. Sonny spotted the look of disappointment on Ren's face. He grinned so wide he showed off his tonsils. And he laughed. 'I'm just playing you. Milton's a bully and he got what he should've.'

'He gets a hard time at school because he's so fat.'

'Don't matter. You're smaller than him. He should have gone after someone closer to his own size. There was enough of them standing there. He picked you out because you're the smallest. What time you leave for school in the morning?'

'When I get out of bed.'

'Me too.'

'You ever late doing that?'

'Not always.'

Sonny scraped the toe of his shoe across the ground. 'Milton could come hunting you before school. Tomorrow, if I'm out of the house first I'll wait here for you. You do the same, if you're out first.'

'Okay.'

Ren offered Sonny his hand. 'Thanks for saving my life. I reckon he would have killed me if you didn't come along.'

Sonny shook his hand, shrugged and turned his back on Ren. He opened his front door and went inside.

That's the way it would be between the friends. Whenever Ren needed him Sonny would be there, standing by the front gate, looking like the loneliest kid in the world without realising it. Except for Ren, other kids steered clear of Sonny.

He had only his father for company, if you could call it that. Once he came to trust Ren, Sonny told him a story about his mother running away with his baby brother, Lucas, and leaving him behind with his father. He hadn't seen her or heard a word since the day she left.

'I knew soon as I walked in the house from school she was gone, without my old man saying a word.'

'How'd you know?'

'Not sure. But I could feel it. The house was empty of her and it made me feel empty inside.'

Ren decided he should share something of his own story with Sonny.

'I don't have a dad. I mean I've got Archie, and he's okay most of the time. But no real dad.'

'Your mum and dad split? I bet you miss him.'

'Nah. They never got together in the first place. I don't miss him at all. More like he never was. Or a ghost.'

Differences between the boys could have set them apart, but their shared loss drew them together. Sonny and Ren were also the only kids around the neighbourhood without brothers or sisters living under the same roof, which was unusual. Most families had three or four kids at least, and often more. The Portelli family, two doors along from Sonny, had eight kids, and Mick O'Reagan around the corner had eleven. Mick was a lucky man. He had a job as a milkman and got his cream, butter and milk for free, which helped him to keep his tribe fattened over the cold months of winter. Before Sonny came along, Ren had been friends with a couple of Mick's boys, but from the day he'd been rescued in the schoolyard it became the two of them, for better *and* worse.

CHAPTER 2

Loretta Renwick knew her son was a dreamer from the day she spotted him looking up at the sky as a small boy. He was sitting on a rug in the public gardens, watching the flight of a bird above his head. He soon began drawing them with crayons, on the rough concrete ground in the backyard, or on the footpath in the street. As he grew he took his sketchbook everywhere he went, drawing train wrecks in the railyards, and mighty ghost gums growing along the banks of the river. It was where he spent most of his weekends, alone, roaming as far as he liked. Ren had a loose contract with his mother, one that Archie went along with despite his grumbles. As long as he was always home before dark, and, as his mother would remind him, he brought no trouble to the family door, he was given a free rein.

Only weeks after Sonny moved into the street Ren decided it was time to share the river with him. The water was not easy to find and local knowledge was vital. The dirt track leading to the river lay in the shadows of the mill, hidden among a forest of wild thorn, scrub and overhanging trees. At the bottom of the steep riverbank another track skirted its edge. In one direction lay an iron bridge, which carried traffic to and from the high side of the river where the moneyed people lived. In the other direction, a wooden pontoon nudged the bank, bobbing up and down with the current. The pontoon nestled next to the ruin of a wheelhouse. When the gates of the mill were shut the giant wheel that drew water from the river to supply the mill seized with rust, the wooden floors and foundations rotted and the building slowly sank into the muddy riverbed. From a distance it resembled a red-brick boat floating on water.

Further upstream a low waterfall stretched the width of the river, topped with a concrete ledge, maybe three feet wide. When the wheelhouse had been in operation, an iron handrail had been bolted into the ledge of the falls to transport workers from one side of the river to the other. The handrail had been swept away in a flood many years before, leaving the crossing dangerous, particularly after a heavy rain when the water from upstream swept across the falls with ferocity.

Ren knew *his* river as good as anyone and better than most. As well as drawing birds and other animals, his exercise books were increasingly filled with maps of the river, including sketches of the swimming holes, the hollows where rabbits burrowed into the ground, the fox holes hidden beneath the barbs of blackberry, and the drainways spewing out rubbish from the streets above. Ren's thoughts of the river were so constant he sometimes woke in the night, recalled an image of his most recent visit, opened one of his books and began drawing.

★

On one of Sonny's early visits to the river with Ren they came across the river men. It was a Sunday, and they had spent much of the morning in the grassed laneway behind their yards, doing what teenage boys do when they're bored, resting against Ren's back fence and talking about nothing in particular. Sonny was teaching Ren how to roll cigarettes. He was a slow learner. The wind blowing from the north suddenly gusted. Ren could smell the water calling them.

'Come on, Sonny. Let's go.'

'Where to?'

'Follow me.'

They ran beside the wall separating them from the mill and negotiated the maze of thorn bushes before sliding down the steep track to the riverbank.

'The falls or the bridge?' Ren asked.

'The bridge. I've got an idea,' Sonny said. 'Them pigeons that make a home under the bridge, I'm gonna catch a couple and start my own flock. I could race them. There's prize money in that. And you can make even more betting on your bird. Or against it.'

'You don't have any place to keep birds.'

'I could build a coop outside my bedroom window, over the kitchen roof.'

Ren didn't doubt Sonny had the skill to build a coop, there was nothing he couldn't do with his hands. Just the same, he didn't like the idea at all.

'I don't know about that.' He frowned. 'Keeping a bird in a cage. I reckon it's cruel.'

'It's a coop, not a cage. If I can find enough wood and wire I'll make it as big as a house. Anyway, you train pigeons and

13

you don't need to keep them locked up. They fly away and come back home to you. No harm to the bird in that.'

'S'pose so.'

'Is so.'

As they approached the iron bridge Ren heard hollering up ahead. He whispered to Sonny to keep low and stay quiet. They moved off the track and lay in the long grass, Sonny's knee digging into a length of metal pipe. He pulled it out of a tangle of weeds, put one end to his shoulder and pointed it at Ren.

'You're fucken dead.'

Sonny stuck his head up above the line of grass and saw a group of men underneath the bridge stomping around a campfire. They looked like a long-lost tribe. The men passed a flagon of wine between them while they sang and kicked up dust.

'We have trouble,' Sonny said. 'We're gonna have to take them, Ren.'

'You'll be doing it on your own.'

'Please yourself, coward.'

Sonny stood up, lifted the pipe to his shoulder, moved forward through the grass and took aim at the men. One of them saw him coming, nodded to the others, took a couple of steps forward himself and raised his hands in surrender.

'Don't be shooting at me, youngster. Are ya from the authorities?' he asked Sonny, humouring the boy.

'We're outlaws,' Sonny answered.

'Thank Jesus Christ for that one.' The man smiled, relaxing his hands at his sides. 'So are we. How about you be polite and come over here and introduce yourselves?'

After some coaxing the boys walked closer to the camp. The man offered them a seat, which they refused. The other men took no notice of the boys and went on shuffling around the fire, humming a tune and continuing to pass the bottle.

'This is my camp,' the man said. 'So you can end the poor manners and stop pointing that weapon at me,' he ordered Sonny. 'If not, I'm as likely to take it and shove it up your arse.'

He made the comment with a smile on his face, but it was enough of a threat for Sonny to throw the length of pipe to the ground. The man clapped his hands together.

'Good boy. That's what I like to see. They call me Tex and I'm boss down here.' He pointed at Sonny. 'What name do ya go by?'

Sonny wasn't accustomed to providing his name to a complete stranger but he offered up *Sonny Brewer* without thinking about it.

Tex took a step closer and studied Sonny's face. The man was delighted by what he found. 'That eye you have there, I believe it may be a true wonder. Come take a look at this,' he barked at the others. 'We have someone special visiting this morning. How'd you earn such an eyeball as that, son?'

Sonny rubbed the knuckle of his thumb over his eye, unhappy with the attention it was getting.

'I was born with it.'

Tex gently patted him on the shoulder. 'Good for you. It's a true beauty. I have never seen an eye like it. And it's a sign, we can be certain of that.'

'What sort of sign?' Sonny asked.

'Can't say right yet,' Tex answered, seemingly holding something back.

Neither Sonny nor Ren was sure what he was talking about, but they would soon get used to Tex speaking in riddles.

'And you would be?' He turned to Ren.

'Ren,' he answered, through a mouthful of dust and woodsmoke.

Tex skipped back and then forward, reminding Ren of a circus clown he'd seen perform at the town hall one Christmas.

'Wren! The name of a bird. I like that one. You are a free spirit, boy.'

'I'm not a bird. It's short for my last name. Renwick.'

'Don't talk yourself down, boy. The wren is a bird I know from another time. And you're that one. Don't go forgetting it. One day ya will need to fly.'

Tex stepped forward and rested an open hand on Ren's forehead. 'There is no doubt you are a bird. I can feel you have heart and spirit in you, boy. Don't matter that you know nothing of it now. You will sometime in the future.' Tex lifted his hand from Ren's head and straightaway the boy felt different than he had before the old man had touched him, lighter somehow, as if his body might leave the ground.

Tex dusted off his ragged clothes. He had a rich dark face and what looked to Ren like a film of milk across his eyes. He stood a little straighter and cleared his throat. 'Let me introduce you to my companions.' He circled the fire. The men walked in one direction, Tex in the other, and one by one he announced them as if they were about to step up for a boxing title bout.

'First off here we have Big Tiny Watkins, hailing from the heat and sweat of the north, where as a young man he made his mark in the snowdropping trade.'

16

Big Tiny, who was as wide as he was tall, bowed his head gracefully and went on pacing the fire.

'Falling in behind Tiny we have the mighty, mighty Tallboy Parrish, our camp cook, who was at one time the undisputed champion tea-leaf across the state of Victoria.'

Tallboy waved and smiled at the boys. He wore a friendly face that Ren took an immediate liking to.

'And that skinny fella trailing him,' Tex said, moving on, 'is my own second-in-command, the silent but deadly Mr Cold Can Jonson.'

Cold Can, who looked more like a child than a man, and had to weigh something less than a starved jockey, avoided the unwanted attention of the newcomers by turning away.

'And this here is the Doc,' Tex said, completing the introductions in a flat voice, pointing to a silver-haired man wearing a full three-piece suit and no shoes or socks. 'There's nothing more to say about this one.'

Ren couldn't take his eyes off the man's filthy, scabbed and bloodied feet.

'They're some weird names,' Sonny said.

'They are,' Tex answered. 'There was a time when we went by everyday names, until we ditched them and took up with new autographs from no public record. Most of all the police and vagrancy record.'

Sitting around the fire that afternoon Tex told the boys the story of how the men had recently shifted camp after being forced out of their home some distance upriver. Their old campsite had been destroyed by workers from the Water Board laying a run-off channel to deal with flooding. The men had been marched out of their camp, with nothing but the possessions they carried in their arms.

'The camp was burned down on us,' Tex told them. 'They said they done it to kill off the bugs and germs. But we got no germs. If you don't include the Doc.' He chuckled. He explained that the site for the new camp had been carefully chosen, as it would be shaded from the sun on warm days and protect them from the wet weather when it rained. The men had built themselves a humpy between the web of iron supporting the bridge, out of whatever bits and pieces they could scrounge, scraps of timber, an old tarp that had blown off a truck crossing the bridge above, and sheets of iron roofing found in the scrub. The structure was held together with wire and old rope and a handful of rusty nails. Although the humpy swayed like a boat at sea whenever a strong wind came through the valley, it held together well enough to provide what comfort they needed.

Tex ruled the camp, and rule number one was that any man in need of a warm fire and a meal could not be turned away. While sharing the fire and food, Tex would observe a newcomer until he came to what he described as an *understanding of character.*

'I got to read a man's soul. Takes some time and thinking, that one.'

'How'd you misread the Doc?' Tallboy asked him, raising his eyebrows and smiling across the fire at Ren.

'Was gone on the grog the night he turned up. By the next morning he'd settled in like a stray pup and I didn't have the heart to turn him away.'

As camp boss, Tex also demanded that any man who shared his fire and shelter came and went by three commandments:

Never call a man a dog unless he is one. Never take another man's food or bed unless he offers to share. And never touch another man's fire.

Tallboy, the most capable of the men when it came to repairs and maintenance, fashioned a stove from a cut-down 44 barrel he found along the bank and rolled back to the camp. It sat out the front of the humpy and the men worshipped around it of a night, seated on fruit boxes or old car tyres, cooking up a feed, passing the bottle, belting out a tune and sharing stories. Baked beans or canned sausage and vegetables were number one on the camp menu, as they were easiest to lift from the milk bar and could be heated and eaten straight from the tin. When things were on the up, the river men feasted on bacon bones, provided free of charge by sympathetic local butchers. Tallboy boiled the bones in a pot of river water and served them up with potatoes roasted in the fire.

The men possessed a single blunt knife between them – a precious item – which they used to hack at a tin–loaf of stale bread, or split the chest of a rabbit whenever they caught one. They didn't carry a spoon, knife or fork between them and ate with their fingers.

'Licking these stumps after a feed,' Tallboy often pronounced, 'is the best tasting tucker you're likely to come by.'

Big Tiny, always in a hurry to get his food down, had a habit of eating with his face, sticking both his snout and full lips into the can and coming out with a mess of food woven into his scraggy beard.

Cold Can, although he looked like he couldn't lift fresh air, had a shotgun throwing arm and could hit a retreating rabbit with a rock up to a distance of fifty yards, in the old measurement. He'd pass the concussed rabbit over to Tallboy for necking, skinning and roasting over the coals. Rabbit hunting was restricted to mornings though, as once the grog took hold he wasn't capable of hitting the side of a tree trunk, even a few feet out from the mark.

Sonny would soon come to believe there wasn't a creature on the planet as unlucky as one of those rabbits. 'You know, not one of them fellas can even leak straight. I've seen them piss on their own feet,' he would later say to Ren.

'That's no accident. It's for the chilblains,' Ren explained to him.

'The what?'

'Chilblains. It's why they piss on their feet. They all got them from getting round with no shoes and socks on. The only way to get rid of chilblains is piss between your toes. My stepdad, Archie, does it all the time. I seen him do it in the backyard, in his vegie patch.'

'Your stepdad pisses on his own feet? He don't even drink.'

'It's nothing to do with the drink. *Home remedy* he told me when I caught him one time and asked what he was doing.'

Other than rabbits the only occasional meat brought to the fire were chickens that came off the convent farm, two bends along the river. The men would occasionally try their hand at chicken rustling. It was a tricky business and not always successful. The convent birds were slick and shifty-eyed. They also made a hell of a noise. The racket would wake the nuns, who'd come out into the night, each of them swinging a kero lamp in one hand and some sort of fearsome weapon in the other. On one raid Big Tiny backed out of the hen house with a bird tucked under one arm, only to see the lamps swinging across a field in his direction. He slipped in a bog and got stuck. When the *Sisters of Charity* caught up with him they laid into him with picks and shovels, rescued the bird, and sent him back to the camp covered in cuts and bruises.

The river took such good care of the men that Tex called it their *mother*. She kept them safe from those who would do them harm, be it young bucks from the streets above, out for a night of menace, or the local police steaming with grog themselves. Coppers loved the drink as much as anyone and went hard at it any opportunity they got. Their amusements came cheap, and most often involved kicking a wino around the back lanes on a Saturday night. Down on the riverbank, tucked up in their shelter, the men were able to charge on in peace.

It soon became obvious to the boys that Tex organised all camp business. He was in charge of the fire and announced the menu each night, although he did none of the cooking himself. That was a job left to Tallboy, with Cold Can in assistance. As well as possessing the ability to sniper rabbits and cook, Cold Can drew beautiful pictures. Sometimes, as they gathered around the fire, he drew the face of one of the men with a piece of charcoal, or nothing in particular but swirls and lines mapped in the dirt. Ren would watch him closely and later try to copy the same drawings into his sketchbook.

Tex was also an accomplished musician. He played the gum leaf and could belt a song as good as a professional singer on a record album. He liked an audience and was soon performing for his newfound young friends. When he stood up from the fire for a song he transformed into a man from another time, strutting about in his boots, wearing a moth-eaten pair of woollen pants and jacket, and a hat worn back on his head with a magpie feather poking out of the band.

All the river men loved a tune, be it country and western or gospel. The singer would wail over a friend he'd lost to the grog, or a woman he'd busted up with and the kids he'd left in his wake after taking to the road. They had so many children between them the river men could never have recalled all their names, even when sober. Tex would sometimes choke on a lump of pain, and for a moment would be unable to go on with his song. He'd smudge the tears across his face with the sleeve of his jacket, cough and splutter, take a good swig of the flagon and clear his throat.

Most days of the week, bar Sundays, they'd gather of an afternoon out the front of the local wine shop and chip in for a flagon, a pair if one of them had done particularly well on the twine. They were connoisseurs of a cheap brand of red that went by the dubious name of *Captain's Table*. Tex was usually good for a dollar or two, picking up loose change by singing and playing the leaf outside hotels or on the railway station platform. Tallboy, who had at one time been a trump pickpocket, working the markets and racetracks, held his reflexes steady enough to shoplift goods for campfire dinners. And Big Tiny wasn't too bad at the snatch and grab, usually fruit and vegetables. He might have been as fat as a house but he was also as quick as a rat on the run over a short distance. Tex once referred to him as *the refrigerator on ballet shoes.*

The only one who never weighed in was the Doc. He contributed little to the camp other than the miserable look on his face. He was called a *lazy old cunt* any time his back was turned and more than one of the men wanted him barred from the camp every other week. The Doc and Tallboy had come to blows many times. The same day the boys showed up at the camp, they fought over a missing flagon of wine, which Tallboy claimed the Doc had ferreted away for his personal enjoyment. While the Doc denied the theft, as soon as he got up to take a shit in the blackberry Tallboy fronted Tex demanding he be expelled.

'His con ... con ... tree ... bution is fuck all.'

Tex listened to Tallboy carefully before answering, 'I know it myself, Tallboy. Many times I want to be rid of him. But the Doc's been here with us too long. It'd be like throwing a relation in the street. I can't be doing that.'

'But he's no relation of mine.'

Tex raised a hand in the air, which was enough to indicate the conversation was over. Tallboy dropped his head. Tex knew to banish the Doc, for all the selfishness he possessed, could bring bad luck to the camp and he'd have no part of it.

In the weeks after Ren and Sonny first came across the river men, they spent more time around the campfire listening to stories than they did exploring the river. They'd race down to the camp after school and leave late of an afternoon wearing the campfire smoke, envious of the life of freedom and adventure the men enjoyed. Late at night, from his open bedroom window, Ren would sometimes hear the men singing down on the river, listening to the drunken choir wage a battle with the water tumbling over the falls. A breeze would sweep along the river valley, roll up the hill and carry the music and the scent of the water with it. Ren would look up at the same stretch of sky the river men were resting under and wish he was at the water's edge with them.

The river men told prison stories, drinking stories, lost dog stories, and tales of their years on the road. Ren was a good listener and quickly understood there were strict rules governing how a story was told and listened to. Interjections were occasionally allowed, by way of a jeer or a hand shooting into the air, requesting a *point-of-order*. Big Tiny was the most common culprit in that regard. Other stories were sacred, recited in hushed tones and observed in silence, except for the crack and groan of the fire.

Ren soon became so familiar with particular stories he knew them by heart. A favourite was the story of the wreck of a drunk who supposedly dug himself out of the hole he'd been in for years, got himself back on his feet and eventually became a rich man. The story lit the eyes of those around the fire, no matter how many times it was told. While none of the men had personal experience of the story, or the character himself, each of them would have been prepared to swear on the bottle the story was true. Big Tiny went as far as to claim that he'd once crossed paths with the reformed drunk. 'He come out of one of them big banks in the city dressed up like a pox doctor's clerk and got into this shiny new car. In the back seat, of course. He owns the bank and has his own driver.'

On another occasion Ren and Sonny were sharing a rusted car rim one afternoon when Big Tiny and the Doc got into an argument about the truthfulness of a story about a famous strong man from the old days – the Mighty Apollo. Tiny was nearing the end of the story where Apollo had dragged a tram *up the Collins Street hill fully loaded with passengers, by his bare teeth*. Tiny got overexcited and began stuttering and spitting. The Doc, impatient with him, started muttering quietly to himself, 'Fuck me … fuck me.' He picked up an empty wine bottle and hurled it across the fire. The bottle missed Tiny's head by inches before shattering against one of the bridge pylons.

'Shut the fuck up, will ya, Tiny. He didn't drag nothin by his teeth. Apollo *ate that tram*.'

'Fuck up ya self,' Tiny screamed back. 'I'm talking here. Ya know the rules. Apollo dragged the tram with a line of piano wire *in his mouth*. No man can eat a tram, ya fucken imbecile.'

'And nobody drags one through the street by his gob. It was ate. *Piece by piece*. Don't worry about that. I got an old mate, mechanic out there, that took the tram apart at the Preston depot. Apollo lived off that fucken tram for two years. Ate nothing but it. He drunk the sump oil and all.'

Big Tiny threw his arms in the air. 'Fuck me. I give up,' he said, looking across the fire to Tex for support. 'How much longer we got to put up with this fucken lunatic?'

With Tex ignoring his pleas, Tiny turned to Sonny and Ren.

'Don't ya be listening to a word from his trap. If a government man was able to track down anyone in the Doc's family they'd have papers signed and he'd be certified and put away for good. The Doc wouldn't see daylight again.

They found no one to put him away cause he had become an orphan. When he was a kid his own mummy put him out on the street one day with a sign round his neck begging someone to take pity on the bastard. He weren't wanted, by no one. Not even the shirt-lifters would take him home. And no one wants him now.'

'Up yours, elephant arse,' the Doc spat. 'Only one that was left for dead is you. Your old girl looked at you the day you was born and sent a telegram to the fucken circus, hoping for an earner from the sideshows.'

The Doc stood up, hitched his pants under his armpits and mimicked the performance. 'Come see the whole world's fattest baby – also born absent of a brain.' He bowed, sat down and waved a finger at Tiny. 'What Apollo done was in all the papers, with a picture of him tucking in the upholstery off a seat. Horsehair, it was. That's what the sump oil was for. To wash it down. You ever tried eating the stuff?'

'Horsehair can't be eaten!' Tiny screamed.

The Doc pointed at Big Tiny's stomach. 'Was eaten. You'd give it a run yourself, fatman. Could eat your own fucken leg. Between ya mouth and the gut ya could knock the *Southern Aurora* over. What they call that thing on the back of the train? The caboose. You'd do that for dessert.'

Tex smiled and Tallboy laughed out loud, while Cold Can giggled quietly to himself. Tiny didn't find the Doc's attack on him funny at all. He got to his feet, slammed a foot into the dirt and kicked dust across the fire.

Ren and Sonny joined in the laughter, thinking the river men were enjoying a joke between themselves. But before they knew it, the joke had got out of hand.

26

'Ya know nothing, Doc. Why don't ya tell these young fellas something of ya own life? Bout the poor kiddie ya killed way back.'

'You cunt!'

The Doc charged at Tiny, head-butted him in the guts and knocked him to the ground. The two men rolled around in the dirt like a pair of mongrel pups. The others laughed, until Tiny rolled over and crashed into the coals and the sleeve of the Doc's suit-coat caught fire. Tex had had enough. He picked up an iron poker and belted the Doc across the back of the legs with it.

'Knock it off. Both of ya. Fuck this fire up and ya both barred. For life.'

He gave the Doc a second whack with the poker and turned on Tiny. 'You fucken goose.' He raised the poker in the air. 'Say sorry for what ya said or it's the same for you.'

While Sonny seemed to enjoy the spectacle, Ren was shocked by the sudden violence Tex displayed.

Tiny rolled the Doc onto his side and stripped him of his smouldering coat, stomping on it as he apologised for what he'd said. 'I went too far there, Doc. You got my temperature going.'

The Doc picked himself up and brushed the dust from the knees of his pants, which hardly seemed worth it, seeing as the arse was caked in dry mud. 'You don't know what ya talking about there, Tiny. I have never dealt with no kids.' With that, the Doc lay down by the fire, turned his back on the other men and soon went off to sleep.

Many stories circulated as to how the Doc came by his alias. A popular telling was that he'd once earned a living as a street quack with no medical training and had posed as a doctor going door to door across the city selling the *medicinal powders* he prepared himself, with a claim they cured colds, pains and *general ailments*. The powders were a risky remedy, seeing as the Doc purchased the raw ingredients from the hardware store – various chemicals and dyes mixed with warm water. It was claimed that he'd once sold a powder to a mother nursing a baby screaming from a gut ache and throwing up its own insides. Not more than ten minutes after the mother administered the medicine provided by the Doc the infant went off to sleep. When the mother went to fetch the baby the following morning she saw that it had turned a sickish green colour. The baby was dead.

While they had no idea if the story was true or not, the thought that the Doc may have interfered with kids scared the boys a little. After hearing Tiny's story Ren backed away from the campfire and pulled Sonny by the shirt. Tallboy was watching and saw the worried look on Ren's face.

'Hey ya, boys, listen to me. Old Tallboy's got a real good story to tell yas.'

He held up a half-full wine bottle and took a long swig for lubrication.

'I remember one day I been drinking in town, by the Banana Alley there, with a couple of boys who was labouring casual on the railway, chasing some drinking money.'

He stopped and did the best he could to gather his thoughts before he continued. Ren and Sonny listened closely.

'We had a good drink under the palm tree there. Could have been on a tropical fucken island if it weren't for all the noise of the trucks. We finished off the grog and I wished them fellas best and went walking through town on my way to Gordon House for a feed and a bunk. I was going by the department store there. Myer. No good reason why but off I went inside. Ya know, to look at the wristwatches, smelling the perfumes in the air. The women. I took the moving stairs, up and up, to the furniture. Fancy wardrobes and tables. I see this bed with the big mattress on top of the other mattress. Two mattresses. Can you believe it? Would sleep all of us here, I reckon, it was that big. You ever slept on a mattress like that one, you kids?'

Ren answered 'not me', and Sonny shook his head from side to side.

'Wouldn't have thought so. Well, I'm standing there eyeing the bed and this young buck comes along with his shirt and tie. Haircut. Shaved clean. Nametag on. Could never forget it. *LEE*. You know, like Lee Marvin. The kid, he seen me looking at the bed and come over. Gonna say *fuck off*, I was thinking. But nup. He points at the bed. *Would you like to try it, sir?* he said to me, like we was both gentlemen. I look down at my dirty boots and ask if I have to take them off and he says, *I'm happy for you to leave them on.*'

'Must have been looking to get the arse from his job,' Tiny speculated.

Tallboy ignored him and took another drink, emptying the bottle. 'I said to him, *well thank you, Lee*, and lay down on the bed. None of you here ever felt a bed that way, laying in the clouds there. Then he says to me, *would you like to try a pillow, sir?* And I says, *thank you, Lee*, a second time.

Tallboy looked around the campfire, searching for a response from his audience while gathering confidence in his story. 'The next minute he sticks the pillow behind my head like he's my own nurse. Well, I rested my head down and was off to sleep before I knew it.'

Tallboy peered down the neck of the empty bottle. The others, including the boys, waited for him to go on. But he didn't.

'Then what happened?' Tiny finally asked.

Tallboy lifted his head, opened his eyes and gave Tiny's question some serious thought. Ren suspected that maybe Tallboy was making the story up as he was going along. He didn't mind.

'Well, I open my eyes and the young fella had a shop girl with him, they was over the top of me, shaking me awake. I'd give a ton of gold dust right now to have that old bed down here. I'd share it with all of you, I would.'

The Doc, who'd been laying across the fire, stealing the heat from the others, lifted his head from the ground. 'And what the fuck does this story have to do with anything?'

Tallboy looked across the fire at the Doc, with half a mind to choke him to death. He took a deep patient breath and answered in a quiet voice. 'It's just a story bout a good day I had one time. And a young kid who didn't treat me like shit. That's all it is.' He pointed directly at Ren. 'It's like these two young fellas here.' He winked at the boys. 'I see friendship in them.'

'And it's a good, good story,' Tex said, by way of instructing the Doc to keep his mouth shut.

The campfire went quiet until Tex began humming a tune. The other men quickly joined in singing.

After the boys had left the camp Sonny asked Ren what he

thought about the story of the Doc and the mother. 'You reckon he would have killed someone? He don't look like a killer.'

'Nah. Not a child. Anyone who kills a kid, and if others know about it, they wouldn't be walking round free. He'd be in prison. Maybe even hanged.'

'They'd hang him for that?'

'They hung that fella, Ronald Ryan, last year, for shooting a prison guard. And Archie says he didn't even do it, was the other fella who broke out with him!'

'You afraid of these men?'

'Could be. But Tex, I reckon he'd keep them in order with that poker. See how hard he whacked them two for fighting? Anyway, I can't give up the river cause of some old men. It's our river too. And I like the stories they tell.'

The boys would come to know how much the river men loved their storytelling and singing. The only time they went totally quiet was whenever a snoop passed by the camp, sometimes an official from the Water Board, or a fisherman they hadn't come across before. Tex would give the others the nod to go *deaf and dumb*. Anyone passing by who didn't know better would have sworn the men were clapped-out mental cases. And that was the way Tex liked it. He didn't care that outsiders looked down on them. Silence was a valued lesson he learned during his years *away*, a reference to a stint in prison for which he provided no detail, except to say, 'It was where I come to know to keep the mouth shut and lay doggo.'

CHAPTER 3

Stories of the river were told across the city. There wasn't a child living within reach of the water who hadn't grown up warned away from it with tales of dead trees lurking in the darkness of the muddy riverbed, ready to snatch the leg of a boy or girl braving its filthy water. Rusting skull and crossbones signs, hammered into tree trunks around the old swimming holes, warned of infection. There were also the horror stories of children who disappeared on sunny afternoons never to be seen again, leaving piles of clothing behind on the riverbank, waiting for a parent or the police to discover the telling evidence. It wasn't only children who drowned. As well as the suicides there were the accidents. People fishing fell out of boats from time to time and went straight to the bottom, weighed down by heavy clothes and boots. A dark joke claimed that drowning was a more fortunate end, as eating a fish caught in the river would cause a slower and more painful death.

On calm days, when the current moved slowly towards the bay, and the sun sparkled off the water, it would have been easy to mistake the river's gentle disguise. During Sonny's first summer on the river he decided nothing was going to stop him from going for a swim. He put the idea to Ren, who was less eager. If only half the horror stories he'd heard about the river were true, the riverbed was a graveyard he'd rather stay clear of.

'I dunno, Sonny, about swimming here,' Ren said, sitting on the pontoon, dangling his feet in the water.

'I reckon you're scared.'

Although Sonny was right, Ren wasn't about to confess.

Sonny stripped to his underpants, pumped his arms backwards and forward as if he were an Olympic swimmer, and willed himself for the challenge. 'It's only water. Not much different than diving in the deep end at the baths.'

'It's nothing like the fucken baths. You can see the bottom at the baths. Here, you wouldn't know if your own hand was in front of your face. Could be anything down there.'

'Like what?'

'Like stuff you can't see. You wanna know what Archie calls the trees at the bottom of the river?'

'What?'

'When he was a kid they called them preachers.'

'Preachers?'

'If a person got caught in the snag of a dead tree and they never came back the family would have to get a preacher to stand over an empty coffin and pray for the life and soul of the dead person. Burying an empty coffin. Fucken spooky.'

The image of a rotting corpse lurking below the surface was enough for Sonny to step back from the edge of the pontoon.

'I think old Sonny's chickening out now.' Ren laughed.

'Bullshit, he is.' Sonny let out a screech and dived into the water.

Ren couldn't see any sign of him, except for a trace of bubbles, until he bobbed up halfway across the river, grinning. Ren realised he had no choice but to follow his friend into the water. He stood up, closed his eyes, crossed his heart twice and jumped in. He swam to the middle of the river and flipped onto his back. As the current caressed his body Ren noticed the shifts in water temperature, from warm to ice cold. He trod water and watched as Sonny let the current carry him downriver until he reached the shadow of the iron bridge and headed for the bank. Ren swam back to the pontoon and stood watching as Sonny circled the campsite and searched the empty humpy. He walked back along the track, jumped across to the pontoon and lay his body in the sun.

'No sign of Tex and them?'

'Nah. They're probably up at the wine shop.' Sonny was so happy he laughed out loud.

'What's funny?' Ren asked.

'This is good.'

'Yep. It's the best.'

Ren sniffed his arm. The water smelled like nothing he'd expected. It was a rich scent, the same that was given off by the back garden after he'd watered Archie's bed of tomatoes for him. As his skin dried he noticed specks of dirt, fine as baby powder, covering his body. From that day on, the boys carried the river home with them. They went to bed of a night with the scent of river on their bodies and through their hair, no matter how hard they tried to wash it out. And it was with them the next morning when they woke.

In the days after their first river swim the boys couldn't stay out of the water. They explored the banks both upstream and downriver, trying out every swimming hole and increasingly testing their courage, jumping from rocks, out of trees, and eventually off the bridges that crossed the river. Their first bridge jump was from Kane's, a cable bridge that swayed from side to side in the slightest breeze. It was no more than twenty feet above the water, but was challenge enough. Having conquered it they moved on to others, testing their bravery, each bridge higher and more dangerous than the last.

Late in the afternoons, Ren would sneak along the lane behind his house, slip into Sonny's yard and stand under a hose, trying to wash the silt from his body before returning home. If he thought he'd deceived his mother about what he'd been up to, it was only himself Ren was fooling. When he brought the river home Loretta knew immediately he'd taken to the water. She pinched her lip and held her tongue, worrying over her boy as a mother would, but unwilling to crush the free-spirited nature she quietly admired.

The day of their first swim Ren dried off in Sonny's yard with an old towel. It was stiff and felt like sandpaper against his skin.

'Hey, Sonny, I better wait until my hair dries. I can't go home with it wet or she'll know where I've been.'

Sonny held a thumb over the end of the water hose. Once it had built pressure he squirted Ren in the face with it.

'We can go to the signal box for a smoke.'

An abandoned signal box in the railyards had become the classroom where Sonny taught Ren to roll cigarettes. Sonny's cigarettes were so perfect, Ren told him that if it was a national sport he'd be world champion. They left by Sonny's gate that day, walked the length of the lane to the railyards, climbed the fence and scaled the ladder into the box. Sonny sat in the signalman's chair rolling and instructing. Ren lay on the floor flicking through the pages of an old *National Geographic*.

'That's your problem, Ren. It's why you'll never roll a decent smoke. You can't concentrate.'

Ren *was* concentrating, on a centre-spread photograph of a large bird gliding across a clear sky. The bird was magnificent. He carefully tore the photo from the book, folded it and put it in his shirt pocket.

'What have you got there?'

'A picture of an eagle.'

'Eagle? What you want that for?'

'I'll put it on the wall near my bed so I can look at it.'

Sonny was dumbfounded. 'Look at it? You do some crazy things, Ren.' He lit the cigarette he'd rolled, took a couple of drags on it and passed it to Ren.

A train whistled in the distance, rounded a bend and sped through the yards. Sonny held on tightly to his seat as a diesel-powered coal train thundered along the tracks below him, shaking the signal box from side to side and rattling the windows like an earthquake. The box filled with smoke and fumes. Sonny spun around in his chair and kept an eye on the train until it disappeared around the next bend.

'Hey, Ren, you ever been on one of them trains to the countryside?'

Ren could hardly see and was rubbing his eyes.

'I got no reason to. I don't know anyone who lives out of the city. You been there?'

'Once, when I was a small kid. My gran lived in a town in the bush where my pop worked in a garage fixing cars and trucks. After he died she stayed on in the house by herself. She fell over one day and hurt herself and my mum took me on the train, just me and her, for a stay and to take care of her.'

'Did you like it?'

'Yeah, the train had leather seats like big couches, and when I had to go to the toilet it had a hole in the bottom straight down to the tracks. Splattered the shit at fifty miles an hour. Maybe faster than that.'

'How long did it take to get there, the town she lived in?'

'Hours. They had a shop on the train for sandwiches and cups of tea. Ham and pickle. And sausage rolls and lollies.'

'And your gran, what was she like?'

'She was okay. But strict. She was crazy on keeping everything clean and tidy. I had to wash my hands any time I touched myself and scrub my nails clean with a laundry brush after I'd been playing outside. She could cook better than anyone. When we were there relatives come over and we had a big lunch. She was in a wheelchair, me pushing her round the kitchen, and her giving my mum orders and telling her what to do.'

'What else did you do in the country?'

'Not much. There was an old truck rusting away in a shed in the yard. I'd climb in that and pretend I was driving some place.'

'Where to?'

'Just places. Anywhere, as long as it wasn't back to the city where my old man was waiting for us.'

'Have you seen her since, your grandmother?'

'I don't even know where my mum and little brother went to. My gran could be dead and I wouldn't know.'

He threw the tobacco and papers to Ren.

'You gonna try one or not?'

Ren did, and rolled a cigarette that bulged around the centre and tapered at both ends. When he finished he handed it to Sonny for approval.

Sonny looked at it in disgust. 'Fucken spastic.'

Walking home, Ren saw a furniture van parked out the front of the vacant house next door to Sonny's. Two men were unloading cupboards and tea chests from the back of the truck. The house had been empty for months, left to a battalion of cockroaches that moved in after the tenants did a moonlight runner, a pair of con artists who kept Salvation Army uniforms and a tambourine at the ready when they were broke. They dressed up and stood on street corners belting out hymns and passing around the hat. After hearing that police had been knocking at their door while they were out, the couple disappeared one night, tambourine in hand, rattling along the street as they went.

The complaints started when the cockroaches spread from the vacant house and marched into neighbouring homes, including Sonny's. A health inspector from the council was called. He broke the door down with a sledgehammer and trapped a pair of roaches in a glass jar. He then stood out front of the house examining the insects, with a crowd gathered around him.

The inspector took a magnifying glass out of his briefcase, studied the roaches closely and declared that the house had been invaded by cockroaches of the *Argentinian variety*. The landlord was ordered to fumigate the building, fix the leaking roof and clear out the rubbish. The old stable in the yard behind the house, which had been used as a blacksmithing works for years, was also cleaned and given a coat of fresh paint.

The boys stood on the footpath watching the removalists wrestle with a piano. The men lifted it up and strapped it to a trolley, swearing at it like it was someone they were fighting with. 'Fucken iron frame,' one of the workmen grunted to the other. 'We're marking the job. Double time.'

'Triple time. Bad enough as it is, working Sundays.'

They were beaten and stopped for a cigarette. One of the men looked over at the boys.

'What you two looking at?' he snapped at Sonny, wiping sweat from his neck with a dirty hankie. 'You wanna try carrying this?'

Sonny folded his arms, smiled and whispered something under his breath, words of cheek the removalist couldn't quite hear.

'Wouldn't reckon so,' the removalist jeered, 'you can stop being smart-arses or piss off.'

As far as the boys were concerned the street belonged to them as much as anybody and they weren't about to piss off anywhere. The removalists finished their smoke and dragged the piano into the house.

Sonny stepped into the gutter and tapped the toe of his foot against the bluestone edging. He looked up at Ren and back down at his toe. He whacked it hard enough that it was bleeding. He went on tapping as he spoke.

'My mum used to play one of them. A piano.'

'You had a piano in your house?'

'Nah. She had a cleaning job before she … she used to pick me up after school and take me to this kindergarten where she cleaned, after all the kids had gone home. It was before my little brother was born. I'd lay down in one of these tiny beds, where the little kids slept in the afternoon. Or I'd go in the kitchen and make my own cup of tea while she worked. One time I was sitting at one of the tables, they were tiny too, same as the chairs, and I heard music and somebody singing in the hall next door. I thought it must have been one of the teachers practising for a show or something and went to take a look.'

Sonny stopped kicking, lifted his toe in the air and watched as blood dripped from the wound into the gutter.

'And?' Ren asked. 'What happened when you got to the hall?'

Sonny kept his head down and eyes on the injured toe, a ploy to stop himself from looking at Ren. 'It was my mum, playing the piano, like she owned it, and singing a song.'

The front gate of the empty house creaked. The workman who had told them to piss off was standing at the back of the truck watching them.

'Do you remember the song she was singing?' Ren asked, only because he could think of nothing else to say.

'Yeah.' Sonny smiled. 'It was an old song, *Wheel of Fortune*. She used to sing it around the house too sometimes, when my father wasn't home.'

'And what did she do when she saw you watching her at the piano.'

Sonny shrugged. 'Not much. Closed the lid of the piano and picked up her mop and bucket.'

The removalist walked across to where they were leaning against Ren's front fence. He noticed the man had a limp.

'How'd you kids like to earn a couple of dollars?'

'You just told us to piss off,' Sonny reminded him.

'I was mucking round.' He smiled, front teeth missing. 'Name's Jack.'

If he was waiting for the boys to introduce themselves it would be a long day.

'We have a load of chairs in the back of the truck, and my mate, Henry, and me, we want to get away. You give us a hand and there's an earn for you. A couple of bucks each.'

'How much is a couple?' Sonny asked.

Jack held up two fingers. 'Same as it's always been.'

Sonny held up four fingers. 'Two's not enough. It's Sunday. We work double time, same as you.'

'Jesus, you running a union here? You're not getting four. Three dollars each.'

'Only if you pay up front.'

'Bullshit! Nobody gets paid up front. Not in full.'

'Then we're not doing it.'

Three dollars is good money, Ren thought. He wanted Sonny to shut up and take the deal.

'Fuck me. Next time I'm chasing a pay rise, I'll give you a call,' Jack said. He dipped into his back pocket, pulled out his wallet and paid the boys three dollars each.

The chairs were made of solid wood and were heavy. The

boys struggled with two chairs apiece, one under each arm. They followed the removalists through the house – it smelled of fresh paint – and crossed the backyard into the open door of the stable. The walls were painted white and the wooden floor had been sanded clean. Ren looked down at the boards, marked with deep scars. The piano sat at one end of the room, next to a brass cross atop a wooden pole. Picture frames rested against another wall. They reminded Ren of the prayer cards the fake Salvos had given out on street corners, except these ones were bigger. He read aloud the gold lettered inscription running across the bottom of one of the cards. *There Can Be No Being Before God, As God Has No Mother.*

'What do you reckon that means?' he asked Sonny.

'Fucked if I know.'

One frame was covered in a piece of green cloth. Sonny pulled it away, revealing a portrait of a man in a dark three-piece suit, a round-collared shirt and spotted bow tie. He had shining black skin and wore a pair of round sunglasses that hid his eyes from view. He was seated in a carved wooden chair. A young woman in a white wedding dress knelt alongside him. She held the man's hand in hers and looked up at him, smiling. She had golden curls, flowers in her hair and skin as white as his was black. Across the bottom of the painting were the words *Father Jealous Divine & Mother Purity Divine – the Younger.*

Jack whistled and called out to his mate on the other side of the stable. 'Henry, take a look at these stagers.'

Henry was lining up the chairs in straight rows. He shuffled across the room, picking at his arse through his overalls. He stood next to Jack, folded his arms and studied the painting with his head tilted to the side, as if he was an art expert.

'She's not bad looking, Jack.'

'Not bad at all. See the way she's eyeing the old black boy. I bet he's fucking her. Put my house on it.'

'If you had a house.' Henry laughed. 'What you think, boys? The old buck fucking her or what?'

Ren was sure the man in the painting had to be old enough to be the girl's father, if not her grandfather. He didn't want to think about Henry's question at all.

Heavy footsteps echoed across the room behind him. He turned and was frightened by the sight of a tall thin man standing in the doorway of the stable, casting a shadow across the room. The man wore a long suit coat over a white shirt. A silver head of hair sat on his shoulders, and his skin, pulled tight across his face, was lined with pulsing veins. The removalist began rubbing his chest with a hand, as if the man's cold blue eyes were boring a hole in Henry's heart. His face tightened with pain.

The man strode across the room and stopped inches from Henry, who looked down at the floor, at the pair of black leather shoes the man was wearing.

'Your remark?' the man asked, raising one eyebrow.

Henry flicked his tongue out and licked his bottom lip. He tried getting his mouth moving, but it had seized on him.

'That weren't no remark,' Jack offered. 'We were having a joke here with the youngsters. Weren't we, Henry?'

The man set his eyes on Jack, who suddenly seemed as uncomfortable as his workmate.

'How often do you feel a need to speak on behalf of your co-worker?'

Jack appeared insulted and spoke up for himself. 'I don't

feel any particular need. Like I said, we were just mucking about. No harm done. Is there?'

The man ignored the comment. He took a stiff white handkerchief from his jacket pocket and dabbed at the corners of his mouth. Ren, listening closely to the man's voice, heard an accent. *American*, he thought.

'Set the chairs in rows, an equal number of chairs per row, separated by a clear centre aisle of three feet. You will move the piano to the right side of the room. You will also need to hang the psalms, and ...'

He stopped and looked down at the cloth that had been pulled away from the painting of the old black man. He picked up the green cloth, folded it neatly, tucked it under one arm, raised the other and pointed to the wall behind the piano. 'Mount the portrait of the Messenger in line with the centre aisle. At a height on the wall.'

He took another step forward and stood so close to Jack they almost touched. He handed the folded piece of cloth to him. 'Are you able to complete these tasks?'

'No worries.' Jack smiled. 'It'll cost a little more though. Mr Beck, weren't it?'

'Reverend Beck,' the man smarted.

Jack offered his grubby hand. The Reverend ignored it and wiped his hands with the handkerchief. He put it back in one coat pocket and took a small black leather Bible from another and held it in one hand. He opened the Bible and ran his eyes down the page before suddenly flicking them to one side. *As sharp as a bird in the sky spotting the prey it was about to snatch and kill*, Ren thought. A girl had appeared at the stable doorway. She wore a long chequered dress reaching to her ankles and a scarf on her head, hiding most of her blond hair. She was around the same age as the boys. Ren snuck a look at her face. The girl glanced at him and just as quickly, for only a moment, before turning away.

'Della,' the Reverend said, 'what are you doing in here?'

She answered by bringing her hands together in prayer. 'The followers have arrived and they are asking what work you need them to do.'

The Reverend spread his arms, raised his hands in the air and closed his eyes. 'There is work for them in our church. Return to your mother and ask her to escort them here.'

Jack and Henry were staring at the Reverend as if he was a freak. Sonny caught Ren's eye and nodded in the direction of the stable door. As the boys slipped past the girl, Ren stole another look at her and decided on the spot that she was pretty, even though half of her face was covered by the scarf. Her skin was as a clear as the young bride's in the painting except for the dark rings under both eyes, which gave her a look of deep worry.

Ren followed Sonny through the house. A thin woman stood in the middle of the kitchen wearing a uniform similar to the young girl's. She wrung her hands together and said nothing as the boys walked by. In the next room a group of men, dressed similarly to the Reverend, were gathered in a circle. They had their heads bowed in prayer and did not look up as the boys passed the doorway. Once they were out in the street the boys began firing questions at each other.

'What a nutcase,' Sonny said. 'Did you see his crazy eyes?'

'The black man in the picture? He didn't have eyes. Just them circles. His glasses.'

'No, I mean the Reverend fella. They are the eyes of a killer, for sure. He was so white he looked like someone had stuck him in a freezer for a week. He had a strange voice. And the girl, she was afraid of something. I could see it on her face. Come into the yard with me. We can sneak a look through the fence.'

Sonny was peeping through a hole in the side fence when the back door swung open. It was his father. His hair stood on end and he was wearing only a pair of stained underpants. He didn't look at Sonny or Ren, or say a word as he leaned against the fence. He supported himself with one hand, pulled his dick out of his underpants with the other and pissed in the dirt. When he finished, he spat against the fence and shuffled back into the kitchen, scratching at his unshaven face.

'Sorry,' Sonny said, as embarrassed for Ren as much as for himself. 'He's been hitting it hard.'

'It don't matter to me,' Ren answered. 'I don't care.'

Ren truly meant it. He felt bad about most things that happened to Sonny — his mother up and leaving him, and his father treating him poorly. He wanted to offer words that might help his friend feel better. 'I have to get home or my mum will kill me. But tomorrow, I reckon it will be hot again. We could swim at the falls?'

Sonny was staring at the open doorway his father had just walked through. 'Sure. We'll swim at the falls.'

Ren went into the house and up to his bedroom. He took the photograph of the eagle out of his pocket and smoothed the creases in the paper as best he could. He took two drawing pins from a matchbox and pinned the photograph to the back of his bedroom door, where he'd be able to look at it from his bed. He heard footsteps on the stairs. His mother's.

Loretta walked into the bedroom, stood alongside Ren and admired the bird.

'Where have you been all day?' she asked.

'Nowhere. Hanging around with Sonny.'

She moved closer to him, sniffed the air and raised an eyebrow. A clear sign she was giving Ren the opportunity to confess that he'd been swimming in the river. He declined the offer.

'Nowhere, you said. Must have been doing something with your time?'

Ren dug into his pocket and pulled out a one- and a two-dollar note. 'New people moved in next door to Sonny and we got a job helping move the furniture. Sonny earned the same as me. That's what I've been doing. Working.'

Loretta kept her eyes on the photograph of the bird as she spoke. 'Is it a family moving in? I hope we get more decent people than the last lot of frauds.'

'I guess they're a family. But they're strange-looking.'

'How?'

'Well there's a girl and a woman, her mother, I guess. They dress strange. Old-fashioned. And there were these men in one of the rooms, praying I think. And one fella who must be in charge. Sonny reckons he looked like a dead man. They're making a church out the back, in the old stable.'

'A church? Archie won't be happy about that. He's got no time for religion. Are you sure it's a church they're thinking of?'

'That's what I heard him say to the removalists. He's got a piano in the back and some holy pictures and lots of chairs.'

Loretta took a step closer to the photograph of the bird. 'And where'd you get this?'

'In a magazine. I found it laying on the road,' Ren lied. 'Do you know how they do that, Mum?'

'Do what?'

'Take photographs like that. That bird is way up in the sky, but the picture is close. How do they do that?'

'Oh, they'd be professional people with special cameras, almost like telescopes. Have a look at the photographers on the boundary line next time you go to the football. They use cameras like that.'

Loretta poked a finger through a lock in Ren's hair and stuck it behind his ear. 'You need a haircut.'

'No, I don't. All the kids have it long now.'

Loretta frowned. She thought her son looked scruffier than he ever had, but she wasn't going to argue about an issue that didn't mean a lot to her

'Fair enough.' She laughed, 'I hate to think you're not up with the trend. I best get tea started.'

She sniffed the air again before leaving the room. 'I'd swear I can smell the river in this room.'

'Yeah, it's the wind,' Ren said, faking a sniff of his own. 'You know, coming off the water.'

Loretta did know. She'd only just come inside from hanging the washing in the yard. She knew a change had blown in and the wind was coming from the opposite direction to the river.

CHAPTER 4

The next morning, Ren sat on the front fence waiting for Sonny. Archie came out of the house not far behind him. It was a warm morning and Archie fell into his chair with a novel in his hand. He held it up for display. 'Haven't seen you with your head in one of these for months. They have you reading books at school?'

'I read, at the library. About birds.'

'And what about stories?'

All the stories Ren needed were told on the river. 'Sometimes. We have to read for tests.'

'Tests is one thing. But reading for yourself. You could do with more of it.'

'I'm busy.' Ren frowned.

'Oh.' Archie laughed. 'I can see that. Sitting out here on the fence doing nothing. Waiting for your shadow next door.' Archie tapped the side of his head. 'Up here, in your head. Books can take you places.'

Ren looked up at the sky. 'I go places. Plenty of places.'

Reverend Beck came out of his gate and marched by the house. His wife walked several paces behind him, holding the hand of the girl, Della. She looked at Ren a little longer than she had the day before. The family crossed the street and turned the corner. Archie rested the book in his lap.

'That the new people?' he asked.

'Yeah. He's some sort of minister. I think they're gonna have a church in the back.'

'A church? Don't reckon they can do that. Not legally.'

'They already have. And he's an American, I think.'

'That's all we need. A fucken know-all.'

Sonny came out of his house, wheeling his bone-shaking wreck of a pushbike. He knew Archie didn't have much time for him. It didn't stop Sonny niggling him.

'Hey.' Sonny waved. 'I see you got a book.'

'You being cheeky, Sonny?'

'Nah. Just talking.'

'You read books yourself?'

'I don't have time for books. I'm busy.'

'So I just heard. What are you planning today?' Archie asked. 'You gonna change the world would be my guess.'

'That's my plan,' Sonny answered. 'You guessed right, Mr Kemp.'

Archie craned his neck forward and looked up at the shimmering ball of morning sun. 'If I were you two, at your age, you know what I'd do on a hot morning like this?'

'What would that be?' Sonny asked.

'I'd get busy on the river.' He winked at Ren. 'And I'd get going before your mother finds something for you to do.'

★

50

Sonny wheeled the bike between him and Ren. When he reached the ridge above the water, he mounted the bike, took off and held on as best he could down the steep treacherous track to the bottom, the bike bucking and shifting in the loose ground. Ren had warned him that one day the brakes might fail and he'd ride straight into the river, a real possibility that never held Sonny back. His other trick on the bike was to ride it across the slimy ledge of the falls to a swimming hole on the other side. He'd slipped from the bike more than once, and had gone close to falling onto the rocks below, though no accident had ever stopped him trying the trick again.

It was a beautiful morning on the river. The boys jumped again and again from a tree hanging over the swimming hole until they wore themselves out. Ren sat on a low sandstone step at the river's edge. With no wind in the air, the water above the falls lay flat and still as a sheet of glass. He watched as the sheet nudged the falls and shattered as it tumbled over the ledge. Sonny lay stretched out like a cat further up, his T-shirt covering his face from the hot sun. Ren stood up, climbed the steps and collected Sonny's tobacco and papers. He produced two cigarettes, one fat and the other thin, with tobacco trailing from one end.

'Here's your smoke, Sonny.'

When he didn't answer, Ren picked up a pebble and threw it at him. It missed Sonny, bounced off the rocks and tumbled into the water. He tapped Sonny on the ankle.

'Smoke?'

Sonny pulled the shirt away from his face, looked up at the pair of cigarettes and chose the fat one.

'Matches?'

Ren handed them to him and he put the smoke in his mouth, lit it and took a long drag. Ren sat next to him, lit his own smoke and looked down at the water. 'After we finish here we should call by the camp.'

'Why?'

'Check on them. Make sure they're okay. Maybe ask Tex for a story. He hasn't told one in a while.'

'He's not remembering them so well. He's drinking too much. Doesn't know his own name some days.'

'He's always been drinking.'

'Maybe. But not what he's been on lately. I smelled it all over him last time we was at the camp. *White Lady* they call it.'

'What's that?'

'Metho and water. I heard about it one time from an uncle of mine, Rory, my old man's big brother. He knows a lot of stuff. He told me that when the winos get desperate they mix the water with the metho to calm its fiery kick. Turns the metho white. Rory said it can *strip the insides of a man's throat, roast his guts and cook his brain.* Send a man blind, even kill him. No wonder Tex can't see proper. And he forgets all the time. He's gone crazy.'

'Leave him be. He always gives us a seat at the fire. And he shares.'

'Not hard sharing when you got nothing.'

'You have it the wrong way, Sonny. Those who have the money, rich people, don't share. Think of the times you've had a feed round Tex's fire. That's his own he's giving us. And don't forget, he found the river long before we did. He knows more about it than anybody, and shares stories with us too.'

'Tex don't own the river. This is a free country, Ren.'

'Never said he owned anything. I said he shared.' Ren puffed at his cigarette, held the smoke in his mouth and blew it out. 'And this is no free country. You're wrong there too.'

'Course it is.'

Ren stood up, picked up a hunk of rock and shot-putted it into the water. 'You think so? Get yourself lost on the street late one night and see if you can make it home without police tracking you for a belt. Only way you'd make it in one piece would be through the lanes. If you was lucky.'

'It's not like we're crims, Ren. They got more to do than hunt kids.'

'Hunted you when you smashed that window.'

'Right. But not because I was walking down the street.'

'Before you come here there was a robbery at the TAB, next door to the paper shop. The robber put a gun to a lady's head and told her he was gonna kill her. The next day the police pulled this kid off the street for it. He wasn't much older than you and me. They took him to the cells and bashed him and the kid died. It was one of the detectives that did it. Foy. You heard of him?'

'I don't know any detective.'

'He jumped on that kid, from a table, and killed him. Everybody knew it was him. Didn't stop the judge finding him not guilty. Other police who come to the court to watch the case laughed when it was over, in front of the boy's mother. So don't tell me this is a free country.'

Sonny stood up and waved his T-shirt in the air. 'I give up. It's no free country. But the river don't belong to Tex. That's all I'm saying. And he's a wino.'

'So what? There's plenty of winos round here. He's not the only one. Tex is a better person than most of em.'

Sonny stubbed his cigarette butt against a rock. 'Enough. I said I take it back. Hang on. Let me do better.' He stood up, cupped his hands around his mouth and screamed along the river valley. 'Old Tex … is … not … useless.

'That'll have to do. You want a statement from me you'll have to belt me with a telephone book and wet towel.'

'If I was police, I would. After that I'd drop you at Snaky Bend, from the divi-van, give you a crack and let you walk home in the dark.'

By the time they'd rolled and smoked another cigarette the hot sun was directly overhead. Ren climbed the tree and dived into the water. He was the cleaner diver of the two boys but couldn't get near Sonny when it came to bombing. After half-a-dozen more dives he stood in the sun drying off, examining the hairs on his arms, covered in a sprinkling of fine dirt. It was also in his hair, his ears and under his fingernails.

Sonny stood on the bank flexing his arm muscles. 'Do you reckon they've got bigger? I been doing push-ups every morning.'

'The only part of you that is any bigger is your fucken head.'

Sonny went on flexing. 'That Reverend Beck, you think he's a real churchie? Looks more like an undertaker.'

'He'll be doing both jobs if he's gonna run his own church out the back. Dead bodies might turn up before long. All I know is he's a creep. Them workmen were scared of him.'

54

'The girl too. I could tell by looking at her face.'

'How?'

'Because I seen that look before.'

'Where?'

Sonny ignored the question, picked up his T-shirt and scrambled up the steps where his bike lay. He looked up at a winding narrow pathway that led to a cliff-top high above the river.

'Hey, Ren, you ever been up there?'

'A few times. It's a good spot for watching birds. They come downriver from the mountains and fly along the valley on their way to the bay, chasing fish, I reckon.'

'You and your birds.'

'You and your dick, Sonny. The diver. He's up there too.'

'The diver?'

'Yeah, the diver. I bet you'd like to meet him. Come on.' He skipped ahead of Sonny, who was picking up his bike. 'You can leave it here. There's only the one way up and down. We can fetch it on the way back.'

'I'm not leaving this behind. Someone might knock it off.'

'Nobody would steal that bike, Sonny. Not in a million years. And there's no one round anyway.'

'Maybe not. I'm not taking any chances.'

'Please yourself. You're lugging it, not me.'

It was an old railway bike and weighed a ton. The railyards captain rode it around at night, turfing drunks out of empty carriages. The frame was made of cast iron and the tyres would fit a tractor. Sonny had stolen it, hand-painted it red and put new transfers on it. His attempt at disguising the bike was not a success. It looked exactly like what it was, a stolen railway bike that had been painted red. If the yard captain came across Sonny riding it through the streets he'd kick his arse and maybe have him charged. Ren had warned him about it, but Sonny being Sonny, he shrugged and said he didn't give a *half a fuck* about the yard captain, which was true.

By the time they reached the cliff-top Sonny was exhausted. He rested the bike against the trunk of a tree and lay on the hard ground. Ren walked on ahead, to where the path ended.

'Come take a look at this.'

'At what? I'm fucked.'

'I told you. The diver.'

Sonny dragged himself to his feet and walked across to where Ren was standing, in front of a pile of rocks, crudely cemented together. A brass plate screwed into the rocks was engraved with a picture of a young man gliding through the air high above the river. Down below, boats filled with people waited in the water. The riverbanks were lined with faces looking up at the diver.

'Let me read this,' Ren said, running a finger across an inscription below the image. '... as the crowd gathered, numbered in their many thousands, the diver fell through the sky, plunged into the water completing the world record dive. The feat has not been attempted since.'

Ren brushed a cobweb from the plate. 'In the library, next to the town hall, they have a photo in a frame that this drawing was taken from. And a news story. The diver come here from some island in the Pacific Ocean where they dive from cliffs into the sea with ropes tied to their legs. Twenty thousand people were watching him when he dived here, screaming and crying after he took off, then cheering like crazy when he hit the surface. He was in the nude when he come up, cause his bathers were torn off him when he hit the water.'

Sonny walked a little closer to the edge of the cliff.

'No one could dive from this high and live.'

'Well, he did it.'

'Have you looked over the edge?'

'Yep. We got to lie down, to be safe.'

Ren got down on his stomach and Sonny lay alongside of him. They slowly crawled to the edge of the cliff. Sonny rested his chin against the rock and looked down to the water and across to the far bank, to the remains of an ancient swimming pool that had been carved into the river decades earlier. Strips of bark, newspapers and rubbish were trapped in the rusted metal frame separating the pool from the river.

'What's that?'

'Deep Rock. The same man who put the money up to bring the diver here paid for the swimming pool to be built. People used to swim there every weekend, when the water was clean. A long time ago.'

'Why haven't we swum there?'

'It's dangerous. The bottom of the pool is full of broken glass. It was done on purpose to stop kids swimming there.'

Sonny worked up a full gob of spit and shot it into the sky. He watched it fall through the air. 'Sure is a long way down.'

From where they lay the boys were able to trace the journey of the river, snaking towards the city from the hills in the distance. The wheelhouse and the pontoon lay to the other side of them, and further on, factories and narrow houses along the river.

'Would you try jumping from here?' Sonny asked.

'If I could fly.'

'I reckon I could do it.'

'I would bet you that you couldn't do it, except I'd never get my money cause you'd be dead.'

Sonny moved away from the cliff edge, sat on a stump and rolled himself a cigarette. As Ren crawled back to join him, his heel clipped the front wheel of the bike. It rolled forward. He threw a hand out to grab hold of a wheel, but the bike picked up speed and shot by him. Sonny watched, his mouth open, as the back wheel of the bike tumbled over the cliff.

'Grab it,' he screamed.

'Too late. It's gone.'

'Gone?' he said, as if he hadn't just seen it disappear.

'Gone as it gets.'

'Fuck! You should have grabbed hold of it, Ren.'

'I tried. It was moving too fast.'

While Sonny swore and spat Ren realised something wasn't right. 'Listen.'

'Listen to what?'

'To nothing. There was no noise. No splash of the bike going in the water.'

He crawled back to the edge of the cliff. The front wheel of Sonny's bike was hooked over the branch of a tree growing out of a crack in the rocks on the riverbank. The branch had almost snapped in half and the bike was swinging precariously over the water.

'Whoa!' Ren yelled. 'Take a look at this, Sonny.'

Sonny crawled across to him, a cigarette hanging from his bottom lip.

'What a shot! Can we get down to the bike from here?'

'There's no way down. We'll have to cross at the falls and swim over from Deep Rock.'

'We have to be quick, before the branch breaks off and I lose the bike to the river.'

Deep Rock was bordered by a concrete ledge separating the pool from the river. Sonny stood on the ledge and looked across to his bike, dangling from the tree above the water.

'How we gonna get it down?'

'Easy. We swim across, one of us climbs the tree and unhooks the bike and lowers it to the water. We tow it back across the river between us.'

'I don't reckon we have much time before that branch snaps.'

'After you then, Sonny.'

Sonny dived into the water, swam to the far bank and rested on a tree stump at the bottom of the cliff-face, waiting for Ren.

'Hurry.' He waved.

Ren dipped his hand in the water and scooped out a bug. It swam in circles in the small pool of water cupped in his hand. He was about to slam his hands together and squash the bug, but changed his mind and dipped his hand into the water a second time and watched as the bug swam away. He stood up, dived, turned under the water and swam across the river backstroke, catching the sun on his chest. He threw his head back as far as possible, until he could see the hanging bike. He flipped over onto his stomach and swam the last few strokes to the cliff edge.

Sonny welcomed him by spitting a mouthful of water in his face. 'Could you be any slower, face ache?'

'Don't be calling me names, Sonny. Or you can get the bike on your own.'

Sonny spat another mouthful of water at him. 'I reckon you should climb the tree. That branch looks like it's about to snap. You weigh less than me.'

Ren scaled the tree quicker than a cat. As he got higher he wrapped one arm and both legs around the tree trunk and tried to guide the front wheel of the bike over the end of the branch it was hooked on. The bike was too heavy. He let go of the wheel and collapsed against the tree trunk.

'I can't do it, Sonny.'

'Yes, you can. Climb a little higher and get a better grip.'

'I can't get higher.'

'C'mon, Ren. One more try.'

Ren shifted his weight and stretched out his arm, grunting and swearing until he'd lifted the wheel over the top of the branch. The bike slipped from his grip at the moment he called out to Sonny, 'In the water! Grab it!'

Sonny dived from the bank as the bike was about to go under, and hooked a leg through the frame. Ren jumped out of the tree, landed next to the front wheel and wrapped an arm around the handlebars. He roped a leg through the frame and tried swimming breaststroke with his stomach resting on the handlebars. He wasn't sure how Sonny was doing, but he felt like he was getting nowhere. He was about to give up and let the bike sink, when between them they got into a rhythm, making their way to the opposite bank until they could stand, their feet sinking into the muddy riverbed.

'Hold on to it, Sonny,' Ren spluttered, coughing up water. 'I've had it.'

Sonny dragged the bike the last few feet and tried lifting it onto the bank. He couldn't do it on his own. Ren waded across to him and grabbed the front wheel.

'One ... two ... three.' The boys hurled the bike onto the riverbank, where it landed with a heavy thud. They stood in the waste-deep water laughing. Sonny crouched down, brought a handful of mud up from the bottom and slung it at Ren. The ball of mud hit him in the centre of his forehead and slipped down his face. Although they were worn out they got into a celebratory mud fight until Sonny called a truce, ducking below the surface and washing the mud from his body. Ren paddled to the edge of the river.

Sonny waded across to him and whispered, 'Ren, look at this.' A brown snake, no more than a couple of feet long, slid between them.

'Which snake's poisonous? The black or the brown one?' he asked.

'Not sure. One of them. I forget which.'

They didn't move an inch until the snake had slipped away. Ren got out of the water and picked up the bike. He noticed someone further along the bank, midway between where he was standing and the falls, a man dressed in army greens, crouching forward and peering into what Ren thought looked like a telescope.

'Sonny, take a look at this fella.'

'Can't see nothing.'

'Not from there, you can't. Hop out of the water. There's someone spying. See him now?'

Sonny scrambled onto the bank. 'Yeah, I see him. What's he doing snooping down here? I'm gonna ride over and ask him what he's up to.'

'You can't do that.'

'Course I can. This is our river.'

Sonny took the bike from Ren, straddled it and pedalled off.

The workman spotted the two boys heading his way. He waved at them and smiled. When they got close Ren read the words sewn into the pocket of his shirt – *ROAD TRANSIT AUTHORITY*.

'How are you going, lads? Warm day.' He smiled, looking up at the sun. He had straw hair and wore sunglasses. He seemed friendly enough to Ren.

'What are you looking at with the telescope?' he asked the workman.

'It's not a telescope. We're surveying along here. This instrument provides accurate measurements of distance, height and the contour of the land. Would you like to take a look?'

He smiled again. Sonny was having none of his friendliness. He leaned back on the bike and crossed his arms.

'I'll take a look,' Ren said.

'Good. Hang on a second.' The workman pulled a walkie-talkie from his belt, pressed a button and spoke into it. 'Stan, give us an upright, mate.' He put a hand on Ren's shoulder. 'Okay. You take a look through the level and you'll see my mate holding an upright pole.'

Ren bent forward and closed one eye. He could see numbers and lines, and in the distance another workman standing on a rise, dressed in the same uniform, holding a striped wooden pole.

'Can you see him?'

Ren stood up. 'What's he doing?'

The man pointed to the words on his chest pocket. 'We're from the RTA, and we're doing the survey ahead of the excavation for the freeway coming through here. It's our job to measure and peg the ground before the explosives team come in and begin their work. Once the powder monkeys have done their job it will be over to the bulldozers. We can't lay a major new road without knowing exactly where it has to go. We don't want to blow up the wrong hill.'

He laughed out loud, as if he'd told a joke. But there was nothing funny about what he'd said as far as the boys were concerned.

'But there's no roads down here,' Ren said.

'Not yet. But there will be soon enough. Five lanes of freeway, each way, stretching from here to the eastern suburbs.'

Ren couldn't make sense of what the man was saying.

'Going where?'

'Exactly where you were looking through the level. We're going to gouge out that hill and excavate through here, and …' He turned and faced the other way. 'See the marker ahead, through the trees there?'

He was pointing towards another striped pole, pitched in the ground on a low hill above Deep Rock.

'The freeway will head in that direction.'

'How they gonna do that?' Sonny interrupted. 'You can't put a road next to the old swimming pool. There's no room for it.'

The workman's smile disappeared. 'It's a freeway, son, not a road. And it takes up a lot of land. Accordingly, the hill

63

here will be dynamited, the ground will be bulldozed, and a stretch of the river will need to be realigned. The derelict swimming basin you're referring to will be dynamited and demolished. As will most of the land you see here.'

Sonny's face expressed the bewilderment both he and Ren felt. 'You can't go and blow it up. Tell him, Ren.'

'It *will* be demolished,' the workman interrupted. 'And it's a good thing too. You boys shouldn't be swimming anywhere along this section of river. The water here is contaminated.'

'No, it's not,' Sonny protested. 'We swim here all the time and we've never been contaminated.'

The man packed up his gear and rested the tripod on his shoulder. 'Oh, it is contaminated. Our scientists have tested the water along here. Whether you like it or not, you won't be swimming here for much longer. All of this land, all that you can see, will be bulldozed and built over within the next three years.'

He studied the boys a little closer, their muddy faces, scrawny hair and Sonny's prehistoric bike. 'I don't know how it happened, but somehow the world has passed this place by. These old tracks and pathways don't appear on any of our survey maps. This whole area has been a dumping ground for too long. The job has come to us to clean it up and prepare it for the future.'

He turned his back on the boys and walked away, whistling as he went.

Sonny leaned over the handlebars of his bike. 'Can it be true, what he said?'

'Course not. Nobody can blow up the river. He's a smart-arse.'

'He looked like a smart-arse, alright. And did you hear the big word he used? *Accordingly*. Only a smart-arse would use a word like that.' Sonny defiantly spat on the ground. 'Nobody's touching our river.'

Sonny dinked Ren along the track, passing the falls, the wheelhouse and the pontoon. The sun had fallen behind the cotton mill. It left a sawtooth shadow across the river, biting it in half. Ren could smell the campfire ahead and saw someone moving about under the bridge.

'We should tell Tex about the road, Sonny. If the bulldozers are going to come through here they'll be thrown off their camp again.'

Tex was resting in an old car seat. He was mumbling to Tallboy and sharing a drink. Big Tiny and Cold Can were curled up in the humpy, and the Doc was resting on his haunches over the fire, warming his hands. Tex shielded his eyes with one hand. He had trouble seeing anything at all from a distance.

'Who are yas?' he called, as the boys rode towards him.

'Cool Hand Luke,' Sonny called out. 'Shaking it here, boss.'

'Ya can fuck off then. I don't know any Luke.'

The boys jumped off the bike and let it fall to the dirt. Tex pointed a finger at Ren. 'And you'd be?'

'Come on, Tex. You know who I am.'

'Is the bird,' Tallboy shouted across the fire. 'Young Wren and the Sonny Boy.'

'Oh! Good then. Me own outlaws. Be good to me and fetch some wood for the fire,' he said. 'Old Cold Can's hit it hard today and gone useless on me. Can't hold his drink no more, that one.'

The boys ran around the campsite and along the riverbank picking up dead branches and short logs until they'd built a decent pile of wood next to the fire.

'You after any food?' Ren asked.

Tallboy pulled a tin of baked beans and two potatoes out of one coat pocket and a large can of beer from the other.

'You're some magician,' Ren said. 'You got a rabbit in there?'

'Might have.' Tallboy grinned, showing off a pair of black pegs that passed for his front teeth.

Sonny loaded the fire with wood and Ren dropped the potatoes in the coals. He also helped Tallboy out, piercing a hole in the baked-bean tin with a rusted screwdriver.

'You want me to open your beer for you too, Tallboy?'

'No need for that, Wren. A feed comes first. Then me and old Tex here will kick on.'

Ren kneeled next to Tex's car seat and told him about the surveyor and the plans he'd talked about. 'He said some of the river will be blown up to build a road here. He called it a freeway.'

Tex shook his head furiously from side to side and slammed a fist into his open hand. 'What the fuck is a freeway, Tallboy?'

'Oh, it's a big wide road and the cars drive real fast on it. I seen one of them up north one time. Frightening, it was.'

Cold Can woke, stood up and staggered over to the fire. With Tallboy's help Tex got to his feet. He tugged Ren by the sleeve of his shirt and waved Sonny over to him. 'Two of you. Outlaws. Fight's coming and Tex needs you to be ready.'

He rested a palm on Ren's head just as he'd done the first day they met. He lay the other hand on Sonny's shoulder. 'The river. Now, she needs you most of all. Tex's time is nearly up and there's nothin I can do. That's all I can say. Are you ready to help me?'

Ren didn't know what to say. He loved the river, but didn't know what he could do to stop any change that might be coming.

'I'll stop em,' Sonny said.

'Good boy,' Tex said. 'You got some mongrel in ya, Sonny. I like that.'

Big Tiny stuck his head out of the humpy. 'Neither of them can do bugger all.'

Tex picked up the end of a fiery log from the fire and threw it in Tiny's direction. The log landed in front of the humpy and sparked to life.

'Shut your mouth. Ya done nothing for this river. Anytime. She don't forget. Don't you be having an accident and fall in. Ya do, Tiny, and she'll thieve the last breath from your body.'

Tiny backed into the humpy, fearful of Tex's words.

The boys said goodbye and headed for home. Although the air was warm Ren shivered as he neared the wheelhouse, sure he could hear a tangle of snakes slithering in the cellar water. They dragged the bike up the track between them, reached the top, then turned and looked down at the campfire smoke-signals rising in the air. Ren looked further on to Deep Rock. He couldn't make sense of the idea that someone would want to destroy the river just so people could go for a ride in a car.

'Last smoke,' Sonny called. 'Pass the tobacco.' He fixed his eyes on the water the whole time he rolled his cigarette. 'They can't do it. Blow it up. There must be a law to stop them doing something like that.'

'Maybe they can. One of my aunties used to live in a house she and my uncle paid money for. They owned it. Never stopped the government coming along and taking the house away from them. Knocked it over with all the other houses in the street.'

Sonny stuck his head between his knees and took a deep breath. 'This is our place. We can't let them do it.' He passed the cigarette to Ren. It was perfectly rolled.

Ren looked up at the sky and watched as a hawk lifted from one of the girders of the iron bridge. It swooped down and glided along the river, its wings tipping the surface of the water. The bird suddenly dipped its beak and plucked something out of the water. Ren couldn't be certain from such a distance, but it looked like the bird had a rat in its mouth. The hawk flew into the sky and hung over the river before turning and flying back to the bridge.

Ren left Sonny at the back gate and sat sulking in the backyard toilet, thinking about the damage that might be done to the river. A little while later he heard the sounds of digging in the lane. Except for stray dogs nobody used it but him and Sonny. He went into the yard and opened the back gate. Della was scraping mud along the lane with a shovel and tipping the mess into a rubbish bin. She was without her scarf and her hair hung across her face.

Ren was surprised when she looked up at him and smiled. 'My father doesn't want the bad smell entering our church. We will begin services soon.'

'Services?'

'Yes. We have been sent here by the Messenger to hold the Gatherings.'

'From where? Your father, he sounds like an American. You too, sort of.'

'Oh, we've been there, to the United States. My father trained there, with the Messenger himself. When the time came for my father to be tested, and he passed the test, he was sent to mission. We've been to many places across the world, my father speaking His word. And now, he has been called here to save.'

'To Collingwood? Good luck to you. People are too far gone to be saved round here. What was the test your father passed?'

'A test of pain.'

'Like what?'

'Another follower held one of my father's hands on a wooden table and stood a nail on it. We watched as my father drove the nail through his hand with a hammer.'

Della spoke the words with no more drama than if she were telling Ren how to thread needle and cotton. He was sure the story couldn't be true, but was polite enough to say nothing. He watched as Della collected a shovelful of muck. 'It's dog shit,' he offered, which wasn't really necessary, he thought, as soon as he had made the comment, seeing as Della was the one shovelling it. 'It's dumped mostly, out of the backyards.'

Della didn't seem interested in Ren providing her with the history of local dog shit. She tucked her fringe behind her ears, grabbed hold of a broom leaning against the stable wall

69

and began sweeping. Ren couldn't think of anything better to do so he grabbed the shovel and worked the shit and mud towards the broom. Della swept muck onto the shovel and he tipped it into the bin. It wasn't long before the section of lane behind the stable had been swept clean.

'I saw you, just now, coming across the road from behind the factory wall, with your friend. I've seen you coming from there before. Where do you go?'

Her eyes blinked a little nervously, as they'd done when Ren first saw her in the stable. He was caught off-guard and wasn't sure what to say.

'Where do we go?'

'You don't have to tell me, if you don't want. I'm sorry for being curious. My father tells me that curiosity leads to sin.'

'I must be a big sinner myself,' Ren said. 'I'm always curious. My mum reckons it's a good thing.'

Della raised a corner of her mouth. Ren was pleased. It wasn't quite a smile, he thought, but he'd get one out of her soon enough.

'We go to the river, down behind the mill.'

Her eyes lit up. 'There's a river close by?'

Before he knew it, Ren was sharing stories of the river with Della. 'It's a secret river, almost. Sonny and me are the only ones who use it. Except for the river men. They've been down there longer than anybody. There's wild cats and foxes and bats, and a waterfall. If you open your window of a night and you shut your eyes, you can hear it, the water coming over the falls and crashing into the rocks.'

'I have heard the noise. I'd like to see it.'

Ren wasn't sure what to say. Talking about the river was one thing. Showing Della the path to the waterfall would be something else. He was certain that Sonny wouldn't like it at all.

'Della!'

Reverend Beck was standing at the rear gate of the stable. He looked down at the cleared lane and back up at his daughter. The look on his face cut her in half.

'Collect the bin, empty it in the garden and dig it into the earth.'

Della picked up the bin and shovel without looking at Ren. Her father stood to the side and she disappeared into the yard. She'd left the broom leaning against the stable wall. Ren picked it up and offered it to the Reverend. 'This is yours.'

The Reverend Beck snatched the broom from him. As he did so Ren noticed a clean rounded scar on the back of his left hand. The Reverend snapped the broom handle across his knee and threw it to the ground.

'Remain clear of my daughter.'

Ren wanted to run but couldn't move, he was so frightened. The Reverend fixed an eye on him until Ren turned away. When he looked back the man was gone.

CHAPTER 5

The new school year started with a heatwave. Straight after last bell Sonny would run to the bike shed and dink Ren to the river for a swim. Afterwards, he would lay on the pontoon and wish he wasn't in school at all. It took only weeks for his wish to be granted. While he had only himself to blame for much of the trouble he found himself in, the science and chemistry teacher, Mr Crooke, took aim at Sonny every chance he got, whether the boy deserved the attention or not. On the first day of term Crooke separated Ren and Sonny, and ordered Sonny to sit at the front of the room, directly below his own desk on the platform. Each time he asked a question that couldn't be answered by anyone in the class, Crooke would single out Sonny. The more he focused on him, the more agitated the boy became, returning the teacher's bullying behaviour with a snarl.

The term was only two weeks old when Sonny reached boiling point. He complained to Ren as he rode with him to school in the morning. 'We got science first up?'

'You know we do.'

'I fucken hate that Crooke. Why's he always picking on me?'

'Because you stand up to him and he doesn't like it. None of the teachers like it when you do that. You need to learn to keep your head down.'

'Well, fuck that. I'm not a coward.'

'Nothing about being a coward. Archie says that pulling your head in is all about being sensible when you need to.'

'And fuck that too.'

'Please yourself, Sonny, but it's not gonna get Crooke off your back.'

By the time first bell rang out across the schoolyard Sonny was angry enough to be clenching and unclenching his fists and slamming them into his thighs. Before the boys could take their seats in class, Crooke was already getting stuck into them. 'Shut up the lot of you.'

The room groaned when he announced a closed book chemistry test. The first few questions were answered easily enough. He then asked for an answer to 'the molecular structure of sulfuric acid'. The classroom went quiet as bodies shifted nervously and wooden desks anxiously creaked. Several boys looked out of the window into the asphalt and treeless schoolyard, hoping to avoid the teacher's gaze. Crooke stood up from his desk, walked around to the front of it and looked down at Sonny.

'Brewer, I hope that you are alert enough this morning to enlighten the class with the breadth of your knowledge on the subject of chemistry. Would you please provide the class with the answer?'

Some of the boys sniggered with relief, until Sonny turned to see who was laughing at him and they fell silent. Crooke stepped down from the platform and stood over Sonny's desk.

'Look at me when I am talking to you. The answer? Speak up now.'

Sonny refused to look at him. Crooke reached out and grabbed hold of him with both hands, by his school jumper. A few of the boys in the room gasped. Sonny looked down at the teacher's hands. Crooke addressed the class as he pulled Sonny towards him. 'Do you know what we have here? A stupid boy. Brewer is a stupid, stupid boy, who knows only trouble.'

Sonny turned his head towards Ren, seated in the third row, and winked at him with his good eye. Before Crooke knew what was happening, Sonny managed to slam the heel of his fist under the teacher's jaw, leaped onto the desk and tumbled over the top of it, onto Crooke. Boys in the front rows stood up from their desks. They were afraid to move any further. Except for Ren. He got up from his desk and paced the aisle, watching as Sonny threw windmill punches at Crooke. All the teacher could do to protect himself was cover his head with his hands. Hearing the commotion, the woodwork teacher from the classroom opposite, Mr Hearn, burst into the room and tore Sonny away from Crooke. He dragged Sonny into the corridor.

Mr Hearn was one of the few reasonable teachers at the school. He had a soft spot for Sonny and was prepared to speak up for him to the headmaster that day. Ren was also called to the office. He sat in the corridor and listened as Mr Hearn complained that Crooke had been provoking Sonny. 'He's been giving him a hard time for weeks. The man is a sadist.'

The teacher's testimony wasn't enough to save Sonny. He was expelled the same day and a letter was delivered home to his father by one of the prefects.

At lunchtime, Ren saw Sonny walking across the schoolyard with his bag over his shoulder. He ran and caught up with him at the bike shed.

'Where you going?'

'Home.'

'Early?'

Sonny threw the bag over the handlebars of the bike and hopped on. 'Nah. For good. I've been chucked out.'

'Shit! What will you do? Your father will ...'

'You don't need to say it, Ren. My old man is going to skin me. Then he'll kill me, if I'm not dead already.'

'This is bullshit, Sonny. And it's not fair. Crooke started on you because you couldn't answer the chemistry question. No one in the room knew the fucken answer.'

'H_2SO_4.'

'What?'

'The answer to the chemistry question is H_2SO_4.'

'You knew it all along?'

'I did. Can hardly believe it. Maybe the first time ever I knew the answer. Don't know why, but it stuck in my head from last week.'

'Why didn't you tell him then? It would have saved you from all this trouble.'

'Nah. He would have kept going until he got me for something else. This was always gonna happen, Ren. I'm glad it's over and done with.'

'But your dad?'

'He'd find something else to whack me for as well.' Sonny smiled, as if he wasn't bothered at all. He slammed his foot on the bike pedal and hoisted his bag onto his back. 'Fuck Crooke. And fuck this school.'

Loretta Renwick, while never a gossip herself, had a habit of picking up news of importance to her. The following night she asked Ren to help her with the washing up. The only time Loretta asked her son to help clear up was when there was something serious she needed to talk with him about. They washed and dried the dishes in silence. Loretta wiped the kitchen table, set a fresh tablecloth and asked Ren to sit down with her.

'What happened to Sonny? I hear he's been expelled.'

Ren told her about the incident in the classroom. 'Crooke wasn't going to stop picking on him until Sonny went for him.'

'So, you think it's okay for a boy to hit a teacher?'

Ren did think it was okay. Standing behind Sonny as he punched the teacher about the head, Ren didn't want him to stop.

'I don't know.' He shrugged. 'Dunno what else he could do.'

'You planning on spending time with him now that he's out of school?'

Ren wiped his nose on his sleeve. 'He's my best friend.'

She pulled at the sleeve. 'Don't do that, you grub.' She leaned across the table and took Ren's hands in hers. 'Do you really believe Sonny can stay out of trouble? The way he's going, it could be the lock-up next.'

Ren looked down at his feet, swinging back and forth under the chair. His only thought, at that moment, was that if Sonny could stay out of trouble he could also fly to Mars. 'Crooke's been riding Sonny since he started at the school. He was bullying him in front of the class and Sonny'd had enough.'

Loretta stuck a finger under her son's chin and lifted his face until they met, eye to eye. 'Why didn't he go to someone and talk about it?'

'Because there's no one to go to. The headmaster's as bad as Crooke. So's his dad. None of this is fair on him.'

'Maybe not. But I can't help it. I have no say in what Sonny gets up to but I have to answer for you, Charlie. Archie too. We're responsible. I heard a racket in there last night. What went on?'

'His dad was waiting with the letter in his hand, from the school. He gave Sonny a belting, buckle out.'

'How long's the father been hitting him?'

'He's always hit him. Before they come and lived here. He blames Sonny for his mother running off.'

'Rubbish. A man can't blame a child for his own misery. And that one's as miserable as they come. And he drinks too much.'

Loretta stood up from the table. 'I won't stop you seeing him. For now. You'd only go behind my back anyway. But you find yourself in trouble, Charlie, it will be over. No Sonny. And no river.'

Ren found Sonny the next day sitting on the backyard step in the lane. He was a mess. He had a swollen face and a dark bruise on his neck where, he told Ren, his father had choked him. After he'd beaten Sonny he told him that he had a week to find a job or cop another belting and be put on the street to look after himself any way he could.

'What are you gonna do?'

'Don't know. Go round to some factories and ask if they have any jobs.'

Sonny didn't pick up a factory job, but with a day left on a ticking bomb he got lucky for maybe the first time in his life when he saw an ad in the newspaper shop window, for a paperboy. He went inside and was offered the job after a talk with the owner, Brixey Booth. The man was a walking repository of news and local history. He knew who Sonny was the moment he walked into the shop. Brixey had come up through the same streets the boys lived on. He wore a deceptively owl-like face behind a pair of rounded glasses. If anyone were to see him in the early hours of the morning, stripped naked in front of his shaving mirror readying himself for a day's work, they would have noticed the untidy scars across his body, war wounds from his younger days when he'd been not such a soft man.

Brixey possessed the uncanny ability to read people and saw something in Sonny that most missed. He chanced his judgement on the boy and gave him the job. Ren walked to the paper shop with Sonny the next morning when he went to collect his locker key and leather money pouch. Ren recognised one of the other paper boys, sitting atop a pile of magazines reading a comic. It was Spike, a kid who'd gone to the same school as Ren and dropped out a couple of years earlier. The best compliment anyone paid Spike was that he was *slow*. He'd had an accident when he was younger, falling from the roof of a factory he was trying to break into. Spike had been knocked unconscious, fractured his skull and spent six weeks in a coma.

Brixey handed the leather money pouch and belt to Sonny with advice and a warning. 'You know last night the wife said to me that maybe I'm a soft touch for taking you on.' He looked across the shop at Spike. 'I have a habit of collecting no-hopers, she says.' He knocked on the top of the shop counter with a pencil to get Sonny's full attention. 'She best be wrong. For both our sakes.'

He then handed Sonny his locker key. 'Listen to me, kid. I was around your age when a bloke give me a job, jockey on the ice truck. Heavy work for a boy my size.' He grabbed hold of a fist-full of gut fat. 'Believe it or not, I was as skinny as you in those days. You know what the boss said to me the first day on the job? *Fuck up youngster and you'll be gone in a flash.* So don't be offended. But I have an investment here and I need to give you the same advice. You fuck this up and you'll be out of here faster than a champion greyhound needled on fizz.

'You got that? All of it?'

'I got it.'

'By the way, you got a pushbike of your own?'

'Sort of. I mean, yep.'

'Good. Never know when you have to get somewhere in a hurry. You do good and I'll give you the afternoon newsstand under the rail bridge at the bottom of the ramp at the station. Be here at six on the button tomorrow morning and I'll have Spike take you through the round. Follow his lead real close because the next morning you'll have to get around on your own.'

Sonny looked across at Spike, studying his comic book. It was left to Brixey to reassure him.

'Yeah, I know. He's got a metal plate in his head. But he also happens to be a walking street directory. Young Spike knows every back street across the concrete jungle. By heart.'

The job was a godsend for Sonny. With tips he made near the same money he would have in a noisy factory or hosing down coal dust at the railyards. And he saved, hiding his pay packet away so his father couldn't get hold of it and gamble it away. Or spend it on the drink. Within a month, as Brixey promised, he also took charge of the afternoon newsstand at the railway station.

Ren missed Sonny's company at school and began hanging out at the newsstand with him. He helped out by delivering the afternoon papers to the stationmaster and shopkeepers along the arcade at the station. After dropping the papers at the bookmakers and the dry-cleaners, Ren would stop at the pawnshop and pore over the secondhand cameras in the front window.

'You must really want one of em?' Sonny said one afternoon. 'You spend all your spare time looking at them.'

'Don't matter what I want. They're too expensive for me. Even the secondhand ones.'

'You could do a smash and grab.'

'Yeah, and have my own photo taken at the lock-up. Only way to get one of them cameras is to save for it. I don't even have a job.'

Sonny thought about what Ren had said and the next day put an offer to him. 'How'd you like to become a sub-contractor?'

'What's that mean?'

'Means a job. I work for Brixey and you come and work for me of a morning on the paper round. I pay you from my wage and you save up for one of them expensive cameras.'

'How much would you pay me?'

'Fifty cents a morning, times six. Three dollars a week.'

It was better money than Ren would have expected. The offer appealed to him. 'I'll have to ask my mum if it's okay.'

That night Ren lay on his bed looking across at the photograph of the majestic bird on the back of his door. He could hear the TV in the room below. Loretta and Archie were watching the nightly news. They never missed it. Ren couldn't stop thinking about a camera. He wrote some figures in his sketch book and calculated how much he'd save from what Sonny was willing to pay him. As soon as he heard the music from the TV announcing the end of the news he took the photograph off the back of the door and marched downstairs with it. Loretta was changing the channel and Archie had his head in the newspaper. Ren lay the photograph on the coffee table, sat next to Archie on the couch and coughed to get his attention.

Archie looked over the top of his paper at the bird. 'An eagle. A beautiful bird, that one.'

'It's a wedge-tail. It's taken with a special camera, isn't it, Mum?' Ren said, looking to Loretta for support.

She glanced from the TV to the photograph and up at her son, wondering where he was heading with the conversation.

'I seen some cameras in the shop at the train station,' Ren explained to Archie. 'I'm going to save up and buy one.'

'But you don't have any money to save,' Archie said.

'A photograph like this one would need a decent camera. And it would cost a packet. Then there's money for film and developing. How would you save money for that?'

'With a job,' Ren answered.

He told them about his plan to work with Sonny on the morning paper round. Loretta turned the volume down on the TV.

'I don't know, Charlie. How you going to get out of bed so early in the morning?'

'Sonny'll wake me. He's got an alarm clock. He's been getting up early for a month now. At five-thirty.'

'But it's dark out that early.'

'Not for long,' Ren countered.

Archie picked up the photograph from the table and studied the bird. 'You really think you could take a photograph like this one?'

'One day. I've been looking in the library next to the town hall. They have books on birds and others that are all about cameras. I could teach myself.'

'Books.' Archie laughed. 'You mean you're looking at books that aren't for tests at school, for your own interest?'

'Yep. I borrowed one. A book about birds that move from one part of the world to the other. Every year. Some of them come all the way here from above Russia. And other places.'

'Loretta?' Archie asked.

While she knew it was her decision that counted most, Loretta could see that Ren's enthusiasm had already won Archie over. 'Sonny's behaving himself?'

'Yep. He works in the morning and afternoon and is saving up too. That's what gave me the idea.'

'I let you do this, you save every cent. No wasting money on lollies and comics.'

'Every cent.'

The next morning it was raining. Sonny hopped out of his window, crossed over the roof and knocked at Ren's bedroom window. When he couldn't wake him, he opened the window, jumped into the room and tore the blankets from Ren's bed. Ren rubbed the sleep from his eyes with the sleeve of his pyjama top and looked up at Sonny. He was soaked through.

'You wash with your clothes on?'

'It's pissing down. You try walking across a roof in the rain without getting wet. Come on, we have to go. You wanna work for me, Ren, you can't be late. Or I'll get my arse kicked off Brixey. Meet you out the front.'

Ren dressed, went downstairs and grabbed two rolls from the bread-bin, which the boys ate as they rode through the streets in the rain. At the shop they swapped the bike for an old pram. Sonny loaded it with the morning papers and magazines and covered the pram with a plastic sheet. He picked up an elastic band and flicked it at Ren, stinging his neck.

'Sonny!' Brixey called. 'If you want your mate helping you out here, don't be fucking around.'

'I won't.'

He handed Sonny a raincoat. 'Take this.'

One raincoat between the two of them wouldn't be much help keeping them dry. It was fortunate that, as they were delivering the first papers, the rain eased to a drizzle, and had stopped completely by the time they got round the first block.

The early morning streets were dead quiet except for passing trains, the tinkling of Mick O'Reagan's milk bottles and the clip-clopping shoes of his sturdy horse, Tim, hitting the bitumen. During the first week of the paper round Sonny had been stealing milk from the back of the milk cart, until Mick caught him tearing the foil cap off a bottle. Rather than clip him behind the ears he offered Sonny an exchange, the morning paper for a half-pint of milk. A fair deal, Sonny reasoned. As he drank from the milk bottle he asked Mick why he was still using a horse when most other milkmen drove round in vans.

Mick patted the horse along the mane as he answered. 'I been with this old fella for ten years, and was the last milky left using a horse a year back when they offered me one of them electric trucks that make no noise. I was about to change over. Then my eldest boy, Daniel, he'd been grooming that horse in the milk yard since he was younger than you, he got conscripted. Last thing he said to me before he got on the bus to start his Army training was *look after Timmy for me*. And that's what I'm gonna do. Look after this boy until he gets back.'

'What's conscripted?' Sonny asked.

'For that war in Vietnam.'

Sonny barely understood what Mick was talking about. He'd seen images on the TV, of the war, but had paid little attention. 'Why'd they pick him to go to war? Your son?'

Mick looked into the horse's eyes, as if searching for an answer. 'Part of it's luck, like playing the lottery. His number come up and he never got a prize. And part of it is because he's a milkman's son and not a politician's.'

★

'I got to tell you, Ren,' Sonny said, as they took it in turns pushing the pram through the streets, 'you see some weird stuff round the time the sun's up.'

'What sort of stuff?'

'Keep your eyes open. It won't take long.'

They were walking up the hill behind the Catholic Church when a woman coming from the opposite direction limped towards them. She was wearing a pink dressing gown, slippers and a white turban on her head. She had a smoke in her mouth and was carrying a cage with two small birds inside. Zebra finches.

The woman blocked Sonny's pathway and jabbed a pair of nicotined fingers in the direction of the pram. 'You got my *Women's Weekly*?'

Sonny lifted the newspapers and pulled out a copy of a magazine he'd hidden earlier. 'It come in this morning, Vera.'

She rested the birdcage on the ground and stuck a hand in her dressing gown pocket, like she was going for her purse, Ren thought, watching her. She pulled out a packet of cigarettes, took three smokes out and handed them to Sonny. He put one in his mouth and the other two in his shirt pocket. Vera took a silver lighter out of the other dressing gown pocket and lit Sonny's cigarette for him.

'There you go, lovely boy. Have a good suck on that.'

'Ta. What about my best mate here? He likes his smokes.'

'I just give you three, you cheeky bugga. If he's your mate you can look after him yourself.'

'One *Women's Weekly* equals three cigarettes, Vera. I can't be sharing on that. I give him one and I've only got one left. Maybe he can do you a favour?'

Vera looked Ren up and down. 'You're only a little fella, aren't you? Poor urchin. They forget to feed you in the orphanage or something? What do they call you?'

'Ren.'

'Wren. A beautiful bird that one.' She picked up the cage, brought it to her face and tried making bird sounds, which wasn't easy with a cigarette hanging from her mouth. She blew smoke over the finches. 'Look at this boy,' she said to the birds. 'Here's another birdie for you, lovelies. He's a wren. Hold on to this for me.' She handed Ren the cage, opened the packet and silently counted the number of cigarettes she had left. She took a cigarette and handed it to Ren along with the lighter, in exchange for the bird cage. She watched closely as he lit up and took a decent drag.

'Now, nothing's free in this world. You remember that, lovely boy. That ciggie I just give you is all about incentive. You want a big smoke from Vera, you got to work for it. You bring me a magazine, like my number one paper boy here, and I'll take care of you.'

She reached across the pram and tried stroking Sonny's face. He pulled away from her.

'I love my *TV Week*,' she said, turning back to Ren. 'You bring me that one.'

She stuck a hand on the back of his neck, pulled him into her body, took the cigarette out of her mouth and slopped a wet smoky kiss on his lips. Ren wouldn't have admitted it to anyone, even Sonny, but he felt his dick jump in his pants.

'Don't you forget. One magazine a week and I'll look after you.' She winked and laughed out loud, then turned around and headed back up the hill, chatting to her birds.

'She's mad,' Ren said.

'You're telling me. First time I give her the *Weekly* she stuck her hand down the front of my pants and squeezed my balls.'

'What did you do?'

'Told her it would cost her more than three cigarettes if she wanted to be doing something like that.'

'What did she say?'

'Nothing. But the next morning she gave me a packet of Viscount twenties. Unopened.'

'What did you have to do for them?'

'Can't say. You'll get jealous.'

'How old is she?'

'Old old. Maybe thirty.'

'And you let her play with your dick?'

'Didn't you hear me? A full pack of Viscount.'

'Why's she carrying the birds round with her?'

'They need the fresh air, she says.'

'She shouldn't be smoking round them, then.'

The last delivery of a morning was to Stumpy's place. Sonny knocked at the door of a house on a dead-end street by the railway line.

'Put your ear to the door and listen for the noise.'

Ren heard a low rumble in the distance, a sound that appeared to be coming from miles off. If he didn't know better he would have said it was a train. The noise grew louder until it came to a halt on the other side of the door.

'He's here,' Sonny whispered.

'Who?'

The door opened with a creak. Ren looked down at a man around the same age as his stepdad, Archie. He was kneeling on a wooden trolley and the knuckles on his hands had thick yellow calluses on them. Ren looked closer. He wasn't kneeling at all. The man had no legs.

Sonny handed the man the morning newspaper.

'There you go, Stump. This is my mate, Ren. He'll be helping me out from now on. You need anything from the shops this morning? I could call by later on.'

Stumpy didn't give Ren a second look and never bothered with Sonny's question.

'Okay, Stump. Tomorrow then.'

Stumpy shut the door on them. Ren listened again, to the fading sounds of the cart.

'What happened to his legs?' he asked, as they walked the empty pram back to the shop.

'It's a long story, that one.'

'I've never seen him up the street. Wouldn't miss someone getting along on a cart.'

'He don't go up the street. Says he don't want people seeing him that way, without any legs. He does some work in his garden, crawling round on what's left of his legs. Nobody goes to the house except a woman from the church who drops off his food and does some cleaning and pays his bills.'

'Why don't he get some artificial legs so he can get about?'

'He did have wooden legs one time, when his mother was around. Stumpy liked a drink and would put his legs on and get out to the pub. He'd finish up so pissed he'd fall off them on the way home. Sometimes the cops would give him a ride home. But if no one come across him he'd stay in the gutter until his mum come and found him. In the end she got jack of it. One night, after he went to bed, she threw the legs on the fire and burned them to ash. The next morning she told him he wouldn't be going up the pub any longer. Laughed at him, Stumpy told me.'

'Does she live at the house with him?'

'Nah. She died a few years back.'

'He could get himself some new legs. From the hospital.'

'Yeah, I know. But he says he can't be bothered.'

'Where'd you hear this?'

'He told me himself. Stumpy gets lonely and likes to talk. When he gets used to you, you won't be able to shut him up.'

The boys reached the intersection a block away from the paper shop. They waited at the red light to cross the street. A car pulled in to the kerb, an old blue Mercedes, highly polished and not a scratch on it. The young driver hit the horn and an older silver-headed man came out from a curtained shop front. He got into the passenger seat of the car. As the car crawled to the intersection, the man wound down his window and called Sonny over to the car.

'You have paper?'

Sonny handed him a newspaper. The man offered him a twenty-cent coin, double the price of the paper.

'Keep the change.' He smiled, and ordered the young driver to take off.

The building the man had come out of had originally been a fruit shop. After it had shut down, the blinds were drawn on the windows. Men came and went from the building day and night, although they never seemed to buy anything.

'What's that place?' Ren asked.

'The Greek club.'

'What do they do inside?'

'They run a card game. And the radio's turned up loud on race days. An SP on the horses, I guess.'

'You sell papers in there?'

'Never stepped foot in the place. That bloke who just got in the car, just now is the first time he's bought a paper from me. Usually sends a kid down to the shop of an afternoon for his paper.'

Sonny's job kept him so busy Ren was soon helping him out at the newsstand as well. At the end of the school day Ren would race home, drop his bag in his room and head down to the station. Passing by the Reverend's house he'd often find Della sitting on the front verandah reading from a book. It looked just like the Bible the Reverend had held in his hand in the stable. Her mother would be sitting nearby, also reading, and there was no chance for Sonny to talk to her, which he'd been desperate to do since the day they'd spoken in the lane.

From the day Sonny started his job he developed a work ethic that hardly seemed possible. He even lectured Ren on the best approach to selling newspapers.

'You will need to be here when it's busiest, so you have to come straight after school. And it's important that you learn to smile at the customers. That helps a lot, specially with the women buying magazines. He held up the latest copy of *Woman's Day*, with a picture of Elizabeth Taylor on the front.

'Brixey's been doing this for most of his life and he told me that hard work is number one in the newspaper business.

Manners is number two, and a smile is close third. People are buggered after a day's work. The last face they want to see on their way home is one that looks like a smacked arse, Brixey says. And it's the best way to make tips.'

'How much you earn on tips?'

'Depends on the night. Thursdays, pay-night, is best, followed by Friday when people are out on the street. Early in the week it's not so good, especially in the pub. Most of the drinkers are near broke, and a tip would cut them out of a beer. If the *Truth* didn't come out on Tuesdays it wouldn't be worth showing up. It's dead.'

The boys played handball against the wall under the rail bridge while they waited for the trains to pull in to the station. When one arrived they worked fast, selling the afternoon *Herald* and magazines to the workers pouring from the trains. The *Truth* newspaper, which came out twice a week, was a bestseller. It carried pictures of topless women and stories of girls who'd been caught by police in the back of a car or a telephone box, sometimes naked with an older boy. The stories were not all that different from each other. All that changed were the names and locations. It didn't matter that none of the stories were actually true. They were read religiously.

Ren would recite the stories aloud to Sonny as he sat on a stack of newspapers, smoking a cigarette and nodding his head up and down like he knew what was coming next. Ren had only started reading a story about a *Fourteen-year-old topless girl discovered in wardrobe* when Sonny interrupted him.

'I bet a dollar she comes from St Kilda.'

'It don't say that here. There's no address with this one. It says her name's Ursula. That can't be a real name.'

'Don't matter if it says where she comes from or not. I bet she's from St Kilda. Things are different on the other side of the river. You been over that way?'

'Nah. You?'

'Nup. Maybe we could go sometime? You can catch a tram to the beach. And to Luna Park. It's over that side of the city too. I heard they have river boats and caves at Luna Park.'

'A real river?'

'No, a fake one.'

'We don't have to go then. We got our own river.'

Ren also helped out by dropping a bundle of newspapers on the front bar of the pub next door to the station, The Railway Hotel. On the way back to the paper shop they'd call into the pub, collect the takings and any leftover papers. The barman, Roy, would shout them a lemon squash each, and sometimes a packet of chips between them.

The first time he went into the pub Ren couldn't take his eyes off a group of men, sitting around a table in the corner of the room. The light above the table was out, making it difficult to see their faces through the haze of smoke. Ren soon worked out that the seating arrangements around the table never changed. The same man always faced the double saloon doors that opened into the street, and whenever the doors swung open he'd look up while the other men went on talking and drinking. He had his hair in a pony-tail, a moustache and a goatee, and wore a suit coat like he was off to a court case. Sitting opposite him, with his back to the room, sat a man wearing a similar coat, except his jacket was too tight for his heavy shoulders. He had no neck and an ugly purple scar, the shape of a half circle, in the back of his shaven head.

The barman would regularly load a tray of drinks and take it over to the table without the men having to ask for them.

After the boys had left the pub one night Sonny grabbed Ren by the arm to stop him from walking on. He poked him in the chest as he yelled at him. 'Don't be looking over at the table like that.'

'Like what? I weren't looking at no one.'

'Bullshit. You gawk every time we go in there. You want your throat cut, keep staring.'

'Throat cut?'

Sonny squeezed Ren's bicep, tight. It hurt.

'This is serious. You go looking at that table too long and one of them will pop your eyes out of your head and stomp on them.'

Ren squeezed his eyes tightly together just thinking about it. 'How do you know so much about them?'

'The other paperboys. They hear stuff all the time. That's a gang round that table.'

'The big one, with the mark on the back of his head, is he the boss?'

'Nah. It's not him. He's the bodyguard. Wide enough to take a bullet. That would be his job. Number one is the fella with the long greasy hair. I was in there last week picking up the papers when two men come in. Every head in the bar turned round like in a Western movie, when the gunslinger comes to town and crashes the saloon. I looked over to the table. The one with the big head stood up and spun round. Wouldn't have believed he could move as fast as that. He stuck his hand in his jacket pocket. Ready to go for his gun, I reckon.'

'What happened?'

'Nothing. Turned out they were only the health inspectors. Went back in the kitchen, snooped round a bit and come out. Roy opened the till, give them their sling and they left. Everyone went back to their drinks like nothing had happened.'

'The boss, the one facing the door, who's he?'

'Vincent.'

'Vincent who?'

'Just Vincent. Every one of them at the table are killers, but Vincent is the biggest killer of all. The other paperboys whisper about him. Won't speak his name out loud.'

'Who's he supposed to have killed?'

'For one, some debt collector they found in the waiting room at the railway station last year before I moved here. Had cut his throat from ear to ear. They say that was Vincent that did it. Did you hear about that?'

Everyone knew about the bloody crime. It had been in the papers and on the news. Boys couldn't stop talking about it in the schoolyard. Nobody seemed to know who had done it and there hadn't been anyone charged over the crime. 'I remember Archie saying the reason they got no one for it is because debt collectors have so many enemies the police would have to go through the telephone book to rule out suspects.'

'Well, it was Vincent that did it.'

'Yeah? And why'd he kill him?'

'Over money is all I heard.'

'You're telling me you know he's the killer?'

'Yep.'

'And all the paperboys, they know he's the killer?'

'Yep.'

'But the police don't know? They can't be that stupid.'

'Course they know. The police always know. They would have been paid money to leave it be. They don't own the streets. The crooks do. So don't you be looking across at that table when we go into the pub or it will be your neck. And mine. Don't even speak his name.'

'*Vincent ... Vincent*,' Ren whispered, teasing Sonny.

'Stop fucking round.'

Despite Sonny's warning, Ren couldn't resist a sneaky look across at the corner table when he next went into the pub. A few nights later the boys were at the bar enjoying their free lemon squash when one of the men from Vincent's table walked over and stood between them. He had the ace of spades tattooed on the back of his right hand. The man called out for Roy, who was down in the cellar tapping a fresh barrel of beer. Ren slowly counted the newspaper takings as he looked at the man out of the corner of one eye. Roy came up from the cellar and the man took a brown envelope out of his jacket pocket and handed it across the bar.

'What time's he coming across?' Roy asked, placing the envelope under the bar.

'Due any minute,' the man answered, and walked away.

As the boys got up to leave, Ren bumped into a man coming into the pub. It was the Mercedes driver from the Greek club he'd seen on the first morning he helped out on the paper round with Sonny. The man pushed Ren to one side with an open hand. He was back out of the door a few seconds later, tucking the same brown envelope into his inside coat pocket.

'You see that?' Ren asked Sonny, once they were in the street.

'I seen nothing. And neither did you.'

'I bet there's money in that envelope.'

'We don't know what's in it, so don't be thinking about it.' He slammed the pram into Ren's knees. 'Push that for me. And learn to mind your own business.'

'Learn yourself, Sonny. Between you and the other boys at the shop you have more news to tell than is in the papers. If minding your own business was so important you wouldn't listen to them in the first place and you wouldn't have told me.'

'I was just trying to save you from trouble. Sticking your beak across the bar at them.'

'You worry about your own beak, Sonny, and I'll take care of mine.'

CHAPTER 6

The summer had officially ended but the hot days continued. No one, even old timers, remembered heat like it. The falls slowed to a trickle, and as the level of the water dropped the river gave up some of its old secrets. The skeleton frames of car wrecks reappeared, along with the footings of a pier between the bridge and the pontoon that had collapsed decades earlier. Some of the swimming holes along the river were reduced to mud, forcing Ren and Sonny into the middle of the river for a decent swim.

The heat sucked the life from the city. The streets were deserted and Ren struggled to find a bird in the sky. On Easter Saturday, Sonny sat on a pile of newspapers reading a magazine, having dragged the newsstand into the shade of the train bridge. He'd had only three customers the whole afternoon. People seemed too tired to even read the news. Only the pub did a good trade, packed with thirsty drinkers. Ren nursed a milk bottle full of water. He took a long gulp, passed it to Sonny, who took a drink of his own and handed it back. Directly across the street from where they were sitting, a narrow lane ran beside the railway tracks. Ren watched as a car drove into the lane and stopped in the middle of the road, blocking the street.

'Hey, Sonny, look at this. It's the Mercedes from the Greek club.'

The driver's side door opened and the man who'd picked up the envelope from the hotel got out, rested against the bonnet and lit a cigarette. Sonny poked Ren in the side, nodded, and whispered. 'Look, here comes Vincent.'

Vincent was walking along the footpath on the other side of the road. He was with one of his off-siders, the one who'd handed the envelope to Roy, the barman. They turned into the lane where the Mercedes was parked. As they neared the car, the front seat passenger unwound his window.

'What's happening?' Ren asked.

'Dunno.'

Vincent's mate hung back as he spoke to the man in the car, quietly at first. A few moments later the boys watched as Vincent threw his arms in the air and began shouting. The driver of the Mercedes left the bonnet and slowly walked around to the side of the car. Vincent had already turned his back on him and was walking away. The driver watched closely until Vincent had exited the lane. He got behind the wheel of the car and reversed out of the lane. Neither Sonny nor Ren spoke as Vincent walked back along the main street. He stopped on the other side of the road and looked directly at Sonny and Ren before walking back to the pub.

'What was that about?' Ren asked.

'Not sure. None of them looked happy. I know that much.'

'Maybe it's the hot weather.' Ren laughed. He poured what was left of the water over his head.

'It says here,' Sonny said, pointing to the newspaper, 'that the weather will break and it's gonna turn cold, maybe even by Monday or Tuesday.'

'Weathermen have been saying that for weeks, Sonny. They know nothing.'

'Maybe they're right this time. If they are, then tomorrow is gonna be the last hot day we get until next summer, which means our last swim. You know what we have to do, don't you, Ren?'

'No, I don't. But I'd bet a million it's one of your crazy ideas.'

'We have to jump from the Phoenix.'

The Phoenix was the highest bridge over the river. The boys had stood on the bridge many times, looking down at the water, a little fearful of even talking about what they were both thinking. They'd been on the bridge the day it was being repaired, and watched a carpenter sawing fresh planks of wood to replace the rotting ones. Sonny had asked the carpenter if he knew how high the bridge was above the water.

'Not sure, boys. Why don't we find out?' He dropped a lead weight and string line over the side of the bridge and lowered it until the weight touched the surface of the water. He marked the line and hauled it up, counting each knot in the line under his breath. 'It's sixty-two feet. Why you want to know?'

'Just wondering,' Ren answered.

The figure had stuck in Ren's head. Sometimes he thought sixty-two feet would be a suicidal jump, but on rare days he almost convinced himself that if he conquered such a jump he could turn to thinking about leaping from the cliff-top. In a story he'd written for an English class, one of the only subjects he enjoyed at school, Ren had mentioned the name of the bridge. The teacher, Miss Wills, told him that it was likely that the bridge had taken its name from a *classical legend*. Ren, who liked the teacher a lot and didn't want to disappoint her, said nothing, although the teacher was wrong. *His* bridge had been named after a factory, Phoenix Biscuits, that had been built many years earlier in the shadow of the bridge. Whenever Ren and Sonny visited the bridge they would smell the biscuits being baked in giant ovens and their stomachs would rumble with hunger pains.

The following afternoon, the boys took a short cut through the golf course and met the winding river on the other side. Ren's heart was banging away with excitement. He was in a hurry to get to the bridge before he talked himself out of the jump.

'You know with the river running low, Sonny, we have to jump from the middle of the bridge.'

'Don't be thinking too much about this, Ren. Straight in,' Sonny said.

'Straight in, but from the best spot. No landing in a couple of feet of water.'

They reached the bridge and hid their clothes and tobacco in a tree hollow. Sonny raced ahead of Ren in his underpants.

He reached the centre of the bridge and climbed over onto the wooden rail and balanced on the narrow ledge for only a second or two before he threw himself off, screaming his lungs out as if he was Tarzan. Watching from the safety rail Ren noticed that the long drop took more time than he'd expected. Sonny hit the water with a splash, surfaced quickly and waved up at Ren.

'Fucken easy!'

Ren climbed over the rail and made the mistake of looking down at the water. He froze. He'd never quit on a jump before, but then he'd never felt fear the way he did standing on that ledge. He felt as if his legs might collapse under him. If he'd been on his own he might have climbed back over the rail, but he had no choice but to jump. With Sonny screaming out, 'chicken, chicken', and clucking like a demented hen, Ren looked up to the clear blue sky, took off and fell through the air.

The mighty gum trees lining the riverbank rose above him. For a moment he was sure he was flying and that he would never touch the water. He looked down at the exact moment he shouldn't have and smashed his face against the surface. Water shot up his nostrils with a rush, his eyeballs felt like they'd exploded and the river felt like ice against his skin. As he plunged towards the bottom, a belt tightened around his lungs. His feet hit the muddy silt of the riverbed and he pushed off as best he could. Looking up, Ren scrambled towards the light, desperate for air. When his head broke the surface, except for a circle of light around the edge of a red bullseye, he couldn't see a thing. The best he could manage to do was to swim in the direction of Sonny's hooting and clapping.

Ren felt for the muddy bank with an outstretched arm.

'Jesus fuck me, Ren! You're crying blood!'

Ren wiped his eyes until he could see a little better.

'You head-butted the water.'

'Don't have to tell me.'

'And your face is battered.'

'Don't need to tell me that either. I can feel it.'

River water spewed from Ren's nose and mouth. He pushed the tips of two fingers from each hand against the swollen cheeks under his eyes. More water ran from his eyes. He could see Sonny well enough to know his friend was laughing at him.

'You think it's funny? Almost fucken killed myself.'

'But you didn't.'

Sonny seemed as happy with himself as he'd been in a long time, getting the Phoenix jump finally done. Ren may have felt the same way if it weren't for a pounding headache and a swollen face.

'Not much left for us to do, is there?' Sonny said, as they walked home across the golf course.

Ren thought about the cliff-top again but was in no state to talk about it.

Sonny filled the silence with talk about his father. 'I think he's gone right off with the grog. Not like what Tex and the others go through. I mean really fucken mental. He hasn't been to work for two weeks. He got the sack I reckon, and won't tell me. He falls asleep drunk on the couch most nights and is still there in the morning. The house is a pigsty. It won't be worth living in soon.'

'Do you have other family you could stay with?'

'Only my uncle Rory. He'd take me in, but I don't know where he is. Him and the old man had a blue about a year back.'

'What was the fight over?'

'Nothing. They don't need a reason. One minute they was drinking together and the next it was on. Ended in a swearing match in the kitchen, Rory thumping the table and my old man shaping up to him. He barred Rory from the house and I haven't seen him since.'

They left the golf course behind and were about to take the track away from the river when Ren noticed someone laying outside the wheelhouse.

'Look, Sonny. It must be one of the fellas.'

The ruin was collapsing in on itself. The cellar was home to river rats, snakes and eels that thrashed about in the oily water, making terrifying noises as they went at each other. Three levels above the cellar the wheelhouse roof had long gone. What was left of the open floor was covered in bird shit, solid as a lump of plaster and half a foot deep. The birds, perched in the open roof of a day, left the rafters around dusk, bullied by the arrival of the thousands of bats that wrapped their bodies in leather wings for the night. They hung until sun-up when they took off as one, blackening the morning sky.

The boys walked to where the body lay, curled into a tight ball, across the wheelhouse doorway. Ren recognised the burned sleeve of the Doc's suit coat. He bent forward and shook the Doc's shoulder.

'Doc. What are you doing out here?'

Sonny helped Ren turn the Doc over onto his back. He opened his eyes. They had clouded over, just like Tex's did whenever he drank metho. The Doc tried moving his mouth to say something but no words came out. His cracked lips were caked in dried blood and his breath stank of metho. Ren gave Sonny a hand sitting him up and resting the Doc against the wheelhouse door.

'You stay here with him, Sonny, and I'll find help.'

Ren sprinted along the track towards the iron bridge, calling out, 'Tex! Tex!'

Sonny wasn't sure what to do. The old man's eyes opened and closed a couple of times. The Doc reached out and took hold of Sonny's hand and gripped it tighter than Sonny thought possible for an old man in such a poor state. He gasped for air, closed his eyes, released Sonny's hand and slumped against the door. Sonny was sure there was something terribly wrong with the Doc and nervously looked over his shoulder. He could see Ren helping Tex along the track, followed by Cold Can and Tallboy.

When Tex reached the Doc he stepped forward, stooped down and gently shook him.

'Come on, old boy,' Tex urged.

The Doc collapsed onto his side, his head hitting the dirt. Ren had never seen a dead person before, but he knew straightaway the Doc was gone. Sonny must have known as well because he backed away from the body. Tex sat down in the dirt and put his arms around the Doc and cradled him against his chest. Tallboy, standing behind Cold Can, looked over his shoulder.

'What's wrong with him, Texas?'

'He's dead. Simple as that.'

Nobody moved or said a word until Tallboy lowered his

head and whispered a few words of prayer. Tex eased the Doc's body to the ground. Laying among the weeds, Ren thought he looked like a small child, with chubby sausage fingers and a fringe of white hair falling across his softened face.

'You boys best leave us be,' Tex ordered. 'We got work to do and you don't need to be witness to it. Tallboy, you go tell that fucken bludger, Tiny, to get along here and give us a help with the body.'

Tallboy couldn't get himself moving. He sniffed a couple of times, let out a breath and sobbed. With Cold Can's help Tex struggled to his feet and put an arm over Tallboy's shoulder.

'There's feeling in your heart, I know. But we got to do this. And in quick time. I'll keep old Doc company while you go and fetch Tiny for us. Need the four of us to shift him.'

'Where you moving him to?' Sonny asked, after Tallboy had taken off.

'We gonna carry him to the river. Send him off there.'

Ren wasn't sure what Tex meant. 'Do you mean put him in the water?'

'Where else would we put him?' Tex answered, with a look that implied the boy had turned stupid on him.

'The Doc will get nothing but a pauper's burial otherwise. He would want no part of that. None of us want that end. We made a promise to each other it won't happen that way.'

'What's a pauper's burial?' Sonny asked.

'We got no money for a burial in the ground. Not in our own place, anyhow. And we got no family to pay for us. No one to pray at our graves even if we could pay. Anytime one of us dies up there in the street, or the emergency, he gets put in a hole with all the rest no one wants. With the newborn babies that never made it. Saddest of all, they are. Then comes the hacked off arms and legs from the operations there in the hospital. In one big hole. Together.'

Big Tiny came waddling along the track after Tallboy. He was wheezing and coughing. He looked down at the body. 'Tallboy was telling the truth. I thought he was being tricky on me. The Doc *is* dead?'

'Dead as they come,' Tex lamented. 'Come on. Got to do this quick. Anyone comes by, police will be on us and steal the Doc away. Be no getting him back. Unless he can raise himself up.'

'Don't reckon the Doc would be up for it,' Tallboy said, as if resurrection was a real possibility. 'He believed in nothing but the drink.'

Tallboy and Cold Can got behind the Doc and wrapped an arm under each shoulder. Tex and Tiny took a leg each and they began marching along the track. Sonny and Ren followed the funeral procession, a short distance behind. The men had to stop several times to get a better grip on the body. They passed under the iron bridge and continued marching until they reached the bend on the river below the convent farm, a section of water where the current shifted suddenly from one side of the river to the other and picked up pace. With the level of the water being low the pace was gentler than usual. The men laid the Doc on the bank. Ren looked down at the body. He was a peaceful sight, as if he was sleeping.

'You want any of his stuff?' Tex asked the others. 'You, Cold Can? You'll die a death in your bag of bones come winter. He's got a warm coat on him.'

Cold Can kneeled beside the Doc and unbuttoned his suit

coat. It was covered in dirt and blackberry thorns. He stood up and put the coat on. His frail body almost vanished inside it.

'Any of you fellas want to say some words?' Tex asked the others.

To everyone's surprise Big Tiny stepped forward. He stood at the Doc's feet and looked down at him. 'You was an arsehole sometimes, old Doc. But at the same time, you was one of us.'

Tex patted Tiny on the shoulder, kneeled on the ground and dug both hands into the earth. He smeared the Doc's face with dried yellow clay and patted his cheeks. 'See ya when I join ya, old boy. That's all I have to tell ya for now.'

He looked across the water and studied the flow of the current. 'We gonna need to get him out there near the middle. The Doc will go nowhere if we can't get him moving.'

Tex ordered the others to lift the body again. The four men waded into the water until they were waist deep. Big Tiny slipped and almost went under. He got to his feet and stood his ground. They moved slowly forward until the water lapped at Tex's chest. Poor Cold Can was about to vanish when Tex ordered the men to 'send him off'.

They released the body and the Doc drifted towards the centre of the river where he was collected by a faster channel of water. It carried him away. The men, Ren and Sonny, all of them watched until the Doc slipped below the surface of the dark water. They kept their eyes on the spot he'd gone under for some time.

Tex waded out of the water and sat down in the middle of the track. 'I'm buggered.'

Sonny couldn't take his eyes off the water.

'Tex,' Ren asked, 'won't they find him anyway? The Doc's body? And take him away and bury him with the paupers anyhow?'

'Could do. But not if the river takes good care of him. The water holds the body down so them yabbies and eels can do a proper job. Eat the flesh clean off the bone, between them. Then the bones will fall to pieces and rest in the earth. The way it should be. If all goes right for old Doc, the ghost river, she'll care for him.'

'The ghost river? What's that?'

'Haven't told that one?'

Ren looked over at Sonny. He shrugged. 'Nah. You haven't told us.'

'I been teaching you about this place and I still haven't told you bout the ghost river?' Tex smiled to himself and wiped a hand across his face. 'Well, the time has come, now you seen the Doc on his way. Help me to my feet, Tallboy.'

Tallboy pulled Tex up and propped a dead tree limb under his arm for Tex to rest his body on. Tex beat an open hand on his thigh and stomped the ground. The stomping got faster, then slowed and stopped. He looked to the water, up at the sky and put his open hand on his chest and beat it several times.

'This is a story from the other time when this river she did not end where she is today. There weren't no boats for travel back then. And there weren't no bay at the end of the river. The land was full and the river was a giant. Then one time more water come and stayed. Years and years of rain. The land filled up and there was the bay that come, drowning the old river.'

He stomped the ground again. 'But she's still there, under this one. The old ghost river.' He poked the stick into the ground and drew a swirling snake. 'This is her. And when a body dies on the river, it goes on down, down, to the ghost river. Waiting. If the spirit of the dead one is true, the ghost river, she holds the body to her heart. If the spirit is no good, or weak, she spews it back. Body come up. Simple as that.'

Ren couldn't imagine that the Doc possessed a good spirit but knew it would be disrespectful to say so.

Tex was too clever for him and knew what he was thinking. 'Let me tell you one thing, boy. This one not to be forgotten. The Doc could be a bad old boy. Can't be lying about that. But never as bad as them that turns a man out in the street and leaves him for dead. And the poor woman too, with her young. I seen that nightmare with my own eyes. Starving kiddies crying at the feet of them that have no heart. The fucken money boys. You measure them with the Doc, he comes out a true saint next to them demons.'

Tex threw the stick to the ground in disgust. 'You boys best get on your way. You say nothing about this, to no one. I tell you that for your own good, and the Doc's.'

Sonny and Ren didn't speak until they were almost home. Ren could hardly believe what he'd witnessed. In the days and weeks afterwards he would sometimes convince himself that it had been a dream.

Sonny walked a couple of paces behind Ren. 'That was good for him,' he said. 'I reckon the Doc was lucky.'

'Can't see what was lucky about what happened to him.'

'If it wasn't for the others he'd have no one to speak for him. Say he'd died some other place, like Tex was saying, he'd be buried with the paupers and nobody would know where he'd got to.'

'S'pose so,' Ren said.

'When they're all gone,' Sonny went on, 'they'll be forgotten. There'll be no one left. No family or relations. They won't have no sign stuck to a bit of rock, like the diver has, talking about all that they'd done. It's not right, someone living so long and they die and it's like they were never round in the first place.'

'We won't forget them.'

'Until we're dead. They'll be forgot then. It'll be my turn after that. If I died right now, on this spot, my mum would never find out about it, and my old man don't remember what's gone on from one day to the next. It's alright for you, Ren. Someone will remember you. But not me, they won't.'

'You're making no sense, Sonny. My mother and Archie are a lot older than me and will be dead before me, unless I get some disease or have an accident. They won't be round to remember me either. The truth is, all of us will be forgotten one day. Unless we do something special.'

'Like what?'

'Like you just said. The diver. Something brave other people won't ever forget about. Even people that weren't around when it happened.'

'I'll come up with something then, that people will remember me by.'

'And what would that be, Sonny?'

'Not sure yet. I have to think of something.'

'Maybe you could become the cigarette rolling champion of Australia.' Ren laughed. 'I don't know much else that you're good at.'

'Get fucked. And it don't have to be something good. More people are remembered for the bad they done.'

'Now you're talking, Sonny. Shouldn't be too hard then.'

Sitting at the kitchen table that night, Ren couldn't get the image of the Doc, laying dead in the dirt, out of his head. Later on, he sat up in bed drawing in his sketch book, a portrait of the eagle on the back of his bedroom door. When he finished he got out of bed and held the sketch next to the photograph. It was a good likeness and he was happy with his work. He signed the drawing the way a proper artist would. During the night he woke to the sound of thunder in the distance, the roar of a changing wind, followed by the steady beat of rain on the roof. The long summer had drawn its last breath.

CHAPTER 7

By the end of a full summer on the river Sonny had come to know it well, but his knowledge was restricted to the swimming holes and bridges within reach of home. In the months that followed, Ren introduced him to other stretches and bends in the river that he had not seen before. The boys trekked downriver, to where factories battled for space along the riverbanks. The skinning sheds oozed their own rivers – of blood and animal fats – into the water, while wrecking yards bled dirty oil and spent fuel. The industrial drainpipes were large enough for Sonny to ride his bike through the pitch-black rancid air, chasing an eye of light ahead. Each time the boys entered the drains they ventured further into the darkness, always on the lookout for rats and feral cats that used the drains to move beneath the streets of the city.

Heading upriver couldn't have been a more different experience. They picked up the dirt trail beyond the falls and headed north, aiming to reach the distant hills, a feat they never accomplished. After an hour or more hiking they crossed to the other side of the river, by way of an irrigation pipeline fifty feet above the water and no more than a foot wide. As the grime of the city fell away the river widened into billabongs, the home to thousands of birds. Ren could sit on the bank watching them for hours and not speak a word. And he wouldn't have, except that an impatient Sonny was always pestering him.

Walking home from their excursions upriver Ren would feel a little different. He couldn't make sense of it. He knew it was a feeling he craved, but one in danger of slipping away from him. Even Sonny would be calmer. He would look up at the sky as if he was trying to unravel a mystery. They'd arrive back at the falls around sundown, having been tracked all the way by the glowing eyes of waking foxes. If they spotted the campfire under the bridge they'd call in and visit the river men. Back home, Ren would draw more pictures of birds, count the money he'd saved and dream of a day he might return to the billabong with a camera.

Another attraction of the winter river was the treasure it gave up. The boys came across many decent finds, some of which earned them money. Soft drink bottles that somehow made it to the water without smashing were cashed in at the bottle yard. They also found lots of balls. Tennis balls. Soccer balls. One or two basketballs. But never a football. Not one.

'Why do you reckon that is?' Sonny asked Ren while he was laying on his stomach fetching a lemonade bottle from a drain grate. 'We never come across a footy.'

'Because a kid would risk his life to get a footy back. One time I saw Michael Evans from school, when he was captain of the team. He kicked his footy down a drain, and him and his little brother, Allie, went home, come back with a crowbar, lifted off the grill and got down in the shit and mess to get it back.'

'You don't reckon he'd have done the same for a cricket ball?'

'Why would he? Easy to knock a new one off.'

It was another type of ball that Sonny decided could make him and Ren some money over the winter. He put the plan to him on a wet Sunday afternoon when they'd run out of ideas to get them through a slow day.

'You seen them players at the golf course when it's been raining and the ground is wet?'

'Nah. Haven't spent a lot of time watching golf. Didn't think you had either.'

'Well, I watched enough when we've been walking by. And when it's wet they hit the ball all over the place, into the bushes, skid them across the grass. I bet if we hunted around the course we could find plenty of golf balls and sell them back to the players.'

'That's your plan to make extra money? Sniffing around in the bushes for golf balls? You'd make more in tips with the newspapers.'

'Maybe. But we got nothing better to do. You can come or not. It's up to you.'

They crossed the iron bridge, walked around the golf course and hunted through the bushes, under the low tea-trees and along the road next to the fairway. Ren was surprised that Sonny's plan was a success, at least the hunting part of it. Within an hour they'd turned up six golf balls. One of them looked like a fox had been gnawing on it and Sonny threw it away. Most of the others looked as if they'd never been hit.

Sonny saw a lone golfer up on the fifth green. 'Come on, we'll try this fella.'

The golfer missed a short putt. He looked down at the ball like he wanted to stomp on it. Sonny walked onto the green holding the golf balls in both hands. 'Mister, you want to buy any of these? They're almost new. Twenty-five cents each. Or for a dollar you can have five.'

The golfer looked at the balls, took one out of Sonny's hand, held it to the light and studied it, as if it was a rough-cut diamond. 'This one might as well have my name on it. You look close and you can see a nick in it, where I hit it wide off the tee on the second hole.'

'It could be,' Sonny said, 'but you don't know that for sure. And it don't make any difference.'

'Why not? If it's my golf ball why should I have to buy it back off some kid?'

'Say it is your ball, but we never found it for you. You'd have to go and buy yourself a new ball anyway. This one is like new but you get it much cheaper. And the other ones. Five for a dollar.'

The golfer threw the ball in the air and caught it.

'Fair enough.' He offered Sonny a dollar note out of his wallet. 'I'll take all five.' The man smiled. A gold tooth sat in the middle of his mouth. 'You two from the other side of the river?'

'Yep.' Ren nodded.

He looked across the river valley and on to the factory rooftops. 'I come from over there myself, a long time ago now, before I come good with my cleaning business. Look at me these days. A fat-arsed prick getting about like a poof in a pink shirt and check pants.'

The man reached into his wallet, brought out another dollar note and handed it to Ren. 'A buck each. I've got boys of my own older than you two. Couldn't turn a dollar if their lives depended on it. My fault for softening them, I suppose. You two, you'll never go hungry.' He winked and turned his attention to the golf ball laying two feet off the hole.

Their good luck continued. On the way home from the golf course they found a new pair of rubber boots tied together with string, with the price tag still on them, hanging from a bush like a Christmas decoration. The boots were too big for either of them, so they walked to the camp and offered them to Tex. He'd been getting around in a pair of old leather sandals and his feet had been cut up bad and were freezing with the cold weather. Tex tried the boots on, smiling and humming to himself. He looked down at them and whistled long and low. The others around the fire were as excited as Tex was himself.

'Give us a bit of toe, tap and heel,' Tallboy called to him.

'They look handy for an old jig,' Tiny added.

Tex tried getting himself moving but his body wasn't up for it.

'What do you think, Tex?' Ren asked. 'You happy with them?'

'Oh, these is good. Real good. Thank you, boys.' He smiled. 'I never been so happy.'

The next time they visited the camp Tex was sitting by the fire warming his bare feet on the coals and the boots were nowhere to be seen.

'Where's them boots?' Sonny asked, looking down at Tex's feet.

Tex stared at the scabs and cuts and scratched his head like he didn't know any better than they did where the boots had got to. 'Knocked off while I been sleeping is my belief. Be Big Tiny. The cunning bastard.'

Tex really had no idea where the boots had gone. The metho was digging a deep hole in his brain and twisting his body into knots. He'd slowed to a bare shuffle, could hardly sing a note and was finding it difficult to see. When he spied someone heading for the camp he'd drop his head to the side and squint until he was sure it was a friend visiting.

Life got even tougher for the river men that winter, after a storm tore through the valley and it rained for a week. When the rain was over the boys sat at the falls watching the damage being washed downstream. The water carried uprooted trees, wooden barrels and rubbish of every kind. Sonny pointed out a fisherman's tinny being thrown around by the current. It raced to the edge of the falls, tipped on its end as it went over and crashed against the rocks before careering on.

Ren looked towards the iron bridge, where the water continued to rise. 'We should check on them,' he shouted above the roar, 'see how they're getting by in this.'

The river track was under water, so they were forced to wade through the weeds and long grass. As they neared the bridge Ren saw that the humpy had been washed away. The river men were nowhere to be seen and all that was left of the camp was the 44 barrel stove.

'Where could they have got to, Sonny?'

'Maybe they knew the storm was coming and took off for the street.'

Ren turned and spotted Tallboy in the distance, coming out of the wheelhouse, wrapped in a soggy blanket. He looked dazed and staggered towards the river's edge. Sonny ran after him and grabbed hold of him before he fell into the water.

'Tallboy,' Ren asked, 'where's the others?'

Tallboy eased his body to the ground and wiped bile from his beard with the back of his hand. 'Two nights back, I heard a mighty scream in the dark. Crash. Another one. The tin off the roof was on me chest. I could see up in the sky and the old tarp was gone off the roof and made herself a kite and flew away.' He gestured with his hand, the motion of a bird in flight. 'I was stuck there under the tin weighing me down and called the others. Lucky for Tallboy they was woke up and saved me.' He coughed and sneezed a couple of times. 'We stayed there under one blanket that was left. All of us, together, till the morning come. It was a bad business. Texas said he would have no chance to hunt down all we lost and put the house back together. We had a meeting and picked up what was left and made our shelter there,' he said, pointing towards the wheelhouse.

'You slept in there?' Ren asked Tallboy in disbelief.

'Sure did. Only spot we was able to keep dry.'

'I bet it's creepy in there,' Sonny said.

Tallboy looked up and smiled, a little more like his

old self. 'Nothing special bout that place, except old Doc dropped dead guarding the door. The whole world is creepy at times, boy.'

He tried getting to his feet but couldn't manage it. 'Some of the rooms in there is wet through, but not all of them. The storehouse ain't bad. Got spare blankets and all, in there from the old days.'

'Where's the others?' Sonny asked.

'Oh, they're keeping themselves warm. Sent me for a drink, but I don't reckon I can make it. Haven't been this long off the grog since I was a young fella. Wouldn't say it to the others, but it's not a bad feeling. Not as I would have expected. We got to get up the street for a decent feed. You boys, help me to my feet and I can go and fetch them.'

Ren and Sonny got each side of Tallboy, stood him up and guided him to the wheelhouse door.

'You coming in?' he asked, as if he was inviting the boys into his home. He pushed the door open, releasing a smell of stagnant water, stale air, and what Ren was convinced could only be the stench of rotting bodies.

'We'll wait here for you,' he said.

Minutes later the others surfaced, hugging putrid blankets to their stooped shoulders. They sang a graveyard cough, opening their lungs to the fresh air. Each of them had turned a death grey colour. Tex and Cold Can had also thinned to the bone, and Big Tiny, still on the heavy side, had even stripped a few pounds. Tex stared blankly at the boys as if he had no idea who they were and shuffled along the track. The others fell in behind like the walking dead. They tried climbing the track up to the mill but couldn't manage it.

They were forced to walk as far as the iron bridge to climb a set of stone stairs to the road above.

The cold days continued, but with an end to the rain the ground dried out and Tex decided it was time to move back under the bridge and rebuild the humpy. He asked the boys to help out with materials. They stole a tarp and two lengths of strong rope from a wagon in the railyards, and on the way to the river scavenged lengths of roofing iron and a bundle of wire. Big Tiny and Cold Can were fit enough to gather scraps of wood along the river, and Tallboy set about rebuilding the 44 barrel stove. By the time the new humpy was finished, it was twice the size of the original and looked as if it would hold together well enough to fight most storms. Ren could see some life coming back to the river men. Their colour returned a little, and Tex, even though he'd become crippled that winter, had a bit of step in him.

It was almost dark on the afternoon the boys walked home after finishing the new humpy, tired and wearing blistered hands embedded with splinters.

'I need to tell you something about my old man,' Sonny said, out of the blue.

'What about him?'

'I come home from the paper shop three nights back and he was breaking up the kitchen chairs. He put the wood on the fire in the lounge. When he'd finished with the chairs he tore a door off one of the kitchen cupboards and smashed it up too. And there's no food in the house. Nothing.'

'What have you been eating?'

'Till this morning, dry biscuits and plum jam. I scraped the last of the tin at breakfast. I got up for the paper round yesterday and he was gone from the house. I haven't seen him since. I went looking for him in the pubs. Nobody's seen him. It don't make any sense. It's like he's vanished.'

Sonny stood on a sheet of scrap iron. The sound cracked the air. Both boys jumped with fright as a big cat shot out from behind a roll of old carpet and ran between Sonny's legs. He picked up a rock and was about to throw it but the cat was too fast and disappeared into the bushes before he could take aim. He wrapped his hand around the rock, made a fist and examined it.

'What are you gonna do?' Ren asked. 'Go to the police?'

'I'm not that stupid. If they know I'm on my own they'll take me in and I'll end up a ward with some do-gooder. Or worse. A kid fucker.'

They walked the length of the mill wall and saw Archie getting out of his truck on the other side of the street. He slung a work bag over his shoulder, locked the truck door and walked along the lane to the back gate.

'Shit,' Ren said. 'I don't like getting home after Archie.'

'Tell him you been with me, helping me out searching for my old man.'

'Good idea.'

They crossed the street and ducked into the lane. Sonny opened his gate and looked up to the dull yellow light coming from the upstairs bedroom of the Reverend's house. He noticed a shadow moving behind the curtain.

'Hey, Ren, you see that window. That's the girl's room. She might be getting undressed.'

Sonny went into the yard, propped the rubbish bin against the side fence and stood on it. He watched as the shadow turned to the side and pressed against the curtain.

'It's her for sure,' he whispered. 'And I reckon she's got no clothes on.'

'You don't know that, Sonny.' Whether Della was undressed or not Ren didn't want Sonny imagining that she was.

A second shadow appeared at the window, towering over the girl. An arm reached forward, grabbed hold of Della and pulled her away from the window. The light went out.

'You see that?' Sonny whispered, getting down from the bin.

'Had to be her father,' Ren said.

'Yep. I bet he's doing her.'

'You don't know that.'

'Not for certain. But I'd still bet he is.'

'If he is we should tell somebody.'

'Like who? The coppers? They'd kick us in the arse and tell us to fuck off and mind our own business.'

'He shouldn't be able to get away with it. She's just a girl. And his own kid.'

Sonny looked through the back window into his empty kitchen. 'My mum went to the police one time, over my old man. He was knocking her around more than ever. And other stuff. She waited until he went to work one morning and give me a bath and put me in some clean clothes. We walked all the way to the police station in the cold. She had two black eyes and I was wearing the only jumper she owned, to keep me warm. Come down to my knees. She had this thin dress on, like it was made of paper. It was a long walk to the police station and I was only small. I remember her kissing my cheek when we got there, and saying, *You walked two miles you brave boy, two miles.* She was sat down and had to tell one of the coppers what my dad had been doing to her. She didn't want to talk about it in front of me, but there was no one to look after me and I had to listen to it all. Some stuff I couldn't understand, but knew was terrible. She was crying and all. You wanna know what the copper said to her when she was finished?'

'What?'

'*Go home, love,* he said. *He'll be sober in the morning.* I never have forgot that.'

Ren couldn't think of a single word to say in response. He looked down at the ground and could hear both his own and Sonny's breathing, together in the air.

'They wouldn't even give us a ride home. We walked all the way. When she put me to bed she kissed me here.' Sonny touched his forehead. 'And told me she was sorry. I remember that too.'

'You must miss her a lot?'

Sonny again looked up at Della's darkened window.

'Not as much as I try to forget her.'

CHAPTER 8

Ren woke to a foreign sound the next morning. He put his dressing gown on, went downstairs and opened the front door. The street was full of cars and a crowd was pouring into the Reverend's house, men in suits and women in long skirts with handkerchief scarves on their heads. He went back inside, made himself a cup of tea, went up to his room and heard the piano start up in the stable, followed by the sounds of hymns and prayers. He pulled the curtain away from the window. Sonny's face was pressed against the glass.

'Fuck!' Ren screamed, opening the window. 'You give me a heart attack, Sonny.'

'Let me in. It's cold out here.'

Sonny's hair was standing on end, he had sleep in both eyes, and he was wearing the same clothes he had on when Ren left him the night before.

'You look like a wild kid out of the bush. Tex is in better nick than you.'

'Get stuffed. You're no day at the beach.'

Sonny jumped through the window, grabbed the mug of tea out of Ren's hand and took a long sip. 'You hear what's going on next door to my place?'

'Yeah. It woke me up.'

'Woke the whole street. I reckon we should go take a look.'

'You can go on your own.'

'Come on, put some clothes on and come check it out.' Sonny took another long drink of tea and stared into the bottom of the empty mug. 'You coming or not?'

'Nah. I'm going back to bed. Like you said, its cold out.'

'Your girlfriend, Della, I bet she'll be there.'

'She's not my girlfriend. I've hardly spoken to her.'

'You spoke to her? You never told me that. When?'

'Forget it.'

'Forget nothing. When'd you speak to her?'

'Not telling you.' Ren hopped back into bed and pulled the blanket around his chin.

'Last chance,' Sonny offered. 'You coming or not?'

'Already told you. Not.'

'Please yourself.'

Sonny wasn't halfway out the window before Ren changed his mind. He pulled a pair of jeans and a jumper over his pyjamas and followed Sonny out the window, onto the roof and down the drainpipe into Sonny's yard. The thundering piano lifted the stable roof. Sonny unlatched the back gate and they crept along the lane to the rear of the stable, where Sonny bent down and put his good eye to a crack in a splintered weatherboard. Ren kneeled beside him and tried pushing

125

Sonny out of the way so he could take a look at what was going on. Sonny wouldn't budge.

'Move,' Ren said. 'I wanna take a look.'

Sonny pointed to a knothole in the wood directly below where he was kneeling. Ren lay in the dirt and put an eye to the hole. The ground beneath was muddy. It quickly oozed through his woollen jumper and soaked into his pyjama top. He could see the Reverend pacing the room. The men sat in front of him on one side of the aisle, the women on the other. Ren could see Della sitting between her mother and another girl, who looked a little older. She had red hair poking out of her scarf and looked up adoringly to the Reverend. The music ended abruptly and the hand-clapping and singing stopped. It was perfectly quiet except for Ren's heartbeat and Sonny's wheezy breath. When the Reverend's voice boomed across the room and shook the weatherboards, Sonny jumped with fright and stood on Ren's hand. Ren had to bite into a lump of dirt to stop himself from crying out in pain.

The Reverend's fearsome preaching made no sense to the boys. 'We were brought here, brothers and sisters, to create a place of worship, by the words of the Messenger. God Himself, Our Father Jealous Divine, ordered us to this place from across the ocean where he resides ... and the Good Mother Divine, in her chaste beauty and purity, had also asked that we be in this place, our House of Worship ...'

'You hearing this, Sonny?' Ren whispered.

He nodded his head and stuck his ear to the crack in the wood.

'... and is it not also known,' the Reverend continued, 'that in the days immediate to the Great Earthquake of 1906 the

Messenger attended the city of San Francisco, at that very time a site of pestilence and evil? At the behest of the Holy Spirit, he visited wrath upon the sinful by fracturing the Earth and sanctioned Lucifer to ignite the flames of Hell.'

The words 'Amen, Amen' were chanted across the room.

'And is it not also known that when the Messenger was imprisoned for His holy works the gaolers in attendance to pacify and shackle Him were struck dead by lightning and He was able to free Himself and walk among us again?'

'Amen!'

The longer the sermon went, the louder the Reverend's voice rang out across the stable. Ren could *feel* his words beating against the wall. Women in the audience began to wail and the men called out in agreement with Reverend Beck, 'We are with you ...'

The red-headed girl seated next to Della wiped tears from her eyes, opened her arms and held her hands out. The Reverend stepped forward and took her hands in his. Della couldn't take her eyes off the girl.

'As each of you are with the Messenger Jealous Divine Himself,' he said, smiling down at the girl.

The sermon ended and people in the room stood up and clapped and cried out, 'Be Praised! Be Praised!' The piano struck up again and the gathering sang a final hymn. Sonny tapped Ren on the shoulder and snuck back along the lane. Ren tried to stand up, fell back and slid on his arse. 'Fuck!'

Sonny smothered his laugh with a hand and opened the gate into his yard. Ren followed, one careful step at a time. Sonny bolted the gate behind them.

'Look at you. You been rolling in shit.'

The front of Ren's jumper and the knees of his jeans were covered in a mix of mud and dog shit. When he tried wiping it off, all he managed to do was move it around like a finger painting. 'My mum is gonna kill me for this.'

Sonny couldn't stop himself from laughing. 'And after that she'll kill you again.'

Ren scraped a handful of the muck from his jumper and flung it at Sonny, missing his target. 'Don't go thinking this is funny. She'll flog me.'

'You sling any more of that shit at me and I'll flog you myself. Come in the kitchen and I'll throw your clothes in the twin-tub and wash them for you.'

'Yes, Mum.'

The house was a mess. Broken pieces of furniture lay in the lounge, empty beer bottles were stacked in one corner of the kitchen and Ren's shoes stuck to the sticky lino floor as he walked across it.

'I still haven't seen him,' Sonny said, without Ren having to ask.

Ren sat on the only kitchen chair left in the room, and waited while Sonny found an old football jumper and a pair of Mr Brewer's work pants for him to put on.

'Sonny, you ever hear stuff like that, what we heard in the stable?' Ren asked.

'Yeah. Some of what comes out of Tex's mouth.'

'It weren't nothing like his talk. Them prayers gave me the creeps. And the women crying and babbling. Sounded like another language.' He looked around the kitchen. 'You got any bread for toast?'

'There's nothing to eat. I'll have to use my saved money if I want food.'

'How much you got?'

'Nearly a hundred dollars.'

'A hundred. You could buy any food you want with that. Where you keeping it?'

'I've hid it away from the house so he can't get his hands on it. Shouldn't have worried. He's gone and left me with this mess.'

'Still got no idea where he's got to? What are you going to do?'

'Enough of the questions, Ren. You want to play policeman, get a fucken badge.'

'I was just asking …'

'Well, don't ask. Or you can give the pants and jumper back and piss off home in the nude.'

Sonny lit a fire and strung Ren's wet clothes across the fireplace on a line of string. While they waited for them to dry, Ren tried talking him into coming back to his place for something to eat, but Sonny wouldn't hear of it.

That night, Archie asked Ren if he knew anything about the racket that had gone on in the street that morning.

'You said you were over at your mate's place. You hear anything?'

'Only some music and singing,' Ren replied.

'Couldn't call it singing. Sounded more like the shit I had to put up with when I was a kid in Sunday school. Shouldn't be allowed on our street, where families live. Take their religion some other place.'

'Maybe you could ring the Council?' Loretta offered. 'They'd send the by-laws officer, he'd help himself to the collection plate, and they'd go on with the praying like nothing had happened. Nothing gets stopped around here unless money changes hands. You know that.'

Ren looked down at his half-eaten roast lamb and thought about Sonny sitting next door on his own with no food in the cupboard. He couldn't eat another mouthful.

'Mum, Sonny's dad's gone off some place.'

'What do you mean, gone off?'

'He's left Sonny on his own.'

'The boy's better off without him,' Archie said. 'A nutcase right next door to us. Then again, the kid probably drove him out.'

Loretta glared at Archie. 'Be quiet, Arch. Charlie's trying to tell us something. What's happened in there?'

'His father went crazy on him and shot through. He's got no food and the house is a wreck.'

'And it's none of our business,' Archie added.

Loretta slammed her hand on the table, lifting the dishes in the air, shocking both Archie and Ren. 'Shut up, Arch! Please, shut up! Finish your dinner, get upstairs and try sleeping off your misery.'

Archie went to speak but Loretta raised a hand. 'I said, shut it.'

Archie did shut up, by shoving a whole baked potato in his mouth.

Loretta got up from the table, stood behind Ren and put her hands on his shoulders. 'Now, tell me what you mean, that there's no food in the house.'

'His father's disappeared and there's nothing left to eat. And the place is filthy dirty. Mum, we have to do something to help him.'

'Jesus Christ,' Archie muttered. 'This stuff is for the Welfare Department. It's not our business.'

Loretta flattened her palms on the table and looked across at him. 'Would you mind telling me which one of us is going to ring the Welfare and get the boy taken away? I think you should do it, Arch.' She grabbed her purse from the kitchen bench, opened it and tipped it upside down. Coins poured onto the table. She tapped the tabletop with her knuckles. 'Go on, get yourself down to the phone box outside the milk bar and give them a ring yourself. Tell them it's an emergency. Could have him locked up before you're in bed. Give you a good night's sleep, Arch. Wouldn't that be good? You won't have to sit here and complain about him anymore. Better than that, you won't have to look at the boy again. Just yourself, in the mirror, Arch.'

She picked up some coins from the table and jiggled them in her hand. 'Go on. Ring them.'

Archie stood up and pushed his chair into the table, knocking over a jug of milk. 'Fuck! I didn't say anything about getting him locked up.' He stomped out of the kitchen and up the stairs.

Loretta put her arms around Ren, a rare display of open affection. 'Don't worry about him. He won't be doing anything. Those who have been hurt most can be hardest on others going through the same.'

'What's that mean?'

'Nothing. I don't have time to tell you all that Archie's been through.'

131

Loretta couldn't hide the pained look on her face. She slapped the kitchen table and wrung her hands together, deep in thought. 'You're filthy yourself, Charlie.' She frowned. 'Get upstairs for a shower. Please.'

Ren knew better than to argue when his mother was in such a mood. He stood under the steaming water of the shower with a terrible feeling in his gut. Ren knew Sonny sometimes brought trouble on himself but he didn't deserve what he was going through. He got out of the shower, put his pyjamas on and went downstairs. To his surprise, Sonny was seated at the kitchen table, tucking into a steaming bowl of tomato soup. Two thick slices of buttered toast sat on a plate in front of him. Loretta was standing at the stove. 'You're just in time for a cup of tea, Charlie. I'm shooting upstairs to find Sonny something to sleep in.'

Ren sat down across the table from Sonny and looked at the tomato moustache above his top lip. 'Look at you, grinning like that. And you been bragging all this time you'd be fine on your own, going on how you don't need anyone. And now you're sitting up in Archie's chair.'

Sonny licked his spoon and smiled. 'I would have been a hundred per cent okay on my own. Then your mum come knocking at the door and told me you was feeling lonely and needed me to keep you company.'

'Liar. It was her feeling sorry for you, more like it. Bet you jumped into her arms like a baby.'

Loretta came downstairs with a pair of folded pyjamas under her arm. Archie's. She handed them to Sonny. 'There you are, love. Flannelette.'

'Thank you,' he said, winking at Ren.

Sonny polished off two bowls of soup and an extra slice of toast. Loretta got him to take a shower, his first in a week, which was fortunate for Ren, as Sonny would be sharing a bed with him. The next morning, Archie choked on his tea when Sonny walked into the kitchen wearing his pyjamas. Before he could deliver a word of complaint, Loretta gave him *the look* and shut him up. She sat Sonny at the table and poured him a cup of tea.

'We were talking before you come downstairs, Sonny, and we don't want you next door there on your own.' She turned to Archie for a show of support. 'Do we?'

Ren shifted in the silence of the room, waiting on the reply. Loretta smiled at Archie, encouraging him to say something positive. Ren was relieved enough that he didn't open his mouth at all. Loretta sat down and beat a rhythm on the tabletop with broken fingernails. 'Sonny. Have you got anyone that can take care of you?'

He tried answering but couldn't speak. He felt shamed and wiped his eyes and covered his face with a hand. Loretta took his other hand in her own and stroked it. Ren was a little jealous.

'Your father?' Loretta asked. 'Do you have an idea where he might be?'

Sonny shook his head from side to side and snivelled. 'I dunno where he is. Been out looking for him for days. He's nowhere.' He lifted his head and looked across the table, directly at Archie. 'I'm sorry for making trouble for you.'

Nobody spoke. Ren could hear the tap dripping in the kitchen sink and a dog barking in a backyard further along the street.

'Sonny,' Archie finally said, in a voice softer than the others seated around the table thought possible. 'We will not have you over there on your own. Nobody in this house would be able to sleep at night knowing you were right next door with nobody looking out for you. It's not right. You can stay here with us until something can be sorted out. As long as that's okay with you, of course.'

Sonny nodded his head, just a little, up and down. Loretta squeezed his hand and smiled across the table at Archie.

Loretta was so taken with Sonny, Ren was sure that if she could claim him for life she would've. As it turned out, his stay lasted a week. The following Sunday night the family was sitting in the front room watching TV when there was a knock at the door. Loretta nudged Archie in the ribs. He'd fallen asleep on the couch.

'Who'd that be at this time, Arch?'

'What?'

'There's someone at the door. You get it.'

Archie got up and answered the door. Ren could hear him talking to somebody in the hallway. He came back into the room, followed by an older man with a full head of ginger hair and the bloated face of a seasoned drinker. Sonny jumped up from the couch and smiled. 'Uncle Rory.'

'Hey, it's young Sonny.' The man waddled bowlegged across the room, gave Sonny a hug, reached up and patted him on the head. 'You've sprung up since I last saw ya. I was knocking next door with no luck and saw the light was on here. I knocked on the off-chance.'

Rory explained to Loretta that Sonny's father was his younger brother. She invited him into the kitchen and made a pot of tea. He sat down and took two envelopes from his coat pocket and laid them on the table. He tapped on one of them with a finger, half of which was missing.

'First of all this letter come in the post.' He took a sheet of writing paper from the envelope and ran his finger across the words, written in pencil.

'This is from your father,' he said to Sonny. 'It took over week for it to get to me. I moved house not long after we had a falling out and he sent it to the old address. The post office forwarded it to me. The letter don't say much except that he's going away. Doesn't say where to. Or for how long. But said he needed me, *urgent*, to come here and look after you.'

He handed the letter to Sonny, who also read it, or as much as he could make out.

'It also says not to worry about the rent money. He'll take care of it,' Rory explained before losing his breath in a coughing fit. Loretta handed him a glass of water.

'I thought to myself, *yeah that'll be the day*. Between the horses and a drink he'd always spent more money than he had in his pockets. Then this morning, I get another letter through the mail.' He opened the second envelope and pulled out another piece of paper. It provided both an explanation and more mystery. He placed the piece of paper on the table. It was a receipt. 'This one is from the landlord of the house. The rent on your place has been paid in full, for six months in advance.'

'Six months,' Sonny said, looking puzzled. 'He don't have any money.'

'Well he must have pulled a whack from somewhere. Maybe he kept a trap? No landlord round here plays St Vincent de Paul. And it's not Christmas, last time I looked at the calendar.'

'I don't see that he had any money,' Sonny said.

'Well, maybe you have a guardian angel out there someplace. Don't really matter. The rent's paid in full. All that matters.'

Rory put both envelopes back in his coat pocket, stood up from the table and thanked Loretta for taking care of Sonny. He touched her arm and told her she was a *mighty mighty woman.*

He rested his arm on Sonny's shoulder. 'Come on, Sonny boy. Let's get you home.'

Rory thanked Archie and gently tugged at Sonny's shirt. 'Your uncle Rory's slowed a bit since you last saw me. We got to take care of each other for a time.'

CHAPTER 9

The day after Sonny returned home with Rory, Ren came down with a burning fever. When Loretta put him in the shower to cool him down she noticed spots all over his body. She called the doctor from the phone box. Ren had the measles and was ordered to bed for the next week, which meant no school. Sonny visited him across the roof later that day. He was about to climb into the room when Ren called for him to stop.

'You can't come in, Sonny. Doctor says I'm contagious. I've got the measles and have to stay in bed.'

'What about the paper round?'

'Can't do it. Not for a week. No school either.'

'Lucky for you.'

The next day Sonny knocked at the window again and threw a brown paper bag into the room. 'I brought you a present.'

Ren opened the bag and found two new exercise books and a set of colouring pencils.

'Derwents,' Ren said. 'These are the best you can get. You knock this stuff off from the shop?'

Sonny growled, genuinely offended. 'I'd never steal from Brixey. I paid with my savings.'

'Why'd you go and do that?'

'Because your mum has been good to me.'

'And I put up with your smelly feet in my bed.'

'And I had to listen to you scratching at your balls all night. Sounded like a rat at a cereal box.'

'That was a rat. At your balls.'

Ren spent the following days drawing colourful maps of the river and writing more stories. By the middle of the week he was feeling a little better. He didn't let on to Loretta, worried she might send him back to school early. He waited until she'd left the house for work before he got out of bed, went downstairs and opened the front door.

The morning was cool and the sky was clear. As he sat on the front fence catching the sun and searching the sky for birds, a car drove into the street and stopped outside Reverend Beck's house. A man got out and knocked at the door and waited until the Reverend came out. Ren didn't notice the red-headed girl from the stable seated in the back of the car until it drove off. A few minutes later Della came out armed with her broom. She began sweeping the footpath. She looked up at Ren as she made her way along the gutter and continued sweeping until she'd passed Sonny's house. She stopped in front of Ren and rested on her broom. 'What are you doing wearing your pyjamas?'

'I've been sick with the measles. Nobody can come near me. You better stay away or you'll catch them.'

If the girl was concerned about catching anything from Ren she didn't show it. 'How do you know what illness you have?' she asked.

Ren thought it was a strange question. 'Because the doctor told my mum, after he took my temperature and looked at the rash I had.'

'My father ... we have no need for doctors.'

'What happens when you get sick?'

Della swept leaves into a neat pile before answering. 'Our illnesses are a gift from the Messenger. He administers them to our bodies and eases them once we have dealt with our sins. You would have sinned to contract your own illness.'

Ren was sure Della had to be a little crazy. He didn't really mind. He knew a lot of crazy people. She was just one more. And he wanted to keep her talking.

'I would have sinned, for sure.' He laughed. 'When will this Messenger fella get rid of the measles for me?'

'Maybe never,' Della answered, with complete seriousness. 'Those who have no faith, sometimes they die for their sins.'

'And in your church, no one dies.' He laughed again, angering Della. 'What they call that? A miracle?'

Della rested her broom against the fence and took a step towards Ren. Her eyes narrowed and darkened. 'We die for two reasons only. Either we sin and do not repent, which is a terrible death and ends in Hell. Or we die for the sins of others, which is the pathway of believers.'

Della sounded like her father giving one of his sermons. Ren leaned back on the fence. Her eyes opened a little wider and she suddenly smiled. 'I'm sorry. You're not well. I shouldn't be talking to you this way.'

Della picked up her broom, turned her back on Ren and swept along the gutter towards her house.

The next morning a tremor shook the street. At first, half asleep, Ren thought it was coming from the stable again. He got out of bed and lifted the blind from the window. The side street was lit by the dull yellow eyes of a convoy of tip-trucks and front-end loaders. Each of the trucks had a badge painted on its side, the same name Ren had seen on the shirt pocket of the surveyor.

A worker stood in front of the first truck, swinging a lantern in one hand and holding a red flag in the other. As he walked forward the trucks gunned their engines and drove towards the end of the street and into the open paddock beyond the track leading to the river. Ren got dressed and opened his door. His mother's bedroom door was shut. She had worked overtime into the middle of the night and would be asleep. He crept downstairs, careful not to wake her, left the house and knocked at Sonny's door. There was no answer. He ran along the street and didn't stop until he'd reached the paper shop, his lungs on fire.

Spike was standing in the doorway of the shop biting into a chocolate bar. 'What you doing here, Ren? Sonny says you been poisonous. You look like you're having a heart attack, I reckon.'

'Is he here?'

'Yeah, he stayed back to help Brixey with the count. You looking for him or something?'

'Nah, Spike. I ran all the way here for exercise. Tell him I'm out here. Quick.'

Spike was in no hurry to move. He took another bite out of the chocolate bar, leaving a dangling gob of spit behind. He offered it to Ren. 'You want a bite? I've had three of these this morning and I'm full up.'

'I'd keep it for later if I were you, Spike. Never know when you'll be hungry again.'

The side gate creaked open. Sonny came out, pushing his bike. 'What are you doing here, Ren? You're supposed to be in bed dying.'

Spike laughed so loud he spat runny chocolate down his front.

'Hey, Spike,' Sonny said. 'It weren't that funny. Calm down.'

'It's started,' Ren said. 'They're here.'

Sonny looked up at the bridge as a train rattled across.

'Here? Who?'

'Not *here*,' Ren yelled, his voice breaking up. 'Trucks and machines. They've come to build the freeway.'

Sonny let go of the bike. It crashed to the ground as a news truck sped by the paper shop. The truck jockey dumped two bundles of *The Sun* off the back without the driver slowing. Spike jumped in the air as the bundles hit the footpath.

'What are we gonna to do to stop them, Sonny?' Ren asked. 'It's what you said we'd do. Stop them.'

Brixey came out of the shop to collect the papers. 'Hey, Sonny, don't be distracting Spike from his work. If you and your mate feel the need to hang round the front of the shop you can make yourselves useful with a broom. Or clean the windows. And Spike. *Spike!* Stop feeding your face at my expense. Grab them papers and bring them into the shop.'

Spike licked melted chocolate from his fingertips and strolled over to the bundles of papers. Sonny picked up the bike and walked away from the shop. Ren followed him along the street.

'How many trucks did you see?' Sonny asked.

'A cavalry. At least ten.'

'Hop on. We'll take a short cut through the railyards.'

The bike had no mudguards and water laying on the road shot up Ren's arse as they rode, weaving between the lines of derelict train carriages.

'Maybe this is a bad idea, Sonny,' Ren shouted in his ear, 'showing the bike off here. This is where you knocked it off.'

'The yard boss hardly moves his arse. About now he'll be tucking into tea and toast in front of the potbelly in the foreman's shed. Probably got his feet up in a chair in a pair Hush Puppies.'

'You sure?'

'Sure enough not to be worried about it.'

The bike weighed a ton and the added weight of Ren on the back flattened the tyre. Sonny wore himself out pedalling.

'I need to stop for a smoke,' he said. 'Your turn to roll.'

Rolling and walking at the same time wasn't easy. Ren dropped more tobacco on the ground than he rolled into the cigarette.

'I knocked at your door on the way here. Your uncle Rory must have been out early.'

'He left for the racetrack before sun-up.'

'What's he do there?'

'Helps with the muck out at the stables for an old mate and has his own emu run on race days.'

'What's an emu run?'

'He picks up the betting slips the punters throw away. Collects them in sugar sacks, brings them home and checks them for winners.'

The idea sounded like a waste of time to Ren. 'You say that the punters have already thrown the tickets away?'

'Yep.'

'Why would he go to the trouble of collecting losing tickets?'

'Because some of them are winners. People make mistakes and bin the wrong tickets. He makes money off that. Then there's the big earners after a protest. Plenty of punters throw their ticket away straight after a race, thinking they've lost, before the hooter gives the all clear. If the protest gets up the emus really go to work.'

'He make good money?'

'Rory's a mystery when it comes to money, but it's the only job he's had, as far as I know, so he must make enough.'

'Have you found out who paid the rent on the house?'

'Nah. But my old man must have had a hand in it for the receipt to be sent to Rory's old address. I still can't understand how he could have got hold of that much cash.'

The potholes in the railyards were full of water. Ren slammed his shoe into one of the puddles, splashing water over Sonny.

'Jesus, Ren ...'

'Hey, you thieving pricks!'

Ren turned to see the yard boss running between two

rows of carriages, waving a shunter's bar above his head. 'That bicycle is railway property!' he yelled.

'Go Sonny! *Go!*'

Sonny leaned over the handlebars of the bike, started running and pushed as hard as he could. 'Jump on, Ren,' he urged, throwing his leg over the bike. He mounted the seat and pedalled like mad, all in the one move. Ren leap-frogged the back wheel, onto the rack and spread his legs. The yard boss, even with a wobbly belly to support, gained on them. He was close enough for Ren to see his false teeth jumping in his mouth. And he was wearing a pair of slippers.

Ren slapped Sonny on the back. 'Fucken *pedal*!'

The yard boss reached for Ren's leg just as Sonny picked up enough speed to get away from him. He slipped in a pothole and hurled the iron bar as he fell. It missed Ren's ducking head by a couple of inches and Sonny's – tucked over the handlebars – by the width of a Tally-Ho paper. The boys sped through the yard and turned into the lane. Sonny jumped from the bike and unbolted the gate.

'We'd better wait awhile, in case he comes looking for us.'

Ren hadn't been in the house since Rory moved in. The lino floor in the kitchen had been scrubbed clean and the the room was tidy except for a mountain of betting slips piled up on the table.

'Rory must be a cleaning nut.'

'It's not him. He's got a girlfriend comes over a couple of nights a week to stay. She's mad on the mop and bucket.'

'He's a bit old to have a girlfriend.'

'You think *he's* old. You wanna see her. Like a walking corpse. It don't stop them going at it though. They get the old man's bed jumping off the floor. I'm worried I'll find them dead one morning.'

Ren found it hard to imagine Rory working up the energy to put one foot in front of the other without needing a breather. 'You mean they have sex in the bed?'

'Nah. Fucken ballroom dancing.'

Ren dipped his hands into the pile of betting slips. 'These winners or losers?'

'They haven't been sorted yet. There's a lot there to go through and I've been giving him a hand. If I pull a winner he pays me a commission. I made more last week on the slips than I did on the newspapers.'

'Maybe we could try it out? Go to the racetrack and collect our own tickets?'

'Not allowed. The emu run is a closed shop.'

'What's that mean?'

'Rory's been telling me about it, in case I have to step up. He says that all the workers in the business have their own piece of ground at the track, invisible lines dividing the turf that no one can see except the emus. He says it's always been that way. And when an emu gives the job away or dies, someone in the family takes over the run. There's rules as well. Like the cleaners at the track don't sweep the tickets up. Ever. They leave them to the emus. The most important rule though, according to Rory, is that if an outsider tries snitching a ticket he gets a warning. Second offence and the emus come from all over the track and dish out a kicking.'

'That's tough.'

'It's a tough business. Rory's got the scars to prove it. He took over the run from his old man, my pop, after he died.'

'What happened to your pop?'

'Same as the rest of the family. The grog took him and the run was left to Rory. He was no older than I am now. Had to fight off the standovers who thought they'd take the business from a kid. Rory's shit with my father started back then, he says, when they were kids. The old man wouldn't help him and Rory had to battle for the run on his own.'

The sound of the machines grunted in the background.

'Hear that?' Ren said.

'The coast should be clear now. Let's see what's going on.'

The steel gates guarding the mill hung from their hinges. The lock and chain on the gates had been broken so many times that whoever owned the mill had given up on the battle to keep the scavengers out. The scrap crews had weaselled their way in over the years, cutting through fences, smashing windows and stripping the mill of copper, brass and lead, as well as the porcelain toilets and sinks. Once they'd finished with the scrap they started on the timber. In the end all that was left of the mill were cavernous rooms, cobwebs and pigeons. Ren kicked the gate open. Sonny tried opening the sliding steel door into the main building. It was rusted to the frame and wouldn't budge. He searched the yard for something strong enough to force the lock.

'You find anything?' Ren called from the loading dock.

'Nothing.'

Sonny dragged a wooden pallet across the yard and stood

it on its end against the wall, under a broken window. 'Bunk me up.'

Ren cupped his hands together and Sonny used them as a stirrup. He balanced one foot on the pallet and the other on the ledge of the window. He thumped the frame of a shattered window with the side of his fist. It wouldn't budge.

'Take your jumper off, Ren. I'm gonna have to rest something on the bottom of the window so I don't get cut on the jagged glass when I squeeze through.'

'What about your own jumper?'

'I can't get mine off. I'm lucky to be holding on. Give me yours.'

Ren took his jumper off and threw it up to him. Sonny laid it across the bottom of the window, wriggled through and jumped into the mill. The door shifted and flung open. Sonny was holding Ren's jumper in his hand. He snatched it from him and put it on. It was torn at the shoulder.

'Well, done, Sonny. This is the only good jumper I got. How am I gonna explain this?'

'Looks as if you've been attacked by Zorro.' Sonny laughed. 'Maybe you could sew it up and your mum won't find out.'

Ren popped his head through the hole. 'Sew it, my arse.'

'Forget the jumper. You'll be in more trouble for sneaking out of the house when you're supposed to be sick in bed.'

The saw-tooth roof of the cotton mill was eighty, maybe a hundred feet above their heads. A steel stairway bolted into the brick wall zig-zagged towards the top. They made a racket climbing up and set the pigeons off. Hundreds of birds lifted from the steel rafters, flew in an arc and came together in the shape of a boomerang. The boys stopped on a landing and watched as the birds flew the length of the mill, turned and glided above their heads, close enough that Ren could feel the breeze of their wings. The birds turned again and flew to the far end of the mill. One by one they settled along the rafters.

A small wooden door sat at the top of the stairs. Ren pushed against it. It wouldn't move. Sonny took a couple of steps back, ran at it and gave it a kick. The door flew off its hinges and crashed to the ground below. A cold wind hit the boys in the face and the roar of the machines blasted their ears. Ren stuck his head out of the open window. 'Jesus. Look at what they've done already.'

The paddock was being cleared of every tree and the air was full of dust. A jet of water from a broken water main shot into the sky on the far side of the paddock. Bulldozers had pushed the rubbish to one side of the cleared ground — dead trees, rotting railway sleepers, the wreck of a van that had been dumped years before, and a mountain of old couches, chairs and car tyres. Anything that could be burned had been put on a front-end loader and piled onto a bonfire. Twisted metal and rocks were loaded into the bucket of another loader and dumped on the back of a tip-truck. Another machine was pile-driving deep holes into the ground. Each time the hammer stabbed the earth it shook the ground. Workmen were following behind the machine, laying down metal poles and rolls of wire.

The boys watched from the doorway as a worker circled the mountain of scrap wood and furniture with a can of petrol. He splashed it onto the dry timber, stood back, lay a length of cloth on the ground and soaked it with petrol. Fumes filled the air. He hooked the cloth to the end of a length of wire and lit it with a match. It exploded in flames. He poked the torch into the pile of wood. More flames shot into the air, the wood crackled and spat and black smoke lifted from the bonfire and drifted towards the river.

Sonny was perched on the edge of the open doorway with his legs tucked under him. He rocked backwards and forwards with nothing below him but a gravel driveway. It was a long way down.

'Careful, Sonny. You fall from here and they'll scoop up your broken body and throw it on the fire.'

Sonny ignored him. He couldn't take his eyes off the pile-driver. A pair of workmen stood a metal pole on its end and dropped it into one of the holes that had been made. A third worker followed with a wheelbarrow. With the two workers holding the pole upright he poured cement into the hole and pounded it with a blunt ended bar.

'They're putting a fence up, Sonny. I thought they were building a road. Why would they be building a fence?'

'We'll know soon enough. I never seen anyone work as fast.'

The boys smoked and watched as the work continued. The sky grew dark with smoke from the fire. Diesel fumes from the machines and more dust were thrown into the air as the trucks drove about. A long-load semi-trailer drove onto the cleared ground, its tyres sinking into the dirt. The truck's tray was stacked high with metal panels. More workmen unpacked the panels from the semi and bolted them together. In no time they'd built a workshop. The fence posts surrounding it were knitted together with rolls of cyclone wire, topped with barbed wire and finished off with a set of double gates, ready to be bolted and chained. Other trucks parked in the yard were unloaded and equipment was carried into the shed.

Sonny sat his chin in his hands and sulked. 'I dunno how Tex and the others will get up to the street with that fence in the way. It's hard enough for them now.'

'They'll have to go the long way round. Us too.'

'Bullshit we will.'

'What will you do then? Pole-vault the fence?'

'There's a pair of old bolt-cutters in the toolbox behind the toilet at my place. I'm coming back tonight after dark to cut a hole in the fence. We'll be taking the same track we've always used.'

'And they'll let us walk straight by them, Sonny? Remember the movie we saw last summer, the one about the robbery? They kept all them armoured trucks in a *compound*. It's what this is. A compound. Anyway, they work so fast, we won't have any river soon.'

'Then we have to work quick.'

'At what?'

'Stopping them.'

'No chance of that. One of them bulldozers could crush us to death. Drive straight through the front door of your house and out the back with nothing left standing.'

A workman sitting in a bulldozer turned off his machine. He'd seen the boys. Sonny got to his feet and yanked a metal hinge from the doorframe. He yelled out and waved to the workman, 'Hey, mate.'

The worker lifted his hand and waved back.

Sonny threw his arm back, pitched the hinge as hard as he

could and ran for the stairs. Ren bolted after him, hearing a loud 'ping' of metal on metal.

They didn't stop running until they were at Sonny's gate. 'You have to go home,' Sonny said, 'before you get in serious trouble.'

'Mum's on afternoon shift and Archie's driving interstate.'

'Come in then. We have to make plans.'

'For what?'

'What do they call it? Sabotage.'

CHAPTER 10

Sonny could hear the TV in the lounge room. He put a finger to his lips. 'There's someone here.'

The front room was empty except for one of Rory's sugar sacks sitting on the coffee table. Sonny walked over to the stairway and called upstairs for him. There was no answer. 'He don't usually get home this early. Must be something up.'

Ren wasn't listening. He was concentrating on a game show on the TV. A camera panned along the *Showcase* stage to reveal the winner's loot — a pair of electric blankets, cooking pots, a two-door refrigerator, a tropical holiday, and the biggest prize of all, *a new car*. The boys collapsed onto the couch, unable to take their eyes off the screen.

'You see that car, Sonny? If I won the jackpot I'd drive it down to the river, pick up Tex and the boys and take them on a cruise through the city with the windows down and the radio turned up full blast.'

'But you're not on the show, Ren. And you can't drive a car. And even if you were on the show you wouldn't win the car.'

'How do you know?'

'Because you have to answer the questions. You can't do it.'

'I bet I could answer some of them.'

'Not before one of them contestants hits the buzzer. I bet you can't do that.'

'You're no Barry fucken Jones yourself.'

'Not saying I am. Just setting you straight. Won't be driving no new car. That's all I'm saying.'

'I bet you a dollar I can beat them on some of the questions.'

'You don't have a buzzer.'

'Don't need one. Soon as I have the answer I'll clap my hands together.'

'Okay, but only if you get five, no, six questions right. I bet you a dollar.'

'You said five first. Five and it's a bet.'

'It's a bet.'

Ren sat on the edge of the couch going head to head with the three contestants. He surprised Sonny and himself by getting two questions right in the first round, which was one more than a lanky bank teller, wearing a name tag – *David* – dressed in a chequered jacket with leather pads on the arms.

'See that coat he has on?' Sonny said, during the first ad break. 'He's hoping to make himself look intelligent, wearing that.'

'It's not working. I'm already one point in front of him. They should kick him off and get me on.'

Muriel, the contestant seated in the middle, wore a beehive hairstyle. She was fast on the *Who am I*, but paid the penalty for hitting her buzzer too quickly on other questions and giving the wrong answer. By the end of the second round, Ren had answered only one more question and the carry-over champion, *Bob*, was way out in front. He blitzed the final round with such speed Ren never got to clap his hands once. The champion had the showroom of prizes to himself. All he needed to do to take home the lot was answer one more question. And Ren owed Sonny a dollar.

The losing contestants were shuffled off-stage. The champion stood next to the host of the show, who was wearing a suit that shimmered under the studio lights. Two girls in bikinis lay across the bonnet of a new car. A camera zoomed in on the host opening an envelope holding the last question.

'Look at the champion's hands, Ren. They're shaking.'

'He should stop looking at the bikini girls out of the corner of his eye. He'll lose all his concentration.'

The host took the question card from the envelope, read it to himself and smiled into the camera. He had perfect white teeth. 'I will have to be honest with you, Bob,' he said. 'This is a tough question.'

Bob wiped his brow on the sleeve of his cardigan. The host laid a hand on his shoulder. 'Are you ready, Bob? To take home all of these wonderful prizes?'

The host waved his arm the length of the gift shop. Bob couldn't speak. He nodded and sprayed sweat all over the host, who took a couple of steps back and looked straight into the camera, at Ren and Sonny.

'Bob. For this immaculate six-cylinder Holden car,

equipped with air conditioning – donated by our wonderful friends at City Wide Motors – and everything you see on the floor here this afternoon, with the exception of these two lovely ladies, of course.' He winked. 'We need the answer to the following question … after this break from our sponsors. And don't go away, you good people at home. We'll be right back.'

'Shit! They always do that,' Sonny complained.

Ren was desperate to go to the toilet. He jumped up from the couch and ran out of the room, through the kitchen and out into the backyard. When he got outside he looked up and saw Della at her open window. The rings under her eyes were so dark Ren wondered if they were bruised. A ginger cat was walking across the roof. Della watched it closely.

'Hey, Sonny,' Ren said, walking back into the lounge, 'I just saw Della at her window. I think she has a black eye.'

'Shut up. Bob's back on. This is it.'

'Her face is marked …'

'Shut up! The question's coming.'

A low drum roll kicked off the final drama.

'For the grand prize on tonight's *Showcase*,' the host announced, 'Bob Avon, of Glen Iris in Victoria, we need the correct answer to the following question.' The host turned and directed his attention to the live audience. 'And please, ladies and gentlemen, not a word from you, or Bob may be disqualified.'

He read from the card in his hand. 'The popular brand of dog food, *Pal* – another loyal friend of this program – was the original name of which famous screen canine?'

Bob closed his eyes, as if he was praying. Sonny jumped from the couch waving his arms in the air. 'The answer! I know it!'

'Bullshit.' Ren laughed. 'Bob don't know it himself. Look at him, Sonny. He's fucked. You know nothing.'

Sonny lapped the couch waving his arms in the air like a boxer who'd just won on a knock-out. 'Lassie! It's Lassie!' he screamed.

The drum roll got louder. Bob stuck his tongue out of his mouth and licked his lips.

'Shut up, Sonny. Or we're not gonna hear a word he says.'

The drum slowed and stopped. The host gave Bob a serious look. 'Time's up. We need an answer, Bob.'

Sonny collapsed to his knees, chanting *Lassie, Lassie.*

Bob's eyes suddenly lit up, like someone had turned the switch on. 'It's ... is it Rin Tin Tin?'

The host showed off his sparkling teeth to the TV audience one last time. 'Rin Tin Tin ... Rin Tin Tin ...' he repeated slowly.

Ren threw a dirty sock he'd found between the couch cushions at Sonny. 'Lassie, my arse.'

The host dropped his eyes. 'I'm sorry Bob. Your answer is incorrect.'

The audience groaned.

'It was Lassie. Also know by his handler as Pal.'

Bob went home with the consolation prize, a set of pillows, and Sonny jumped onto the couch and back to the floor, beating his chest.

'How'd you know that, Sonny?'

'Read it on the back page of a comic last week, at the paper shop. *Amazing Facts.* Before Lassie was Lassie, he was Pal.'

'But Lassie was a girl. I saw her have pups in one of her films.'

'Weren't him. Lassie was Pal and he was a boy dog. That was the *amazing* bit. Everyone thought Lassie was a girl dog, but she wasn't.'

A key turned in the front door. Rory walked straight by them holding a chemist bag in one hand and his stomach with the other. He went into the kitchen, banged around in the cupboards and came back into the room. He dropped a couple of tablets on the coffee table and poured a sachet of powder into the glass of water he was holding. He took a long drink of the mixture and let out a roaring burp, followed by a deep fart.

'Fuck me, boys.' He laughed. 'I'm a walking orchestra.'

'You're home early. You crook?' Sonny asked.

'Yeah. Took ill at the track with this pain in the guts.'

He picked the sack up from the coffee table and shook it. The betting slips sounded like dead leaves. 'As luck had it we had a protest in the second. Should be a winner somewhere in this lot. You two make yourselves useful and help me sort through them.'

He tipped the sack upside down. The tickets poured onto the worn carpet, along with a few cigarette butts, chewing gum wrappers and twigs. The betting slips looked as if they'd been screwed up in anger. 'You know how to read a race ticket, young fella?' he asked Ren.

Ren shook his head. 'Nup.'

'Let me give you an education.' Rory picked up a ticket, smoothed it out and pointed to the figures with his grubby stub of a finger. 'See here, you're looking for the race number. This ticket was a bet on race one. Then you look here for the horse,' he said, pointing down the slip. 'Number six. And the bet is written here. On the nose. Or here for each way.'

Rory took a notebook out of his coat pocket and flipped through the pages. 'I've got the placings listed here.' He held the ticket against the open page of the notebook. 'As you can see, this one is worth fuck all.' He screwed it into a ball and threw it into the empty fireplace. 'You still at school, son?' he asked. 'You like it?'

Ren picked up a ticket from the pile. 'I like English and Art.'

'When I was a kid I hated school. Me and Sonny's dad, we went to the nuns. Mad as cut snakes. I'd rather take a belt from the Jacks.'

The machines continued rumbling in the background. Ren was sure he could feel the ground moving under his feet.

'What's the noise?' Rory asked.

Sonny told him about the day he and Ren had run into the surveyors on the river, the convoy of trucks that arrived that morning and the clearing and building work they'd done in just one day. 'We're gonna stop them,' Sonny said, as if it were a certainty.

'Think so?' Rory said. 'They'll be from the government. You think you can put a halt to them? This is no rock fight with a shitty pants kids down the street. You boys got no hope.'

Sonny looked down at the losing ticket he was holding and tore it apart. 'I got some chance. I been saving up my money.'

'And?'

'Maybe I could hire somebody to stop them for me.'

'Someone like who?'

Sonny looked over at Ren. 'Maybe one of them in the Railway Hotel. There's this one fella in there, Vincent. I heard about him. We could pay someone like him to do it for us.'

Rory laughed so loud he blew the tickets across the room. 'You mean the same Vincent who runs the crew from the front bar?'

'Yeah.'

'You're a poor bugga, Sonny boy. Let me tell you a couple of things about Vincent. Firstly, how much money have you got saved up? A thousand? Two?'

Sonny's face dropped.

'I didn't reckon so. That would be your standard fee, right there. Second up, it wouldn't matter what coin you had saved. No crim is gonna deal with a couple of kids.'

He slapped Sonny lightly on the cheek to get his full attention. 'But let me give you some better advice that might help you out when you're a little older. Low types like Vincent pick their mark. That's why he runs his lot from the pub. He's a king pin in a house of stiffs and no-hopers. So fucken what? Most of the drinkers in there are cripples and seasoned alkies. One step off the back lanes. Cunts like Vincent prey on misery.'

'How do you know so much about him?' Sonny asked.

'Because I've been round a long time. Kept my head down and got a street lesson along the way. Better than I could have got in any classroom. Listening and learning and minding my own business. You want to make it, you keep your eyes open, your mouth shut, and don't get too ambitious.'

'What can we do about the bulldozers then?'

'Not a lot, I wouldn't think. But I'll tell you this much, both of you. You got any expectations in life, never pay another man to do the hard graft for you. That's a debt you can never pay back. You'll spend a lifetime round dogs forever sniffing at your pocket, wanting more from you.'

He took a snotty hankie out of his jacket pocket and blew his nose. 'Maybe you don't want to hear this, Sonny, but with your father giving up on you, my job is to teach you, not fill your head with bullshit that will get you nowhere.'

'We're gone then,' Sonny moaned.

'Maybe. And maybe not. You feel strong enough over this, take care of business yourself.'

'How? You just said that the government can do what they like.'

Rory leaned over further and poked Sonny in the chest. 'You do the best you can and go down fighting. Nothing more to it. Why you so upset, anyway? There must be other places to swim.'

'Not if they blow the river up with dynamite,' Ren said.

'Really? They might come across the old tunnels, then,' Rory said, casually, as if the boys would have known what he was talking about.

'What tunnels?' Sonny asked.

'You two have just been telling me how you know everything about the river. But you never heard of the tunnels? Don't know it well enough then. When I was your age ...'

He stopped talking and passed an eye over the ticket he was holding and shook his head. He showed Ren the ticket. 'See this fuckwit? Last of the big spenders. The goose put one unit on number six for the place, and still threw a winner away.'

'What's it worth?' Sonny asked.

'Nothin that will add up to a day's work. But it all counts.'

He smoothed out the ticket and stuck it in his jacket pocket. 'Where was I?'

'You was telling us about some tunnels,' Sonny said.

'Right. The tunnels. When I was a kid, I worked at the paper factory. There's a tip there now. You know it?'

The tip was a few miles upriver. Any time it rained, rotting garbage washed downstream.

'Some of the older fellas on my shift had been in the war. I heard bits and pieces about the tunnels from them. They'd been on the drill that put bomb shelters in.'

The next betting slip Ren picked up was smudged with dirt. He thought it had a number six in the right column, but couldn't be sure. He passed it to Rory for inspection.

'Why would they have dug bomb shelters round here?' Ren asked.

Rory threw the ticket into the fireplace. The pile in front of them was almost gone and Rory had found only the one ticket worth any money.

'It was the Americans. They were holed up at Victoria Barracks, down from the river. They had military speedboats tied up with the idea that if the Japs attacked they'd jump in the boats and head upstream. Couldn't get above the falls, of course. The story is they built a warren of tunnels connecting two bomb shelters for the American command and every politician in the state. And fuck the rest of us good and proper.'

'You believe the story?' Sonny asked.

'Why not?' Rory shrugged. 'It's worth believing. An adventure.'

'But if there were shelters down there, wouldn't somebody have found them by now?'

'They didn't want to be found. Then or now. They would have dug in some hidden entrances. Wouldn't have wanted

161

ordinary jokers fronting up and crowding them out. We're talking top secret here.'

'These fellas you worked with,' Sonny said, 'did they tell you exactly where the shelters were built?'

'I never asked them. But like I said, it had to be this side of the falls.'

Ren didn't want to offend Rory or his story but he couldn't understand why he and Sonny hadn't heard about any tunnels before. 'Hey, Sonny. You reckon if they built air-raid shelters Tex would know about it?'

'S'pose so.'

'Who's this Tex fella?' Rory asked.

'He's the leader of these fellas who live down the river. They're our … friends.'

'Would this be Tex Carter? Blackfella and ex-boxer? That him?'

Tex had deep brown leather skin. But he'd never told the boys that he was a blackfella. Or that he'd been a fighter.

'Maybe,' Ren answered. 'He lives down there with some others like him. They're drinkers.'

'Be the same fella. Knocks around with a big old boy.'

'Tallboy,' Sonny answered.

'That's the one. Blackfella too, that one.'

'And Tex was a boxer?' Ren asked.

'Yep. And a beauty. Lightweight. I seen him fight at the stadium. Like Gene Kelly, on his feet. And quick hands. Could have been Australian champion, maybe world rated. Until he got himself well and truly fucked.'

'What happened to him?' Sonny asked.

'He went out west one time before a big fight. From

162

memory, I think he was visiting family. He took a couple of bottles of beer with him onto the mission where they were living, which weren't allowed. He got caught in possession of the grog and was convicted. Boxing board took his licence away from him for five years. Poor bastard. He was a clean living kid who never touched the drink. Once they'd done him over like that he hit the piss. Fought in the tents after that. Did some time away for hurting a fella in a street fight. How's he holding up?'

Ren was about to answer *not so good* when Sonny waved a race ticket above his head and hollered, 'Number six. Ten units each way.'

'Pay dirt.' Rory smiled. 'You just hit the jackpot, son.'

'How much?'

'I'll have to do the sums.' He got up from the couch and hitched his pants up. 'I'm not feeling too good, boys. I'm going for a sleep.'

Sonny couldn't get the smile off his face.

'Maybe my luck is changing, Ren.'

CHAPTER 11

Ren was over the measles and soon returned to the river with Sonny. It was the winter school break and after the morning paper round the boys would go home for breakfast and meet in the lane. While neither of them were convinced about Rory's story of the tunnels, it didn't stop them searching for them. The old track leading to the river had been destroyed by the bulldozers. On the way to the river, on their first morning in search of the tunnels, they stood on one side of the compound fence and watched the workmen ready themselves for another day of destruction.

Sonny grabbed the weave of wire in both hands and shook the fence. 'Cunts.'

'Yep. Cunts.'

They slipped through the mill gates to the loading dock. Sonny kicked wooden palings out of the fence at the rear of the mill and climbed through. The boys beat a fresh path into the ground, grabbing hold of bushes and tree branches to stop them tumbling forward as they hiked the bank. 'Can't see the old boys climbing up there,' Ren said, once they'd reached the bottom.

Sonny was picking blackberry thorns from the front of his jumper. 'They'll have to take the stairs by the bridge any time they need to hit the street.'

Ren climbed onto a tree stump above the pontoon. 'I reckon we start here and work our way along the bank, up and down, until we hit the bridge.'

'We've walked here a million times before and never come across any tunnel.'

'What are we doing here then?'

'It's like Rory said, a good story is worth the adventure.'

They headed into a tangle of scrub and quickly found themselves up to their waists in weeds. Ren heard rustling beneath his feet. 'You hear that?'

Sonny stopped walking, listened and nodded his head. 'Be rats. I reckon they nest here at night and slip in the water for a swim. Fuck this. I'm not going any further with no weapon.'

He worked ahead of Ren, along the bank to the car graveyard above the camp.

'Where you going?' Ren called. 'Don't chicken out now.'

Sonny forced the boot of an old wreck and dived in, legs in the air. He came out waving a rusted golf club. Walking back he stopped on the track and practised his swing. 'Four!'

He lay the club down and tucked the bottoms of his jeans into his black-and-white striped football socks.

'You've never looked more like a goose,' Ren said.

'I don't care. This'll stop them running up the leg of my jeans. If I were you I'd do the same.'

'Hey, Sonny, how'd you know there was a golf club in the boot of that car?'

'Just lucky.'

'Bullshit. I bet you stole it off the golf course and hid it there.'

'Good thing I did.' Sonny sliced the iron through the weeds.

Ren heard more scattering under his feet. 'They must be close by.'

'One of them sticks its head up and I'll belt it to death.'

'You don't want one of them rats getting its teeth into you. Do you know there's enough poison on the tip of a rat tooth to kill a town full of people?'

Sonny lifted the club in the air, waved it like a sword and jabbed Ren in the stomach with it. 'No, I didn't know that, Mr Peabody. And I don't care. One rat pops its head up I'll smash the teeth out of its mouth before it gets near me.'

The boys worked slowly towards the iron bridge, Sonny slashing and poking at the ground with his club, Ren creeping along behind him, his socks also tucked into his jeans. It was a hard morning's work. They didn't come across a secret doorway or manhole leading into a tunnel or bomb shelter, but they found a lot of rubbish. Bits of rusted machinery, old bottles and cans, and a KEEP OUT sign. Sonny decided the river men might like it.

'Carry it for us, Ren. I'm gonna nail it to a tree at the camp.'

Ren tucked the sign under his arm. 'Never thought there was this much shit in the world. And that most of it would be dumped here.'

166

Sonny made another discovery. He crouched so low in the weeds he almost disappeared. 'Look what I got here.'

He stood up, holding a dead animal by the tail. It was mostly a skeleton, with tufts of dull fur wrapped around its leg bones and shoulders. Weeds were knitted through its rib cage. Ren took a step back. He'd seen plenty of dead rats before, and another time a bag of maggoty kittens in a sack that had been dumped in the lane. He'd never understood why, but he was more afraid of a dead animal than a living one.

'It looks like a dog.'

Sonny held the skeleton in front of his face and sniffed the fur. 'I don't think so. It's a fox. See this red colour along the back. And the teeth. They're longer and sharper than dog's teeth. Maybe we could keep it?'

'Please yourself, Sonny. I'm not touching it. It could have some sort of disease.'

Sonny swung the skeleton from side to side. The back legs of the carcass fell away. 'Maybe I could take the head home and make a necklace from the teeth the way Indians do.'

'I bet it stinks.'

Sonny sniffed it again. 'Smells of nothing.'

'The only reason you can't smell it is because your nose is blocked with snot.'

Sonny threw what was left of the skeleton into the weeds. They went on searching. Ren got a foot caught in a rabbit hole, tripped and fell, and landed on a solid object. 'Something's under here,' he called.

Sonny turned and ran back to where Ren was kneeling. Excited that Ren may have found an entrance to the tunnels he attacked the weeds with the club.

'Watch it, Sonny. You'll take my head off.'

Ren parted the bed of weeds and looked down at the face of a woman half buried in the ground. The tip of her nose was missing and her face was dotted with small holes. 'Jesus!' he screamed.

'What is it?' Sonny asked.

'It's the Virgin Mary.'

'How do you know that?'

'From Catholic school, where I did primary. Pass me the club and I'll dig her out.'

Ren scraped around the edges of the statue with the iron club until he was able to pull it from the earth. One of Mary's hands was missing and the blue paint of her gown had mostly flaked off.

'She's more a broken Mary than a virgin,' Sonny said. 'How the fuck would she have ended up here?'

'Maybe someone who gave up on God?' Ren laughed

'Come a long way to do it. Could have left her on a street corner. You gonna keep her?'

'Not sure yet.'

They walked on. Ren carried Broken Mary under one arm and the KEEP OUT sign in the other. He lost his balance several times and found it hard keeping his feet on the soggy ground. He'd had enough exploring for the day. When they reached the car graveyard he stopped and rested against the bonnet of an HJ Holden. He opened the door and put Mary in the front seat. A pair of older wrecks sat alongside, a VW beetle and a burnt-out Falcon. The graveyard was popular with car thieves, who drove the stretch of road at the far end of the mill to where they could strip a car clean without being spotted.

Sonny noticed a team of roadworkers on the other side the river, climbing the sandstone steps above the falls. One worker drove a metal spike into the ground with a hammer, while another spied on the boys through a pair of binoculars. Sonny rolled and lit two cigarettes, passed one to Ren, jumped onto the bonnet of the wreck and bounced up and down. A flock of white cockatoos lifted from a tree down on the bank. The birds screeched at Sonny to cut it out. He went on jumping until he slipped, fell onto the bonnet and slid off the car. He sat up. The palms of his hands were grazed with rusted metal. And they were bleeding.

'You'll need a tetanus injection for that,' Ren said. 'Or you'll get lockjaw.'

'You got it wrong. That only happens if a dog bites you. There's nothing locking my jaw. Listen.'

He cupped his hands to his mouth and yelled at the top of his voice to the workers, 'Fuck off and leave our river alone.'

One of the workmen called back, 'Fuck off yourself', and the others laughed.

'I'll give them fuck off,' Sonny growled.

He was about to yell something back at them when it started to rain. Ren got into one side of the car, and Sonny the other, with Broken Mary seated between them. The rainwater mixed with flakes of rusting metal created blood-red streaks that ran down the cracked windscreen. Across the river two workmen carried a large box between them. A third man wheeled a piece of machinery on a trolley. They set to work, bolting a cannon-sized drill together and attaching it to a machine on the trolley with a length of hose. When they switched the machine on the roar was heard throughout the river valley. The men steadied the drill, driving it into the sandstone. They quickly disappeared in a cloud of dust.

Once the drilling stopped and the dust settled the boys saw that one of the workmen was on his hands and knees, clearing the hole. He forced something into it and climbed the steps, laying a length of wire as he went. The other workers picked up their equipment and followed him. The team disappeared over the side of the hill.

The windscreen had turned red and it was difficult to see what was happening. Sonny wedged his body out of the side window and wiped the windscreen with the back of his hand. 'Where've they gone?'

Before Ren could answer they heard a loud explosion. Rocks fell from the sky like rain, bombing the river. A hunk of sandstone, the size of a large fist, crashed onto the bonnet of the car. Ren buried his head in his hands and didn't move until he was sure the rocks had stopped falling. Sonny opened the door, hopped out and looked across the river. Smoke and dust lifted slowly from the steps. Or what was left of them. Large branches and strips of bark had been torn from trees.

'Why'd they do that?' Sonny cried. 'There's no road going over that side of the river.'

'Dunno. They could have killed someone.'

Sonny picked up the block of sandstone from the bonnet and studied it like a piece of moon rock that had fallen to earth. 'I bet we could do some damage if we had that stuff. Explosives.'

'*We?*'

'Yeah. You and me. If they go blowing our place up, we could do the same to them.'

He hurled the rock into the bushes and picked up the KEEP OUT sign. 'Grab your girlfriend Mary and let's get going.'

Scaling down the bank to the camp, the boys found the fire low and could hardly see the river men in the gloom. Tex sat in his car seat, wrapped in a blanket, and Cold Can was looking off into the distance. Big Tiny was laying under a tarp spooning beans from a tin can and Tallboy was pacing the fire. They had to have heard the explosion but didn't seem concerned about it. Ren sensed there was something wrong.

'I've got something for you,' Sonny said to Tex, holding up the sign. 'I'm gonna bang it into one of the trees here so nobody can come by without your permission.'

'And look at this,' Ren added. He stood broken Mary in front of the fire and brushed the dirt from her face. 'She is going to watch over the camp.'

Tex looked across at Mary and managed a wave of the hand. 'She some angel?'

'More like a mother,' Ren said.

'Oh. Could use one of them about now.' Tex shivered so badly his bones rattled.

'Fire's nearly out,' Sonny said. 'You want us to build it up for you?'

Tex could barely nod his head. Sonny collected branches, threw them on the fire, and picked up a ratty blanket to fan the flames.

'You're gonna get pneumonia or something, Tex, if you don't take better care of yourself,' Ren said. 'It might be time for you to move back to the wheelhouse.'

'Too late for that,' he croaked. 'Tex is ready for the gun.'

Cold Can looked across the fire at Tex, his face fretting in the low light. He knew he wouldn't survive a week on the river without the old man.

'You're not dying,' Ren said, with no good reason for saying so. 'I heard that you were a boxer. A champion. You never told us that story before.'

'Who told you that one?'

'Sonny's uncle Rory.'

'Oh.' He wasn't interested at all.

Sonny rolled a cigarette, stuck it in Tex's mouth and lit a match for him. The old man sucked hard until he drew smoke. Air whistled through his lungs. He laid his head against the back of the seat and pulled the blanket under his chin, knocking the cigarette from his bottom lip. Sonny picked it off the blanket and put it back in his mouth.

'What can we do to help?' Ren asked.

'Get on home. Take old Tallboy with you,' Big Tiny shouted. 'Just been telling us he's fucken deserting.'

Tallboy stopped circling the fire.

'Fuck up, Tiny. Don't be misrepresenting me. Telling the youngsters I'm a deserter. I got good reason for taking off. Here I was thinking you'd be happy for me.'

'I am.' Tiny chuckled. 'Because I know you'll run back here quick.'

Tallboy scuffed the ground with his heel. 'Won't be coming back. Tomorrow is goodbye for all time.'

'Where you going, Tallboy?' Sonny asked.

'See my daughter. And a grandkid. She got herself a fella and a place. A caravan out back for me.'

'How long since you seen them?'

'Never seen the baby. And my daughter, not sure how long. Years.'

'How'd you find her, after all this time?' Sonny asked.

'She found me. I went for a feed at the Brotherhood. A fella there says a notice been going round from a woman *seeking information as to the whereabouts* of her father, *Michael John Garrett.*'

'Otherwise known as the one and only Tallboy Garrett,' Big Tiny added.

'Quiet down. This is my story, Tiny. There was a phone number for me to call. Welfare fella give me some coins for the call. I walked round the block a coupla times working on my courage before I called up.' He stared up at the web of girders holding the bridge together.

'And what happened when you rang?' Ren asked.

Tallboy straightened his jacket and ran his hand through his hair like he was about to make an important speech. 'We caught up some time we missed. She told me I have new blood. A grandson. Maybe I want to see him, she said. We been on the phone more times since. I'm on the bus to where she is. Tomorrow. Welfare helped me with a ticket. I got a suit coat and clean shirt to collect. Haven't had a drink in three days. I'm ready.'

'Did you tell her you already got a girl of your own, the white lady?' Tiny needled him again.

'Get fucked,' Tallboy snapped. 'You're only jealous.'

Tex tried his best to sit up in his chair. He glared at Tiny until the fat man looked away. Tallboy took a step forward and shook hands with Sonny. 'I'm happy that you boys come by the camp tonight. Both of you is good boys. You been good friends to us.' He shook Ren's hand and held on to it. 'I got to tell you, this grog is no fun. It's made me poor in the head for a long time. You stay away from the drink.'

Tallboy looked down at Tex, who'd fallen asleep. 'I need a favour from you boys. Once I'm gone you call in on Texas for me. I won't be back. Not ever.'

'We will. We always will,' Ren promised.

Tallboy nodded towards Cold Can. 'There are some who care for him like a true brother. Cold Can is up for that. Always been the same way. But others,' he raised his voice to be sure Big Tiny heard him, 'give a fuck bout no one but themselves.'

As the boys walked away from the camp, Ren stopped, turned around and looked at Tallboy's long shadow dancing in front of the fire.

'Take care of yourself,' Ren shouted.

Tallboy lifted a hand and waved back.

The boys struggled climbing the bank. They stopped and looked through the compound fence again. The bulldozers were eating their way into the earth. A canyon was working its way to the river.

'Won't be long before there's nothing left for us,' Ren said.

'Remember what Rory said? We shouldn't give up without a fight. That's exactly what we done. Give up already.' Sonny picked up a stone and threw it over the fence. 'I got to go out with Rory tonight. Into the city to some pub.'

'What for?'

'Since he come home sick from the races, he's been complaining about his guts. He's taking me to meet the gateman from the racetrack. He ticks off the emus on race days. Rory says he needs to endorse me, let the gateman see my face in case I need to cover for him any time.'

'Does he think he's gonna get real sick?'

'Not sure. He says it's all about insurance.'

Ren lay on his bed that night thinking about how poorly Tex had looked, and what Tallboy had said about the drink being no good for him any longer. He understood for the first time that while the river men enjoyed an adventure, their lives could also be miserable, with no warm bed to sleep in on cold nights, no family to take care of them, and the grog killing their bodies. He opened his window, looked up at the clear night sky and remembered reading in a science book that some of the stars, glowing millions of miles away, had been dead a long time.

The thought frightened him so deeply he was about to close the window and jump back into bed when he noticed a soft square glow on the roof above the kitchen of Reverend Beck's house. He poked his head out of his window and saw that Della's bedroom light was on. He hopped out of his window, quietly crawled across Sonny's kitchen roof and perched underneath her window. He slowly raised his head until he could see into her bedroom. She was sitting at a dresser, with her back to the window, brushing her hair in a mirror. It was longer than he would have expected, almost reaching her waist. He could see a large photograph in a frame on the wall next to the dresser and recognised the black face of the Messenger Divine. Standing next to him were Reverend

Beck and his wife. They were years younger. Della leaned forward, stared into the mirror and studied her face. Her own and Ren's eyes met. He ducked under the ledge and tried to scramble away.

The window opened and Della called him back. 'Don't go. Please.'

She moved her chair from the dresser to the window. Ren leaned against the sill, standing on the roof. She asked him where he'd been that day, and he told her about the hunt for the tunnels, finding the statue of Mary, and the deep hole he and Sonny had seen on the way home being gouged by the machines. He also told her how angry it made him feel that anyone would want to do harm to the river. As she leaned forward and listened, Ren looked more closely at the dark rings under her eyes. She also had a deep scratch across one cheek.

'Are you okay?' he asked.

Della raised a hand to her face. 'Why do you care?' she answered, defensively.

'I don't know. I feel sorry ...'

Della cut him off with a sharp look that surprised him.

'My father is doing important work, and everything he does, bringing the church here, he has done at the request of the Messenger and for his family. *We* sometimes feel sorry for you people. Outsiders.'

'You haven't been hurt?'

'Of course not. Don't be silly.'

Hearing footsteps on the stairway outside her door, she turned her head away from Ren. 'You have to leave now. That will be my father coming to pray with me.'

Ren lay awake in bed until the early hours of the morning, thinking about what Della had said. She hadn't seemed troubled at all, which did nothing to explain the scratch on her face. He eventually fell asleep but woke sometime later, thinking he'd heard a loud crash in the distance. The sounds of dogs barking echoed across the neighbourhood. A little later, Ren heard a police siren. It grew louder as it passed the house then quietened and stopped as he fell back to sleep.

CHAPTER 12

Ren woke the next morning, believing he'd dreamed about the police siren, that he and Sonny had found themselves in some sort of trouble and had been chased. It wasn't until he left the house later that he found out that police were swarming over the compound. He walked to the end of the lane and noticed one of the RTA workers talking to a uniformed policeman. A detective was leaning against a car with one hand in his pocket and the other smoking a cigarette. It was the infamous Foy.

Mick O'Reagan, the milkman, was walking along the street reading from a piece of paper in his hands. He didn't see Ren until he was almost on top of him.

'What's going on down there with the coppers? Ren asked.

'Looks like someone has broken in. The fence has fallen over on the far side of the yard and one of the machines is fucked. On its side in the dirt. Serve them right. Messing with the earth that way. Can only be trouble in that.'

Mick waved the piece of paper in his hand. 'Got a letter here from my boy. I snuck out of the house with it when I spotted the postmark. Thought it might be bad news and I didn't want the wife getting hold of it first. But it's good news.' He smiled. 'Good news.'

Ren walked back to Sonny's place to tell him about the break-in at the compound, but when he knocked at Sonny's door a woman opened it. It was Rory's girlfriend. She reminded Ren of Olive Oil. He couldn't look at her without thinking what Sonny had said to him about her and Rory having sex.

'Sonny here?' he asked, looking down at the doorstep.

'Nope. Heard him tell Rory he was off to the paper shop. Shoots through soon as I show up. The kid doesn't like me.' She shrugged. 'He only come in for breakfast and then pissed off again.'

Ren walked around to the shop and asked Brixey if Sonny was around. Brixey pointed to the back room. 'He's just about living here. I'm thinking of asking him for rent.'

Spike was repairing the back wheel of an upturned bike and Sonny was counting a tray of five cent pieces.

'You ready, Spike?' Sonny asked.

Spike spat in his hands and rubbed them together as if he were about to lift a three hundred pound barbell.

'Ready.'

Sonny spilled two handfuls of coins onto the worn and scarred counting board. Spike sat down opposite him, watching closely as Sonny spread the coins. 'Okay, Spike. How many are there?'

Spike ran his eyes over the coins for a few seconds, no

longer. 'Forty-two. That's two dollars and ten cents.'

'Ren, you count them for me,' Sonny asked, 'while I stack the papers.'

Ren counted the coins, to the exact total Spike had announced. 'How'd you do that?' Ren asked.

Spike shrugged his shoulders and smiled. 'Just can.'

'It's not all he can do,' Sonny said. He threw Ren a dog-eared copy of the *Victorian Football League Almanac*. 'Pick any game from that book and ask him the scores. Ask the crowd numbers if you like.'

'Bullshit.'

'I'll bet all these five cent pieces that it's not.'

Ren flipped through the book and settled on round one, 1927. 'Okay, Spike, can you give me the scores for any of the games?'

'Give you all of them.'

Spike closed his eyes and rattled off the points for each game, quarter by quarter, as if he was reading them from a scoreboard. Although he couldn't see how Spike could have tricked him, Ren was convinced he must have. He picked another year and round. Spike answered correctly again. Ren was impressed.

'How'd you do that? That's fucken brilliant, Spike. You should be on the TV.'

'As long as the questions are about football,' Sonny said. 'Try telling him what day is it, Spike.'

'Fuck off, Sonny, I know the day.'

Sonny wouldn't stop teasing him. He poked a finger against the side of Spike's head. 'When they put that plate in your head, you got the wrong one, I reckon. I'd bet all of them coins on the tray that you can't tell us when you were born. The date.' He pushed Spike in the chest and Spike pushed back, just as hard. Sonny pushed him again. 'Come on, tell us your birth date, retard.'

'Don't call him that, Sonny. Leave him be,' Ren said.

'Mind your fucken business,' Sonny snapped.

'What's up with you? Leave Spike alone.'

Before Sonny could say another word Spike threw a punch at him, hitting him square on the nose. Sonny fell to the ground, crashing into bikes and prams. Spike stood over him. 'Don't call me a retard,' he screamed, 'or I'll punch you again.'

'You are a fucken retard.'

Spike dropped his knees into Sonny's chest and grabbed him by the throat. Brixey heard the commotion from the shop and came running into the back room. He dragged Spike off Sonny and threw him across the room. Sonny sat up. His nose was bleeding.

'What are you doing, Sonny?' Brixey demanded. 'Having a go at him like that. You leave the boy alone.' He turned to Spike. 'And you, out of here. Go and keep an eye on the shop.'

Sonny wiped the blood from his nose onto his shirtsleeve. 'It was him,' Sonny lied. 'Look what he done to me.'

'Fucken bullshit.' Brixey looked angry. 'Spike wouldn't hit anyone. Not without good reason. You treat him different than any other kid in the shop and you can fuck off out of here, Sonny. You pull your head in or there's no job here for you. And you apologise to him before you leave the shop. Or don't come back.'

Sonny was lucky that Brixey had come into the back room, Ren thought. If he hadn't, Spike would have near killed him.

He waited until Sonny had cleaned his nose under the tap in the yard before breaking the news to him.

'I need to tell you something.'

'That Spike's not a retard? It's okay, Ren, Brixey already let me know.'

'I just saw the police at the compound. Tons of them.'

Sonny dried his face with a dirty face washer and looked at his nose in the mirror. 'Don't look like it's broken. It was a lucky punch.'

It was no lucky punch and both boys knew it.

'Did you hear what I just said?' Ren was losing his patience. 'The coppers are all over the compound. Someone's got in there and wrecked one of the machines. You know something about that?'

'I know nothing.' He wiped his nose again. 'I got to shoot through. Rory wants me to take home a *Best Bets* for him. Talk to you later.'

But Sonny wouldn't talk about it. At the newsstand that afternoon he buried his head in a comic book and ignored Ren's questions about the break-in. After work, Brixey locked the shop door and sat Sonny on a stool behind the counter. Ren waited in the street, watching them through the window, expecting that Brixey was going to rip into him. He didn't seem to be yelling at Sonny at all. Brixey rested an arm on Sonny's shoulder as he spoke. When he finished, Sonny nodded his head and they shook hands.

Spike had gone off to the fish and chip shop. He came back with a parcel of steaming potato cakes, and was sharing them with Ren when Sonny walked out of the shop and unlatched the side gate to retrieve his bike.

'Hey, Sonny,' Spike called out to him. 'I got a dozen potato cakes here. I reckon you might be hungry. They have vinegar on them.'

He offered the steaming parcel to Sonny, who hesitated before dipping his hand into the parcel, pulling out a potato cake and taking a bite. 'Potato cakes are the best feed ever. Thanks, Spike.'

Spike bit into his own half-eaten potato cake. 'I got no hard feelings for you, Sonny,' Spike said.

'Me either,' Sonny said. 'It was my fault, Spike. Shouldn't have used that word about you. I'm really sorry.'

Sonny rubbed a finger across the tip of his swollen nose. 'That was a good punch you threw, Spike.'

'Don't matter. I don't feel good about it, hitting you.'

A police car slowly passed by on the opposite side of the road, did a U-turn and pulled into the gutter next to the boys. Ren could see Detective Foy sitting in the front passenger seat. He wound down the window, spat into the gutter, reached over his seat and opened the back door. He wore a blunt nose and had bull terrier eyes.

'Brewer,' he called to Sonny.

Sonny took another bite out of his potato cake and ignored Foy.

'Brewer!' he barked. 'Get in the back.'

Sonny wasn't scared of the police like most kids were, even this one. He looked straight at Foy and refused to move. The detective jumped out of the car and fingered Sonny in the chest. 'We're having a word in the car here, or me and my driver are taking you back to the station for a cooking. Do what you're told, or you can burn. Your decision.'

Sonny took the last bite of his potato cake, buried his hands in his pockets and hopped in the back seat.

Foy nodded at Ren. 'You too, girlie. Keep your boyfriend company.'

Ren hesitated. He thought about doing a runner but Foy was onto him. Foy smiled, as if there was something he admired in the boy. 'Don't be a silly cunt. I'm giving you two seconds.'

Sonny slid across the seat and made room for Ren, who left the door open, just in case he was brave enough to change his mind. Spike waited until Foy was back in the car himself before offering Sonny and Ren another potato cake each. 'I'm full up. I can't eat them all.'

Foy looked up at Spike like he wanted to snap his neck. 'Fuck off, you nutter, before I have your head caved in for a second time.'

'I'm going to get my boss,' Spike said. 'Brixey won't be happy bout this.'

'Get who the fuck you like. But piss off before I turn this show into a trio.'

Foy ordered the driver to turn the inside light on. He showed the boys a fist. It was scarred and deformed by calcified knuckles, the broken bones of past assaults. The copper in the driver's seat rested his hands on the steering wheel and looked straight ahead, along the narrow road that led away from the suburb. Foy relaxed his hand and looked closely at Sonny's swollen nose.

'Where'd you get the war wound?'

'Had a fight with the kid just here with the potato cakes.'

'That fucken mental case?' Foy laughed out loud. 'Sonny, isn't it? I heard you had a bit of go in you, but you must be weak as piss to let him stand over you.'

Sonny glared at him and said nothing.

'Enough playing around. Let's get on with business. Where were you last night, Sonny?' Foy demanded, his light-hearted expression instantly shifting.

Sonny pointed to Ren without hesitation. 'I was at my mate's place.'

'Of course.' Foy smiled. He was certain Sonny was lying to him.

'Yep. He was at my place. Watching TV,' Ren said.

Foy laughed softly and didn't seem too disappointed in the game the boys were playing with him. He rested a hand on Sonny's knee. 'You know, I've been watching you for a while now, Sonny.' He ran the hand along Sonny's thigh. 'Admiring you from a distance.'

Sonny shifted in his seat. Foy's hand followed him. 'Some of you arseholes move up the ranks nice and slow. Start with thieving from the milk bar, maybe a couple of larcenies along the way, then the Boys Home. But you, Sonny, you might have come from nowhere straight into the deep end, the damage you did last night. No one else would have picked you. But I did. First time I saw you.' He suddenly snatched at the crutch of Sonny's pants. 'Time's come for us to get to know each other better.'

Foy squeezed Sonny's balls together. He fell forward in agony, unable to breathe. 'Let me tell you, cunt, you're in big trouble. And I don't mean time away at them holiday farms the Salvos run where you get your dick sucked by some poor kid inside for no reason except his family don't want him. They'll do anything for love, them kids. But you, Sonny, you're off to some other place. And you won't be on the receiving end.'

Foy released his hand from Sonny's crutch and turned to the driver. 'Should we take him back to the station? Or break him in here?'

The driver didn't as much as blink.

'The mischief you got up to last night, Sonny, has won you all my attention. What we have to work out now is what I'm going to do with you. So, let's get a start. Did you break in to that yard on your own? Or was fucken Cinderella here with you?'

'Like I said,' Sonny answered, his voice breaking apart, 'I was with him, watching TV.'

Foy took his hand off Sonny's thigh and moved it across to Ren's knee. 'You know who I am, don't you? You've lived around this way all your life. Would have heard all about me.' He grinned. 'And I know you. Your mother, Loretta, she's from one of the old families, the Renwick mob. They go way back. Tough as nails, all of them. You like them?'

Ren was shocked that Foy knew him at all.

'Don't look so surprised. I know every inch of these streets and everyone that walks them. You seem to be a clever kid. Smart enough to know I hate fucken liars. I hate kids just as much, but I'd be wasting all my energy putting time into breaking you. You might as well be an altar boy. But this one, Sonny, we have a future together and I need to start on top. Give him a good fucking.'

He patted Ren softly on the calf. 'Now, you're about to tell me the truth. What did young Sonny get up to last night?'

Ren was so scared of Foy he was about to piss himself. 'He was with me, watching TV,' he answered, his bottom lip quivering.

'You stick fat, you two.' Foy smiled. 'I'll give you that. And loyalty is rare around here. The local crims give each other up every other day.' He clicked his fingers together. 'Pass me the bag,' he ordered the other policeman.

The driver reached down between the front seats and pulled out a brown paper bag. He handed it to Foy, who went on talking while he dipped a hand inside. 'Tell me, where the fuck did you learn to drive a bulldozer, Brewer? You practise stealing cars? You should have taken proper lessons. Putting that machine through the fence, into a ditch. They're still down there, lifting it out with a crane.'

'I can't drive,' Sonny offered. 'I ride my bike. Or walk. Don't I, Ren?'

Before Ren could open his mouth Foy punched him in the stomach. Ren moaned and fell against the back of the seat. He felt the warm piss run down the inside of his thigh.

'Please don't talk, son. Not a word, if it's more bullshit.'

Foy pulled a black-and-white striped beanie out of the bag and stuck a finger through one of two slits that had been cut into it. 'You left this behind, Sonny.'

'It can't be mine.'

'Of course it's fucken yours. Put it on your scone and let me see how it looks on you.'

'It's not mine. I barrack for Carlton. Same as my dad.'

Foy leaned across the seat and took a swipe at Sonny. He threw his head back and Foy's fist grazed his chin. 'Fuck it. I'm jack of this. Let's see how you go down at the station.'

Brixey walked out of the shop, trailed by Spike. He stuck his head in the back door. 'You two okay?'

Both boys were too afraid to answer. Brixey looked Foy in the eye like he wanted to spit in it. 'What are you doing with my workers here?'

'None of your business. They're coming with us for questioning.'

'They are my business. They work for me and I need their help in the shop. Now. Come on, Sonny, you haven't finished the nightly count. You too, Ren, I need you to clean up.'

Before either boy could move Foy jumped out of the car and chested Brixey. 'I told you, mind your own business. These two are wanted.'

'Wanted?' Brixey laughed. 'Come off it. They're just kids. If you want them at the station for questioning, you'll need to give me time to close up the shop. I'll vouch for them and be sure they get there. I'll bring them along myself. With my lawyer.'

Foy gritted his teeth. Brixey refused to back off.

'I said I'll bring them in, if there's a need. What are they supposed to have done? These two are minors and I'll be speaking with a lawyer on their behalf. I'm entitled to know what your interest in them is.'

Foy dragged Ren out of the car, followed by Sonny. 'We'll be having a catch-up, Brewer.' He pushed Sonny with an open hand, got back in the car and ordered the driver to leave.

Although it was a cold night Ren took his jumper off and tied it around his waist, embarrassed by the piss stain on his jeans. Brixey blocked the shop door. He wasn't letting the boys inside until he got a couple of answers. 'What have you two been up to?' he demanded.

'Nothing,' Sonny said.

'Bullshit. That prick is right about one thing. You're lying. Look me in the eye. And don't lie to me or I'll give you near as good a kicking as he'd have done. You been thieving from people, Sonny?'

'No.'

'You sure?'

'Honest, Brixey. I don't steal.'

Brixey turned to Ren. 'Is he telling the truth?'

'Yep.'

'Good. Then I don't want to know any more than that. Whatever it is, you've got yourselves on the wrong side of the wrong man. Foy hands out beltings for sport and has his claws in every business along this street. You better hope he finds something more lucrative to occupy his time.'

'What about your lawyer?' Sonny asked. 'Maybe he could help us out.'

Brixey wrapped an arm around Spike. 'You're my brief, Spike. What can you do to save these lads?'

'So what did you do?' Ren asked Sonny, walking home from the shop. 'Try driving off with a bulldozer?'

'I couldn't stop thinking about that big hole they're digging. I took the bolt-cutters from behind the toilet and cut through the fence at the compound and tried to break the padlock on one of the sheds.'

'Why the shed?'

'It's got this sign on the front, that explosives are kept inside. I wanted them.'

'Explosives? What were you gonna do with them?'

'Blow up the machines.'

'You're crazy, Sonny. You wouldn't know how to use explosives. You'd have blown yourself up first.'

'Nearly did. I couldn't break the lock with the bolt-cutters. I found a metal bar and tried to smash it. Didn't work either. I gave up and climbed back through the hole in the fence. Then I remembered I left the bolt-cutters behind. I was searching for them when I saw one of the dozer doors was open and the keys in the ignition. I got in, turned the motor over, put my foot down on the pedal and drove straight for the shed. Plan was to knock it over, but then the steering wheel locked. I went straight past the shed and drove through the fence on the other side. I had to jump out of the machine before it rolled and slid into that big hole.'

'And the Collingwood beanie?'

'I cut holes in it for my eyes. It was supposed to be my disguise but I forgot to put it on. It must have fallen out of my back pocket.'

A car drove past as they were about to cross the road into their street. Ren pulled Sonny into a narrow lane behind the corner shop. They waited a few minutes until they were sure the car wasn't coming back.

'Why didn't you come get me?' Ren asked. 'To help you break into the compound.'

'In case I got caught. I didn't want to get you in trouble.'

'I love the river as much as you do. You don't reckon I'd take the same risk, to save it?'

'It's not that. I was laying on my bed thinking about how easy it had been for them workers to blow the steps above the falls. You were right all along, and so was Rory. These pricks can do whatever they like to us and we can't stop them. Breaking into the compound was nothing to do with saving the river.'

'Why'd you do it then?'

'To make them pay. Nothing more than that.'

'We're the ones who will pay now. That copper, Foy, he'll come after us.'

'Doesn't matter. You done nothing wrong and all he has on me is a Collingwood beanie. Can't arrest me on that.'

'He won't forget, Sonny. Brixey's right. He won't let this be.'

'What's he gonna do? Give me a kicking? I been copping those for years off my father. I can take another one.'

When Ren got home Archie was at the stove cooking sausages, which could only mean Loretta was out. She refused to let him cook the nightly meal if she was at home. She reckoned what Archie didn't burn or over-boil he suffocated with a bucket of salt.

'Where's Mum?' Ren asked.

'She's gone to the pictures with a couple of girls from the hospital, and then they're off to a caf in the city for a meal. It's me and you. Sausages and eggs okay?'

'Yeah. Ta. You want a hand?'

'You can set the table. Knives and forks. Salt and Pepper. The bread and butter. Sauce.' Archie said. 'You're a little late,' he added.

Although it wasn't meant as an accusation, Ren bristled. 'I was helping Sonny out, fixing a couple of bikes at the shop.'

'He keeping his head down?' Archie asked.

'He is,' Ren lied. 'Working hard and saving money.'

Archie dropped a plate in front of Ren, piled with greasy charcoaled sausages and runny eggs. Just the way Ren liked them.

Archie sat down opposite him, picked up the salt container and went on talking. 'It's just that I ran into Mick O'Reagan at the butcher's and he was asking if I heard any commotion across the back last night.'

He put down the salt, picked up the tomato sauce bottle and drenched the plate. 'I heard nothing. What about you?'

'Pass me the sauce, Arch.'

'You heard nothing either?' he asked again.

'Nah. I slept all night.'

'It's just that Mick was saying that he heard a noise. Crashing and banging that set his dog off. Then today he finds out that somebody broke into the yard where the machines are parked for the roadworks they're doing, and crashed one of the bulldozers. Vandals, he said. You hear anything about that?'

'Nup.'

Archie tucked into his meal. Ren thought the interrogation was over. He watched as Archie mopped up the last of the grease on his plate with a slice of buttered bread. He wiped his mouth on the dishcloth, something he'd never do if Loretta was home, and picked up the earlier conversation. 'Mick also told me he saw you today, on the street. You never saw anything?'

'Didn't say I never saw anything. I saw a police car down the bottom of the side street. Didn't know what they were doing there. Mick was telling me about a letter he got from his son, away in the war.'

Archie collected the dishes and placed them in the sink. 'He said that nasty copper, Foy, was there. You've heard of him, of course?'

Ren picked up the dishcloth to wipe the table down. 'Everyone's heard of Foy.'

'Well, you be sure to stay out of his sights. The man's dangerous.'

CHAPTER 13

Foy had frightened the life out of Ren, and he spent the following days looking over his shoulder, expecting the detective to come looking for him and Sonny. But nothing happened. The week was quiet. He helped Sonny with the morning paper round as usual, and every afternoon he walked up to the station and stood outside the pawn shop looking in the window at the cameras. He'd already saved enough money for a cheap camera, even a new one, but he wanted something better, a camera with a proper lens that would allow him to take photographs of birds in flight. He also spent more time at the public library reading all he could about how cameras worked. At first he understood nothing, but was surprised that as he read more the technology began to make sense to him.

The newsstand was always busy towards the end of the week, as was the pub. On Friday nights the boys moved through the bar selling the newspapers themselves rather than leave the stack of papers on the counter. This earned them more in tips, seeing as the drinkers had been paid the day before and at the end of the working week they were in a generous mood. The regulars who had gotten to know the boys personally sometimes tipped them without bothering to buy a paper. Vera, the owner of the zebra finches, had her own stool next to the dartboard. She was fortunate that the game shut down on Friday nights. She took the birds along to the pub with her, only drank wine shandies and always tipped when she bought a paper, but only as long as she could give one of the boys a deep kiss on the lips in return.

On the Friday night following their run-in with Foy, Ren and Sonny were sitting at the bar sharing a packet of potato chips when Roy the barman, who'd been concentrating on polishing a beer glass in his hand, casually leaned across the bar and whispered something in Sonny's ear. Ren had been chewing loudly on a potato chip and didn't hear a word Roy had said, although he did notice a solemn change come over Sonny's face. He stopped chewing and listened as Roy repeated himself.

'You sure?' Sonny asked.

'Sure as,' Roy replied. 'He says that he wants a word with you. I wouldn't keep the man waiting either, if I were you. He's a busy man, Vincent.'

Vincent didn't look so busy to Ren. He was reading a newspaper, seated in his usual spot, across the table from his neckless bodyguard. The table was crowded with his cronies, swearing and arguing among themselves.

'Is he after a newspaper?' Sonny asked.

'Take a look, my friend, 'Roy said. 'He's reading the paper. It's a calculated guess, I know, but I don't think he'd be after a second one.'

'What's he want then?'

'Vincent don't tell me what he wants.' Roy sighed. 'But I wouldn't test his patience if I were you. You should hop on over there before he decides to send someone across here to fetch you.'

Sonny picked up his lemon squash, finished off the glass, wiped his mouth and hopped down from the bar stool. 'You have to come with me, Ren.'

'No, I don't,' Ren protested. 'It's you he wants to talk to, not me.'

'Ren, I've helped you out plenty of times. C'mon, I need you to help me now.'

'I don't wanna come. You must have done something wrong by him.'

'Can't have. I've never spoken to him. What wrong could I do to a gangster?'

Roy spread a beer towel along the bar. 'Son, let me give you some more advice. Don't be calling him a name like that. *Gangster.* We're not in the movies.'

Sonny pulled Ren off his bar stool and dragged him over to the toilet door. He pushed the door open, went into the room, turned the tap on over the sink and washed his face. 'Fuck it. I'm really in trouble now. Last week it was Foy, and now this. Can't figure out what he'd want with me.'

'Maybe you been swapping too many stories about Vincent with the other paperboys and it got back to him. You know how much crims hate people talking too much.'

'Can't be that. I only *listened* to stories about him. And I told nobody but you.'

'Sonny, it doesn't really matter what it's about. You got no choice but to front him.'

Sonny looked at his face in the mirror. 'If he kills me, Ren, the money I've saved to get away from here, it's in my locker at the paper shop. Number seven.'

'He's not gonna kill you, Sonny. You're only a kid.'

'Have you forgotten about the body at the station, the debt collector with the sliced throat?'

'Course I haven't forgotten. That's the reason I don't want to go out there with you.'

'Help me out, Ren. You come with me and I'll let you have all tonight's tips to yourself. The lot.'

'The lot?'

'Yep.'

They walked out of the toilet. Ren followed Sonny across the bar-room, looking down at the grubby carpet and counting the cigarette burns. Vincent had his head in the paper and an ear cocked to one side, taking in every word around the table. Ren was able to get a closer look at the scar on the back of the bodyguard's head. It was uglier up close. Not the perfectly round circle it resembled from a distance. The scar formed the letter C, carved roughly into the man's skull. Smaller holes were dotted around the scar, as if his head had been mistaken for the dartboard on the other side of the room.

The men sitting either side of Vincent were locked in an argument. 'I'll tell you what, Rodney,' one of the men yelled across the table, 'you want the fucken car back, go and pick it up yourself. You said right here at this table last Thursday night,' he knocked on the table with the knuckles of his fist, 'if you can get five hundred for it, take five. And now you're telling me it wasn't enough. If you're unhappy about it you need to sort it out yourself. But before you do, make sure you're wearing deep pockets. He'll want compensation.'

Ren recognised Rodney as the man who'd been with Vincent at the meeting with the Greek from across the street. He had deceptive puppy-dog brown eyes. He wagged a finger across the table. 'I never said a word about five hundred. You must be fucken deaf, Clive, as well as fucken stupid. The car was worth double that. Fuck, I paid fifteen hundred for it less than a year ago and haven't driven it around the block. Get it back, you say? He'll have ended it by now and spread it round. Be like trying to put a thousand piece jigsaw together. Fuck that. That car is worth nothing to me now. You took five off him. The only collecting I'll be doing is prizing the other five from you. And that'll be like pulling fucken teeth.'

'You're getting fuck all from me. I did you a favour.'

Rodney turned to the bodyguard. 'You were here, Joey. Did I, or did I not tell this fuckwit last week, sitting at this table, to ask for a ton and do not, under any circumstances, bottom out below eight hundred dollars?'

Vincent looked up from his newspaper, over at Sonny and Ren, and then back at the circle of men at the table. 'Knock it off, Rodney. You're giving me a headache. And we have visitors.'

Joey, the bodyguard, slowly turned his body towards the boys. His head moved with it, as if it were bolted to his neck. Ren noticed he had more scars on his face, each of them a mess. He sniffed the air like an old dog on the hunt for prey.

Vincent neatly folded the newspaper and rested it on the table. He ordered Clive to give up his seat to Sonny. 'Over here, son,' he said, quietly.

Sonny snailed his way to the chair and stood behind it. Vincent patted the seat. 'Take a rest. Can I get you and your friend a lemon squash?'

'We're okay,' Sonny croaked. 'We just had one.'

'Well, you wouldn't want to make a pig of yourself by having a second, would you?'

Sonny slowly sat down and shrank into the seat.

'I've seen you around,' Vincent said. 'You're Teddy Brewer's kid.'

'Yep,' Sonny croaked again.

'Joey, get the poor kid a drink of water or something. Sounds like he's got a terrible sore throat. You got a cold or something, kid? Maybe you been out late at night? No good for anyone with the weather we've been having.'

Joey stuck a hand in the air and clicked his fingers. Roy was standing at the table within seconds. Joey ordered another round of drinks for the table and two glasses of lemon squash for the boys.

'I know your old man,' Vincent continued. 'Have known him a long time. Teddy used to come in here like clockwork every afternoon. I could have set my watch by him. Your father is a man of habit, Sonny. You know that?'

'Nup. I don't.'

'He is. Unfortunately, he has one bad habit. Working on the hot-mix. Fucken thirsty work that. The poor bastard got too thirsty, didn't he? He went downhill in a rush, your dad.'

The others at the table sat quietly listening to Vincent, as if he was royalty. He wrapped a large hand around Sonny's neck and gently shook him. 'Where's your manners? I need you to look at me, son, when I'm talking to you.'

Sonny turned to face Vincent.

'That's better. And now I need to ask you a very important question. I need a true answer from you. Nothing like the shit you been trying to sell to that cunt, Foy, over the break-in the other night. I heard all about that fuck-up. Now, I need to know where he's got to, your dad. He hasn't been seen in here or on the street for some time now.'

Vincent shifted his chair closer to Sonny, who couldn't keep his eyes on him any longer. Sonny looked across the table at Ren. He'd never seen such fear on Sonny's face before. Vincent tightened his grip on Sonny's neck and shook him a little harder. 'Where's he got to?'

Ren opened his mouth before he knew what he was saying. 'He went away and left Sonny by himself in the house. He's disappeared and nobody knows where he is.'

Everyone at the table turned to Ren. Except for Vincent, who didn't bother looking up. He patted Sonny on the back, stood up, pushed his chair into the table and stuck his hands in his pockets.

'Come with me, son. There's something important I need to show you. You and your mate. Both of you. Follow me. Don't worry, I'll have your drinks brought up.'

Rodney stood up and opened a door directly behind the table. The bodyguard was about to stand up as well. Vincent smiled at him.

'What are you doing, Joey? Take a rest. We're dealing with a couple of kids here, not hired killers.'

He slapped Sonny on the back. 'You're not gonna kill me, are you, son?' He laughed. 'Rodney, grab the young mascot and bring him along for company.'

Vincent led Sonny through the doorway, marched him to the end of the hallway and up a narrow staircase winding its way to the top floor of the hotel. Ren couldn't move quickly enough. Rodney stopped, waited for him to pass and pushed him in the middle of the back. As they walked along a second hallway Ren could see that the doors on either side were open and the rooms were empty, except for mattresses stacked against the walls. At the end of the hallway Vincent took a key out of his pocket and opened a door. The room had bare floorboards, a beaten leather couch against one wall, and a table in the middle of the room with a pack of playing cards and a telephone sitting on top. A noisy refrigerator hummed away in the corner and a single window looked over the street.

Vincent nodded towards the couch. 'Take a seat and make yourselves at home.' He dragged a chair away from the table and sat in front of the boys. He stared at Sonny for several minutes without saying a word. Rodney walked over to the window, pulled a curtain to one side and looked down on the street. He turned and nodded at Vincent and lit a cigarette. Ren could feel his heart thumping in his chest, convinced it was beating faster than the day he stood on the ledge of Phoenix bridge in the moments before he jumped. Sonny couldn't keep still. His legs were shaking and he was scratching his head like he had nits.

Vincent finally spoke. 'You like a good story, Sonny?' he asked.

'I guess so.'

'Well, let me tell you a beauty. Your father, he came to me some time back. Told me he'd got himself in a heap of trouble. I've never seen a man as desperate as he was that day. Sweating and shaking, he was.'

Vincent tilted his head to the side and stared at Sonny. He couldn't work out if Vincent was waiting for him to say something or was examining his bad eye.

'You're shaking,' Vincent said, putting a hand on Sonny's knee. 'You nervous?'

'Nah. I'm okay.'

'Good. Don't worry yourself over me. Your fucken daddy dropped you in the shit and I'm going to help you out of it.' He took a piece of paper out of his pocket and handed it to Sonny. 'Take a look at that and tell me what it is.'

Sonny took the piece of paper from Vincent and looked down at it. It was a carbon copy of the same rent receipt Rory had shown Loretta the night he had turned up at Ren's door.

'What is it?' Vincent prompted him.

'It's a receipt,' Sonny answered.

'Good. Now let me tell you why I have it in my possession. You're dad came to see me. He sat on the couch, right where you are now, and begged me to help dig him out of the hole he was in. He said he had a rack of debts, gambling and drinking money, and had got himself a long way down on the rent. The landlord had been round to your place and said he wanted the rent back-paid in full or your father and you would be out on your arse. A week's grace the landlord give him. Fuck me. There's no grace in that. Vultures. When the week was up the landlord sent some heavy around to put the threateners on him. Fucken dog. Your old man have a word to you about that?'

'I knew he'd run out of money,' Sonny snivelled, 'but he never said nothing about owing back rent. Or anyone threatening him.'

Vincent took the receipt from Sonny and slowly tore it into thin strips as he spoke.

'He wouldn't want you to know, I suspect. Have you worrying over it. He owed money all over town. That's why he come to me for help. He sat there and broke down and cried, didn't he, Rodney?'

'Like a baby.' Rodney chuckled. 'It was embarrassing.'

Vincent shook his head in mock disgust. 'First of all I thought he was going to ask me to go and pay a visit to the landlord and break his legs on him.' He stood up from the chair, walked across to the window, opened it and sniffed the air. 'A job like that wouldn't have come cheap. But had he gone down that path it would have cost him less in the end, as it's turned out. Rodney here warned me that stepping in and helping your dad out would be a poor investment on my part. My problem is I can be as soft as butter. Against all commonsense I covered his debts. Rodney went off his rocker. *Fuck the cunt and give him nothing.* That's what you said. Am I right, Rodney?'

'Spot on, Vince.'

'Your dad had been near drinking himself to death every night of the week. It got so bad he was pissing his own pants. One of my fellas, Clive, he come across him out in the street after the pub had closed, laying in the gutter. A pathetic sight.'

Sonny couldn't help but show his anger.

'I know, son,' Vincent went on. 'This is a story you don't want to hear. But I need to tell it you in full so you understand the trouble you've been left with. The funny thing is the day he come in for the loan, he was sober. Silly me thought it might be the start of better days for him. That's the reason I covered the debt. I even sent Rodney round to speak with the landlord personally. Paid him the money, every cent your old man owed him. Rodney told the landlord that if he put one of his dogs within a mile of your father I'd have his balls. You paid him a visit, didn't you, Rodney?'

'I did. An old Italian fella.'

Vincent tapped the floor with the heel of his boot. 'I have been more than generous with your father. But the trouble is, Sonny, I haven't sighted him or seen a dollar of my money since that day.'

He slowly walked the length of the room. 'On your feet, boys. Over here. I need you to see something.'

Ren could hardly lift his feet from the floor. He shuffled across the room after Sonny like a crippled pensioner.

Vincent drew the curtain back from the window. 'I need you to take a look down there, over to the other side of the street, and tell me what you see.'

Sonny looked out the window. He didn't notice anything particular about the street. Vincent tapped the glass. 'You see the Greek club on the corner?'

'Yep,' Sonny answered. 'The one where they play the card games?'

'That's the one. Now, you see that white van with the dark window parked down the street a bit?'

A van with a sign – *St Patrick's Meats* – painted on the side, was parked on the corner of a laneway, a couple of car spaces back from the club door. Rodney nudged Sonny in the back. 'You see it?'

'Yep. I see it.'

'Let's test your street nous,' Vincent said. 'Who might be sitting in that van?'

Sonny stuck his hand in the air like he was in school. 'The butcher?'

Rodney chuckled and Vincent smiled. 'Cute, son. But it's the wrong answer. Rotten fucken police are in the back of that van. Gaming Squad. They have one eye on the club door and the other over here, watching me. This snooping has created a problem for me and the owner of the Greek club, Chris. We do business with one another, and from time to time I need to send a package across the street to him. He's been waiting all week on something from me but I haven't been able to get it to him because of the snoops. You think I'm an unfriendly type, let me tell you, Chris can be a very difficult man. Gets himself wound up. Impatient.'

Vincent turned his back on the window, leaned against the ledge and cracked the knuckles of the fingers on both hands. 'If I were to cross the street now, or one of my friends from here were to do so, on my behalf, or let's say Chris sent one of his boys over to the pub to pick up the package, like he usually does, we could have a problem with the pigs in the meat wagon. For all I know they've got cameras in there, and I don't like having my picture taken. So,' he cracked his knuckles again, 'I need to solve this problem. In a hurry.

That's where you come in, Sonny. And your mate, seeing as he's here anyway. What's your name?'

'Ren.'

'What sort of a name's that?'

'Just Ren.'

'Well, Just Ren. As you have just heard me tell your friend, I'm out of pocket on account of being owed money by Mr Teddy Brewer. Do you think his own son has the coin to cover his father's debts?'

When Ren didn't answer Vincent slammed his heel into the floor. 'Do you have it, Sonny. The money owed to me?'

'I have a little,' Sonny offered. 'I been saving.'

'A little bit won't add up to much more than fuck all to me. You'll be about ten lengths off the interest payment just to start with. I don't like to have to tell you this but since your father borrowed from me, the debt has doubled.'

Sonny turned pale and looked as if he was about to vomit.

'You are deep in the shit, son. Chest high and sinking. I feel sorry for you, being put there by your own flesh and blood. But that's why you need to pay. It's your inheritance. Count yourself lucky I'm around to throw you a lifeline. Anyone else might cut you up.'

Vincent held up a finger in the air and left it there, to be sure Sonny got a decent look at it. 'One job. Just one small favour for me and you and your excuse for an old man will be debt-free. I'm ready to wipe the slate. You up for it?'

'For what?'

'For work. All you need to do is push your pram across the street, go into the club and drop a newspaper to Mr Chris. That's it.'

'That all?' Sonny asked, smart enough to know that the man sitting across from him couldn't be trusted.

'That's all. And your debt will be cleared. Every dollar your father owes me, including the interest. Done for a few minutes' work.' He offered Sonny his hand. 'We in business?'

Sonny hesitated before putting his hand out. Vincent shook it. 'Good boy.'

Vincent walked over to the table, picked up the telephone and dialled a number. 'On its way,' was all he said. He put the phone down, opened a drawer under the table and pulled out the morning newspaper, fatter than it should be, and tied together with string. He took a small black pocketbook out of his coat and wrote in it, before handing the newspaper to Sonny. 'Off you go then. You put that with your papers, get over the street, knock at the door and ask for Chris.'

As Sonny was about to take the newspaper, Vincent held it back from him. 'There's something else I forgot to tell you. Part of our arrangement. There's another little story you need to hear from me before you go. I heard that some crazy fucken kid broke into a yard and wrecked a fifty-thousand-dollar bulldozer. Government property it was. You hear anything about that?'

'I heard,' Sonny answered.

Vincent turned to Ren. 'What about you, little fella? You hear about that?'

'Some of it. Not much.'

'Well, the outcome couldn't be worse for whoever done it. Detective Foy is on the case. Fucken psychopath.' He raised both hands in the air. 'I have no time for police. But in the end, they do their job and I do mine. But Foy is something

207

altogether different. The man's a cunt and a half. You get a taste of that when he bailed you in the back of the car the other week?'

Sonny looked down at his scuffed shoes and nodded his head up and down. Ren looked over to the window where Rodney was standing. He seemed bored and was picking his nose.

Vincent rubbed a finger across his bottom lip and licked it with his tongue. 'Detective Foy has the bad habit of behaving like an animal from time to time. I can tell you from experience, I've dealt with some short fuses, but I have never come across a man with a worse temper. So unpredictable. Isn't he, Rodney?'

'He is.'

'But as luck has it, Sonny, I'm in a position to have a word with him. I can shift his attention one way or the other. I can call him off your back altogether with the right word. Or I could have him working like a cross between Sherlock Holmes and Attila the Hun. Which way do you think I should go?'

'I dunno what happened to that machine.' Sonny shrugged. 'It's got nothing to do with me.'

'Good answer, Sonny. It's complete bullshit, but a good answer. Be sure you're just as sharp if anyone asks if you've had dealings with me.'

Vincent pushed the newspaper into Sonny's gut. 'Now use your good sense and get yourself across the street, deliver the paper to the Greek and you're free. No debt and no mad copper up your arse.'

★

The boys stood on the footpath, beneath the glow of the neon light above the hamburger joint, next door to the hotel. The newspaper with the string tied around it lay in Sonny's pram, under a magazine.

'You know we don't have to do this,' Ren said. 'We can wheel the pram straight back to the shop and go home.'

'Maybe you can, but not me. You take off home if you want. If it were me in your place, I would. But I have to do this if I want to keep Foy off my back. And like he told me upstairs, if I do this my old man's debt will be wiped.'

'You gonna take his word for it? I don't trust him.'

'Nothing to do with trust. I'm hoping. It's all I got.'

There was nothing Ren wanted to do less than walk across the road to the Greek club but he didn't feel good about leaving Sonny on his own. 'I'll come with you,' he said.

'You don't need to act brave all of a sudden.'

'Nothing brave about it. Some old Greek fella is not going to give us trouble. I bet he's under Vincent's thumb like everyone round here. Sounds like even Foy is in his pocket.'

They crossed the road. Sonny pushed the pram and Ren looked down the street to where the meat van was parked. The cabin was empty. Sonny stopped outside the club door, turned and looked back at the window above the hotel. The blind was pulled to one side and Vincent was watching the street.

'You see anyone in the van, Ren?' he whispered.

'Nah. They probably have a hidden camera.'

Sonny lifted the magazine, picked up the newspaper and tucked it under his arm.

'Last chance, Ren. If you're thinking of shooting through, go now. Or you can wait out here for me. If I don't come out in five minutes take the pram back to the shop.'

'Why wouldn't you come back out, Sonny? It's not like these Greeks would kidnap you or something.'

Sonny knocked at the door. A boy opened it wearing an apron over a white T-shirt and jeans. Ren had seen him before, hanging around at the hamburger joint playing the pinball machines. 'What do you want?' he sneered.

'We're here for Chris,' Sonny answered. 'We've been sent by Vincent.'

'Stay here. I'll go ask.'

The boy closed the door. Sonny could heard him calling to somebody in Greek. A couple of minutes later he was back. 'Chris says it's okay for you to come in.'

The Greek club consisted of one long narrow room. Men sat at a table playing cards. They didn't look all that different from Vincent's crew, except these men were a little older and greyer. None of them looked up when the boys walked into the club. A younger man leaned over a pool table with a cigarette hanging out of his mouth. He looked as if he was about to play a shot, but didn't. He wore a tight short-sleeved shirt, had muscled arms and an unfriendly face. The walls of the club were covered with posters and photographs of soccer teams. A blue-and-white striped flag hung from the ceiling. The boy who'd opened the front door walked into a back room, through a plastic strip blind. He could be heard talking to somebody, again in Greek.

Less than a minute later the blind parted and a man walked through it. He was wearing a cardigan over a shirt and dark trousers. It was the same man Sonny had sold a newspaper to on the first morning Ren had helped out with the paper round. A heavy gold cross hung from his neck and he wore his thick black hair brushed back. The pool player moved away from the table to the front door and snapped the lock shut. The older man smiled at the boys.

'Hello, young men. You have something for me?'

'Are you Chris?' Sonny asked.

'I am Chris.' He smiled again.

Sonny handed him the newspaper. 'This is for you. We were told to bring it from Vincent.'

Ren was desperate to escape the club as quickly as possible. He turned to leave. The old Greek lifted a hand in the air. 'Now you must wait.'

Chris called the pool player over. 'Nikos.'

Nikos took the newspaper from Chris and went into the back room. Chris invited the boys to sit at one of the tables. Ren did his best not to look too closely at the man. He pretended to be interested in the posters of soccer teams.

'You like the football?' Chris asked. 'This football?' he added, pointing at one of the posters.

Ren knew nothing about soccer but didn't want to offend the man. 'It looks like a good game in the pictures.'

'Ah, you play the other football? Aussie ball?'

The pool player stuck his head through the blind and lifted his hand, just a little. Chris tapped the table. 'All good. Thank you, boys.'

He went behind the shop counter and picked up a large knife. 'Here. Come.' He waved the boys over and stooped to open a cupboard under the counter. 'You hungry?' he asked.

He was holding a square of cake on a tray. He sat it on the counter and began to cut into it. 'The man over there, is he hiding in his castle?' he asked, as he admired his knife. Neither of the boys was sure what he was talking about. He cut two slices from the cake and placed them on sheets of wax paper. Chris looked directly at Sonny. 'Is he King Vincie? Or prisoner in that place?' He seemed to be talking to himself as much as he was to the boys. He handed each of them a slice of the cake. 'Eat this one,' he said, wiping the crumbs from the knife with a cloth. 'I think he is prisoner.' He laughed.

Ren took a bite of the cake. He'd never tasted anything as sticky and sweet.

'You like this one?' Chris asked.

'It's beautiful,' Ren answered.

'Is baklava. The best.'

Chris walked over to Sonny and touched him on the arm. 'I see you go out in the mornings with papers. Every day. Early. You are good worker. Come here another time. More baklava for you.'

Chris nodded to Nikos, who unlocked the front door.

As the boys made their way up the street they could see Brixey was waiting out the front of the shop, marching up and down like a soldier on guard. Spike was leaning against the shop window, listening to him rant. As soon as Brixey saw the boys coming he called out to Sonny. 'Do you know what time it is? I should have locked up and been on my way home by now.'

'I'm really sorry, Brixey,' Sonny said. 'Take it easy. We ran into trouble, didn't we, Ren?'

'Don't be telling me to be taking it easy, Sonny. I'm your boss. What sort of trouble?'

212

'We were in the pub picking up the returns when this kid knocked the pram from the street and took off with it. There was at least a dozen magazines in there. I wasn't going to have them stolen on you. Or lose your pram, Brixey. We chased him all the way to Fitzroy to get the pram back.'

Brixey softened a little. 'What did he look like, this kid?'

'Hard to say. We only saw the back of him. And he was moving real quick.'

'You said you chased him and got the pram back. You must have got a look at him when you caught up with him?'

'Nah. I was half a block off him when he slammed the pram into a wall and kept on running. He took off up a lane and disappeared.'

Ren looked from Sonny to Brixey and back again. He had to hand it to Sonny, the way he could conjure a story out of nothing, on the spot. Brixey looked a little suspicious. He watched closely as Sonny took a bite from his baklava and chewed on it.

'How'd you get your hands on the cake then, if you were running up the street chasing a kid who had your pram?'

'We were given the cake just now. After we got the pram back, we were coming down the street and the fella at the Greek club bought a paper from us. He gave us the cake for a tip. Didn't he, Ren?'

'That's right. He gave us a piece of cake each.'

Brixey wasn't convinced. He wasn't sure if Sonny was bullshitting to him or not, but he raised his eyebrows and decided to let it slide. Spike couldn't take his eyes off Sonny. He wiped a hand across his mouth. 'Do you think I could have some of that cake?'

'Sure, Spike.' Sonny broke off a hunk of cake and handed it to him. Spike slowly chewed on the cake and stared greedily at what was left in Sonny's hand. 'This is a good ... what do they call it?'

'Balaclava. It's a balaclava cake.'

It took only a week for Vincent to go back on his promise. The next Friday night he called the boys over to the table and again ordered them to follow Rodney upstairs where Sonny was handed another envelope hidden inside a newspaper. Rodney wrote some figures in Vincent's book and sent the boys across the road to the Greek club again. The week after it was another envelope, and each Friday after that it was the same story.

While the boys were uneasy around Vincent and didn't trust a word that came out of his mouth they quickly got used to the Greek club. The same kid would always open the front door, wearing his dirty apron, and Nikos, who made a habit of snarling at them when they came into the cafe, would take the newspaper into the back room and count the money. As soon as he'd given Chris the nod the boys were called over to the counter and would leave the club with cake.

It didn't take long for Sonny to realise it would take some time before he paid off his father's debt, if at all. Each week Vincent made a point of mentioning Detective Foy and how he was the only person who could keep the policeman off Sonny's back. Sonny was feeling as miserable as he had in the days between being thrown out of school and landing himself the job at the paper shop. The gloomy weather matched his mood. It rained most mornings when he and Ren were on the paper round. The dark clouds hung so low in the sky Sonny thought he might be able to reach up and touch them.

After they'd done the club run half-a-dozen times Vincent called the boys to another meeting, where he told them he was thinking of giving them other jobs to do. Paid jobs.

'You two don't need to be my errand boys for much longer. You know when I get hungry and want my steak sandwich, a messenger boy from the hamburger place downstairs brings it up to me. If I want something important done, I get one of my own to do it. Somebody I can trust. Right now I'm thinking of making you boys my own. What do you think?'

'What would we have to do?' Sonny asked.

'I haven't made up my mind yet.'

'You don't believe what he said, about giving us paid jobs, do you, Sonny?' Ren asked, after they'd left the pub with the delivery that night. 'Something's up with all this. Haven't seen a van outside the club since the first night. I don't reckon any coppers were watching him in the first place.'

Sonny stuck the envelope in the pram and wheeled it to a vacant doorway three doors down from the hotel. He ducked in the doorway, poked the top of the newspaper open and pulled out the envelope.

'What the fuck are you doing?' Ren asked.

'You reckon there's something up, well, I want to see what's inside the envelope. It's got to be money. Let's see how much.'

Sonny opened the envelope. It was stuffed with large notes. He whistled, stuck the envelope back into the newspaper and re-tied the string. 'Must be a thousand dollars in there. Maybe more.'

'We need to get moving. Vincent will be looking for us from the upstairs window.'

'Why would he give so much money to the Greek?' Sonny wondered as they crossed the street. 'Vincent's supposed to be the heavy.'

'I don't know. And guess what, Sonny? I don't care. All I know is that this means trouble for us. You shouldn't have opened that envelope. If we get caught, we're fucked.'

'Who from? Vincent or Chris?'

'Both of them for all I know. This is the last time I'm doing this, Sonny.'

'You quitting on me?'

'No one's quitting. We're in serious trouble, and we have to find a way out of it.'

'It shouldn't be too hard, Ren,' Sonny said sarcastically. 'Next time Vincent tells me I have to drop the envelope for him, I'm gonna tell him I've retired. You reckon he'll let me walk away?'

'But you paid him back the money, everything your dad owed him, over and over by now. He said it would be just the once. This is bullshit.'

'Remember what Rory told us. With people like Vincent *you never stop paying*, is what he said.'

'And if you'd listened to him, maybe we wouldn't be in this shit now.'

'You reckon I had a choice? My old man got me in all this trouble. I told you the first night I did this you could walk away. You were the one who wouldn't listen. And have you forgotten about Foy? I haven't seen him since that night out front of the shop when he mashed my balls. I bet Vincent can set him on us any time he feels like it.'

Ren had forgotten all about Foy. He felt sick.

The boys dropped the newspaper at the club, returned the pram to the shop and headed home. Sonny knew he was pushing their friendship but asked Ren if he would help him out the next morning on another job.

'Rory's been sick again and hasn't been able to get out of bed all week. He needs me to cover the emu run for him at the races tomorrow. He's already missed the midweek meeting and is worried that if he's away much longer someone will move in on his turf.'

'What time do you need to be at the track?'

'Early as I can get there. You help me with the paper round and we'll take off straight after that. I'll shout you an egg and bacon breakfast in town.'

'If we come up with a winner do we have to hand the ticket over to Rory?'

'Nah. He says we keep everything we earn, except for ten per cent off the top. He says that's a standard manager's fee.'

'Rory's our manager now? We have Vincent running our lives as well.'

'Will you help me or not?'

'Sure. But tomorrow we have to come up with a plan to get out of this trap Vincent has put us in. You told Rory what's going on? Maybe he could help us.'

'I been meaning to talk to him about it, but with him being sick I don't want to worry him. He's already gone out of his way to help me.'

Ren slept poorly that night and went downstairs early in the morning. Archie was getting ready for work, pouring water into a thermos flask. 'What are you doing up?'

'I was gonna make a cup of tea.'

'You look worried. Something on your mind, Charlie?'

'Nah. I'm okay. I woke up and couldn't get back to sleep.'

Archie put his thermos in his work bag along with his sandwiches. He slung the bag over his shoulder. He looked at Ren, sure there was something more going on with the boy than a restless night.

'You change your mind, if there's something you want to talk about, you let me know.'

CHAPTER 14

Once Archie had left for work Ren sat on the couch with a cup of tea thinking over how he and Sonny could escape Vincent's clutches. Backed into a corner, Sonny was likely to do something drastic that would end with him in more strife, Ren thought. He soon fell back to sleep only to be gently shaken awake by Loretta a couple of hours later. He sat up, unsure of where he was.

'What's the time, Mum?'

'Nearly eight. How'd you end up down here on the couch?'

'Eight! I've missed the paper round. And the emu run.'

'What are you talking about? Emus?'

He ran upstairs, got dressed and bolted out of the house. He ran next door to Sonny's and knocked. When there was no answer he loudly called Sonny's name. Nobody answered. He ran around to the back lane, skipping puddles, and picked up a small stone. He threw it at Sonny's bedroom window and waited. Still nothing. Shivering in the cold, he kicked the door open into the yard. Sonny's bike was resting against the rubbish bin. He pushed it into the lane, jumped on and rode around the corner into the street, quickly picking up speed. A terrier ducked under the fence of a house towards the end the street and ran after him, barking madly. Ren turned the corner and almost ran into Spike, trotting down the middle of the road. He skidded to a halt.

'Spike. I'm after Sonny. He finished his round yet?'

'He never turned up this morning and no papers went out. Customers have been coming in the shop complaining all morning. Next time Brixey sees Sonny he will drill a hole in his head. He sent me looking for him.'

'I just knocked at his door and he's not home. You sure he never came into work?'

Nothing angered Spike more than the suggestion that he wasn't quite with the world, mentally. 'I'm not a stupid person,' he grumbled.

'I never said you were, Spike. It don't make sense, that's all.'

'Maybe he's afraid of that copper.'

'Which copper?'

'The ugly one with no hair.'

'Foy, out front of the shop? That was weeks back, Spike. Sonny hasn't missed a day's work since then.'

'But he come this morning too, the copper. He was parked out front of the shop. I saw him and he saw me. Then he took off, driving real slow with the windows down and looking round like he was after someone. I was putting the gum machine out in the street. It was just before Sonny's start time.'

'Did you see which way he drove after he left the shop?'

'Yep. Along the railway line. Same way I've just come. You think Sonny's in trouble?'

'Not sure. If you see him be sure to tell him about Foy. And ask him to leave a note on my window.'

'Your window?'

'He'll know, Spike. Make sure you tell him. I'm gonna try finding him myself.'

Ren rode back along the street to the lane. He was about to open Sonny's gate when he heard a sermon coming from the stable. *The Reverend must be practising*, he thought. He rested the bike against the fence, walked quietly to the stable and pressed his eye to the hole in the timber wall. He could see the Reverend pacing back and forth, looking up at the roof as he spoke.

'Is it known that the Father was the most remarkable scientist?' he asked. 'And though He is a man of peace, is it not a fact that it is Father Divine who is also father of the hydrogen bomb?'

The Reverend stopped, leaned on the back of a chair with one hand and took his white handkerchief from his pocket with the other, wiping his lips before going on. 'And also, when his chosen followers, John the Revelator and Faithful Mary fell, they did so as they had dared to question Him and betrayed our leader, Father Jealous Divine ...'

The Reverend began walking around in a wide circle repeating to himself, 'Is it not known? Is it not known?' and clapping his hands together in time. He stopped pacing, sat on the chair and brought his massive hands together. He leaned forward and repeated the question in a quiet, almost womanly voice. 'Is it not known?'

'Yes,' came an answer. It was the voice of a young woman, although it was not Della's, Ren was certain.

The Reverend stood, stepped back, looked up to the roof again and smiled. He removed his suit jacket and placed it neatly over the back of the chair. He undid the buttons on his white shirtsleeves and rolled them up as he spoke. He took a step forward and disappeared from sight. Ren pressed his ear to the crack in the timber. He could hear the shuffling of feet and what sounded like a chair scraping across the wooden floor. The Reverend whispered what sounded to Ren like a prayer, over and over, and each time the female voice replied, 'Yes, Father.'

Ren crept away, collected the bike and returned it to Sonny's yard. There was only one place Sonny could be.

Ren walked alongside the compound fence on his way to the river. After the night Sonny had broken into the yard and crashed the bulldozer it was patrolled day and night. A watchman walked beside Ren on the inside boundary. He took his cap off, exposing a sweaty comb-over plastered to his skull. 'Where you heading, son?' he asked.

'No place.'

The watchman jangled the chain of keys from his belt, as if it provided him with some authority over the boy. 'You have to be going somewhere.'

'Not me. No place is good enough.'

The watchman trailed him until Ren had scrambled through the gates into the mill. He headed for the camp, but when he got to it there was no sign of Sonny or the river men. From beneath the iron bridge he could see somebody standing at the edge of the river by the pontoon. It was Della. As he walked along the track towards her he could see that the back of her long dress was covered in mud and the hem was weighted down with twigs and leaves. He snapped a stick laying across the track and Della turned around. She had her head scarf off and was clutching it in one hand.

She looked at Ren as if he was a stranger.

'What are you doing down here on our river?' he asked.

'Your river?' she answered, genuinely puzzled.

Yeah, my river, Ren thought.

Even though it was cold Della had rolled the sleeves of her woollen jumper back to her elbows. He could see that she had cuts on both hands and her lower arms. They were so fine he thought that they could only have been done with a razor blade. She noticed him staring at them and rolled her sleeves down.

'What are you doing here?' he asked.

Della pushed her hair away from her face, tucking it behind her ears. She watched Sonny closely but didn't say a word.

'You know this is mine and Sonny's place?' Ren said. 'No one comes down here without our permission.' As soon as he opened his mouth he knew it was a stupid thing to say. He and Sonny hadn't been able to stop anyone coming to the river. It was being bulldozed and blown up in front of them and they hadn't been able to do a thing about it. 'I don't really mind you being here,' he added, gently this time.

She turned away from him. 'This isn't my first visit. I've been here before.'

'You couldn't have. I come here most days and I've never seen you. I know everyone who comes and goes from here.'

She turned back to him. 'I *have* been here,' she repeated. 'Last week I was watching from my window when you and your friend returned home. I waited until you were in his yard and decided to walk here.'

She might just as well have told Ren she'd broken into his house. 'Why'd you do that?'

'You had told me about the river and the waterfall and I wanted to see it for myself.'

After the recent rain the river was running high and fast, and the bank was muddy.

'I'd move back from the edge, if I was you,' Ren warned, 'or you could fall in. That dress will weigh you down and send you straight to the bottom.'

'Straight to the bottom?' Della repeated after him.

'Too right.'

Della concentrated on the passing current as it traced a swirl on the surface of the water and moved towards the iron bridge. The sky had clouded over and it was growing dark. Out of nowhere a flash of lightning tore across the sky. A fresh storm was coming. Ren looked up, sure that the rain was about to arrive.

'We should head for home. Or you'll get caught in the wet.'

She turned and stepped towards Ren.

'I don't care. I'm used to storms. I've lived in places where there are storms far worse than you could imagine. I've seen hurricanes and tornadoes so powerful that they can collect whole houses, crush them and scatter them to the wind.'

'You must have been frightened.'

Della laughed at him as if he were a small boy. 'I was never frightened. My father was doing His work and no harm could come to him. Or his family. You're the one who seems to be afraid of the coming storm. Maybe you should run off home?'

Ren stuck his chest out. 'It don't bother me. I'm always down here. And if the rain comes I know plenty of places where I can keep dry. Like under the bridge with the old fellas that I told you about.'

Della looked towards the bridge. 'What happened to their proper homes and families?'

'This is their home. The river. They've lived here for a long time. It's the only place they got.'

'I want to see these men.'

'You can't. Tex, the boss, he'd have to invite you. And he's gone a little crazy. He don't like new people anymore.'

Della looked defiantly at Ren. 'Well, I want to see them,' she said again, before nudging past him and heading for the camp, without asking his permission.

Ren had walked down to the river in the hope of finding Sonny, with a terrible thought in the back of his head that Foy might have grabbed him in his car that morning and given him a belting. Or something worse. His stomach turned, half out of anxiety at being so close to Della, and the sinking feeling of betrayal he felt towards a friend who could be in danger.

'What's your real name?' Della asked, looking back at him. 'I haven't asked you before.'

'Ren.'

'I mean your true name. I've heard your friend call you by that name. It's not a proper name though, is it?'

'It's the name Sonny calls me. And the old fellas down here. It's proper enough to me,' he said defensively. 'You talk posh. Do you go to a private school?'

'I'm schooled at home, by my mother. It's best for me. And what do you mean by that word? Posh?'

'It's the way rich people talk. And how they act. My mother says that they talk with a plum in their mouths, and Archie, my stepfather, reckons the pole up their arse don't help either.'

'My family is not rich, if that is what you're thinking. We work for the church and keep no money of our own.'

'What work?'

She stopped, turned around and looked at him, again, as if he was a child. 'God's work,' she answered.

Like she means it, Ren thought.

The campsite was empty. It was also a mess. Ren stood the stove up and stacked the pots and pans by the fire. He re-tied the lengths of rope from the tarp to the bridge supports, shook out the blankets and hung them over the string clothesline to dry. Broken Mary was laying on her side. Ren stood her up and cleaned her face.

'You really care a great deal for these old men.'

'They've been the best friends Sonny and me have known.'

'How many of them live here?'

'There used to be five of them. Then one of them, the Doc ...' Ren paused, looked downstream, and thought about the day Tex and the others had put the Doc's body in the river. 'The Doc, he got up and left and nobody has seen him since. And then Tallboy went away to find his family. That leaves Tex, Cold Can and Big Tiny.'

'Your name is Ren. Your friend is called Sonny. And these men have strange names also. Do any of you have proper names?'

'Oh, Sonny does. He was born with that name. Sonny Brewer.'

Della pointed to the ground. 'What are these?'

She was looking at two recent drawings that could only have been done by Cold Can. Two faces. One was long and thin, the other more rounded. The long face had one eye wide open and the other one was sleeping. It could only be Sonny's face. The other, with long full curls sprouting from its head was Ren himself.

Another clap of thunder exploded above them. 'We really should leave,' he said.

Della ignored him. She was full of questions. 'The men who go missing from here, do they come back?'

'Not often. Tex once told us, Sonny and me, that an old man is like a sick animal. When he's coming to the end of his time and he knows he's going to die, he goes off on his own to find some peace and not make a fuss.'

That is what the Doc had done. Ren was certain of it. But he'd only made it as far as the wheelhouse door. He'd *left his run a bit late*, Tex said at the time. When Tallboy had waved goodbye to the boys for the last time, Ren had later wondered if he was really leaving the river to join his family. Tallboy may have known, like the Doc, that he was sick, and went off on his own to die.

'It is not right for people to die alone,' Della said. 'They must be prayed for.'

'There's no one to pray for them and no family to take care of them. And none of them wants to go into the hospital sick. No one would come and visit, except for Sonny and me. Left on their own they'd rot away in a hospital bed. I wouldn't want to be lonely like that at the end of my life. And the river men don't want it happening to them.'

'But if these men have been together for so long and are such good friends they would visit and take good care of each other.'

'They would visit sometimes. But they have the camp to look after and a feed to chase. And the grog. They like a good drink of a night and wouldn't be up to leaving the camp.'

'They would put alcohol before their friends?' She looked over the empty campsite with disgust. 'That's selfish. And sinful.'

Ren felt a need to defend the men again. 'It's the way they are. They understand how the grog works. It's not a sin. It's the way their life is. Nothing more than that.'

Della didn't seem at all interested in his response. She walked to the water's edge and looked beyond the bridge to the next bend in the river. 'I can see a cross and spire on the other side of those trees. Is there a church?'

'Yeah. It's a convent with a stone church and graveyard belonging to the nuns. And they have a farm with animals.'

'Show me,' she ordered.

Ren looked up at the bruised sky. 'If it rains we'll get wet.'

'I don't care.'

Ren was enjoying Della's company a little less each minute.

They followed the bend in the river circling the boundary of the farm. Just for a second Ren was sure he'd spotted Cold Can standing in a row of corn and thought that maybe he was working for his and Tex's supper. When they got closer he saw it was a scarecrow. Della looked across the fields, at the sheep, cows and hens.

'You must enjoy it here?'

'Hardly come here. We're trespassing. Nun's don't cop it.'

They reached the graveyard. The wind tore across the fields and it started to rain. Ren ran for the cover of a weeping willow tree and Della followed him. The branches of the tree touched the ground. They were hidden from view.

'Who is buried here, in the earth?' Della asked.

'Old nuns. And I mean ancient. If you read the headstones you'll see that some of them lived to nearly a hundred years old. Sonny reckons it's because they never had a drink of beer or smoked a cigarette for their whole lives. And they died vir ... vir ...'

'Virgins?'

Ren blushed. 'They say there are orphan kids buried here too. Nobody knows for sure how many of them there are. Because there are no marked graves and no visitors with flowers.'

'That's sad. A grave must be marked for mourners to return and pray for the dead in *waiting*.'

'What do you mean, waiting?'

'The souls of the dead who have yet to be chosen for Heaven or Hell. Prayers must be said for them over the grave if God is to win.'

Ren was tired of Della's religion talk. 'Well, can't find the graves of these kids. Nobody knows where it was they came from, who their family was, and what they did when they were here.'

The rain began to fall through the branches of the tree. 'Maybe we should go into the church?' Ren offered. 'We can shelter in there until the rain stops.'

'I'm not able to do that. This is a Roman church. My father would not allow it.'

Churches were all the same to Ren. Full of prayers and hymns and plates going around chasing money. 'But he's not here.'

'He doesn't need to be. My father is a powerful man. He's able to touch people from great distances. As the Messenger did.'

At that moment Ren thought that Della was just as crazy as her father.

Della parted the branches of the willow and walked into the rain, along a narrow path between rows of graves. She stopped at the foot of each one and carefully read the headstones. She paused longest in front of the grave of Sister Mary Josephine. 'The date of her death is very important. It is April fourteen.'

Ren could feel the rain soaking through his jumper.

'What's important about that?'

'It is Ruination Day. This woman may have done harm in her life and was duly punished. Or, it is possible that she died on behalf of the evil committed by somebody else. She may have been chosen for punishment as a *proxy*. That's what we call it in the church. *Representing the body.*'

'Proxy? She was a nun. She would have done no harm but maybe give some kid a whack on the arse.'

Ren pointed to the headstone. 'What's that mean, the date, April fourteen?'

'It is the day of the year that the Messenger marks to punish those who have sinned in a grievous manner.'

'What sort of punishments have there been?'

'There have been many. Such as the sinking of the passenger liner, the Titanic, on her maiden voyage. She was sunk on the fourteenth day of April in the year nineteen hundred and twelve. A ship of steel was rendered powerless by the Messenger, Father Divine, delivering over one thousand and five hundred sinful lives to the bottom of the ocean.'

'That can't be true, that one person could sink a ship and kill all them people. Or that all of them people on the ship needed to be punished. I bet there were children on the ship too.'

'The Messenger announced such a prophesy before the ship had left port. Besides, it's not a question of truth. It is a matter of faith.'

Ren had had enough and wanted to leave.

Della walked further along the aisle, bent forward and picked a single weed from one of the graves. She noticed a line of bulbs poking the beginnings of their spears through the earth. She stood up and slowly walked between two rows further along and saw more spears.

'Do you see these?' she pointed out to Ren. 'These bulbs. They are most likely daffodils. Look how the lines of plantings form rectangles. They would have been to mark the graves of the children. They will flower.'

Ren looked down at the outline of a row of graves he hadn't noticed before. He felt a little better about the children who had lived and died at the convent.

'We got to go, Della. It's getting late.'

Walking back along the riverbank to the camp Ren saw Tex and Cold Can on the track. Tex was laying in a wooden fuel cart, being pushed through the mud. The cart was bogged and Cold Can was getting nowhere in his attempt to drag it free.

'There's a couple of the old boys,' Ren said. 'I have to help them.'

Cold Can tried forcing the cart forward, with no luck. He shook it from side to side, throwing Tex around like a rag-doll. Ren got behind the cart and pushed. The cart inched forward but fell back in the hole. Ren lowered his shoulder and pressed it against the corner of the cart and counted, 'One ... two ... three'.

With Cold Can's help they were able to free the cart, and together they kept pushing until they'd parked it alongside the 44 barrel stove at the camp.

'Where's Big Tiny?' Ren asked Cold Can.

'Tallboy gone ... Big Tiny gone ...'

'Tiny's gone too?'

'Big Tiny gone ... all gone,' was all Cold Can could manage.

'You seen Sonny down here? Has he visited you and Tex today?' Ren asked Cold Can.

Cold Can mumbled a few words to himself that Ren could make no sense of. He noticed a tear halfway down Tex's face. He took a handkerchief from his pocket and wiped the tear away.

Tex wouldn't take his eye off Della. He shook his head and tried to speak, but was unable to.

'What's wrong with him?' Sonny asked Cold Can. 'He looks real sick.'

'No Tallboy ... Big Tiny gone.'

Ren felt bad having to leave Tex in such a state, but he couldn't stay with him any longer. He pushed the cart as close to the stove as possible, lit a small fire and waited until it was strong enough to add some heavy timber. He went into the humpy and hunted around until he found half a loaf of stale bread, broke it into pieces and laid them around the edge of the fire. He got down on his knees at the side of the cart.

'I have to be going home now, Tex, or I'll be in trouble off my mum. Tomorrow, me and Sonny, we'll come back with food for you.' He held Tex's nicotine fingers in his hands. 'And I'll bring a new blanket for you.'

He watched as Cold Can piled the charcoaled bread onto a tin plate. He held a piece in front of Tex's face, who opened his mouth and flopped out his cracked tongue. Cold Can rested the piece of bread on his tongue.

'This one, Tex. This one.' It was as if he was giving the old man Holy Communion.

'I have to be going now,' Ren said to Cold Can.

He ignored the boy and went on feeding Tex.

Walking away from the camp that afternoon Ren thought about whether he would see Tex again, alive at least. If he did die, he and Sonny might have to help Cold Can dispose of his body. He didn't know if he'd have the courage to put Tex in the water, but didn't enjoy the thought that the old man could end up in the paupers' grave he was so haunted by.

The rain had slowed to a light drizzle. Ren and Della climbed to the car graveyard. She asked if they could stop walking. 'You can go on ahead without me if you need to,' she said.

'I don't mind waiting. I can walk home with you. You don't want to run into any strangers on your own.'

'You must leave me,' she insisted. 'I cannot be seen with you, by my father.'

'You walk on ahead then and I'll keep my distance. That way your father won't see me.'

He looked at the back of her dress. It was a mess. 'How are you gonna explain that to him?'

She grabbed hold of the dress, lifted it, carefully removed some blackberry thorns and tried shaking the dried mud from the hem. Ren couldn't take his eyes off her exposed legs. She saw where he was looking and quickly dropped the hem and straightened the dress.

'I must go.'

Ren leaned against the wreck of the Holden and watched her walk away. He hadn't sighted Sonny at the river and had no idea where else to search for him. If it was true that Vincent controlled Foy, and he'd kept the policeman off Sonny's back, there was no reason for Foy to suddenly come after him. He was almost willing to pray that he was right. He followed Della from a distance and waited until she'd turned into their street before crossing into the lane. He opened Sonny's back gate. The bike was laying where he'd left it that morning. It made no sense. Sonny never travelled far without the bike.

Ren walked around to the front street and knocked at Sonny's door, with no luck. He was sitting on his front step, puzzling over what he should do next, when Loretta opened the front door and sat down next to him. He looked at her and wondered if he'd ever see his mother out of an apron. When she wasn't wearing one at home, she had her hospital apron tucked under one arm coming to and from work.

'What are you doing out here?' she asked.

'Sonny didn't call for me this morning and he didn't show up for work. I been looking for him.'

'Well, you should have stayed around the house. He was just here calling for you.'

'Here? Where's he been?'

'His poor uncle Rory took sick last night. He was in so much pain Sonny had to get him to the hospital, with the help of Mr Portelli from up the street. He laid Rory in the back of his station wagon and drove him to Emergency.'

'What's wrong with him?'

'Sonny doesn't know. All he could tell me was that Rory is going to be moved to a ward tomorrow morning. He was only here long enough to collect a bag for him. Pyjamas, and a toothbrush.'

'Mum, I should go to the hospital and see if Sonny needs my help.'

'All you'll be doing is eating your tea. Come inside and sit down.'

'The truck's not here. Where's Archie?'

'Driving back from the border. He won't be in until late.'

Ren ate quietly, thinking about Sonny and Rory. Nothing was going to stop him getting to the hospital. He could always sneak out later on if he had to, but decided he'd chance honesty instead. He put his knife and fork on his plate and sat up straight.

'Mum,' he said. 'You know Sonny has been trying his best since he got the job at the paper shop.'

'Hmm.'

The statement was more or less true, with the major exceptions of the episode of the runaway bulldozer and the trouble he was in with Vincent, but that wasn't Sonny's fault.

'He's been doing well since Rory come to look after him. And he's been good to me too, giving me work on the newspapers.'

She collected his empty plate and put it in the sink. 'And?'

'And he's my best friend. I know he will be worried over Rory. I need to go to the hospital and see if there's anything I can do to help. I'll be straight back home. I know Sonny'd do the same for me.'

Loretta dug her hands in the front of her apron. 'And how are you going to get to the hospital? Walk?'

'I can take his bike. He left it in the yard. It wouldn't take me more than fifteen minutes to ride there.'

Loretta walked over to her son and stuck an unruly curl of hair behind his ear. 'You look grubbier than a state ward. Don't be giving anyone your name and address at the hospital. I don't need the welfare creeping around here. And don't be away long.'

CHAPTER 15

Ren dragged Sonny's bike into the lane for the second time that day, hopped on and started pedalling. The ride proved tough going. He was pedalling by the railway station before he realised the bike had a puncture in the back wheel. 'Shit!'

He had the choice of pushing the bike back to Sonny's place and running all the way to the hospital or to keep on pedalling, which he did, into a head wind, his arse out of the seat. Halfway up the Parade hill, a truck in the next lane shifted gear and slowly overtook him. Ren pedalled as hard as he could, reached out and hooked onto the back of the truck and soon picked up speed. He could smell burning rubber and looked down at the tyre. It had been reduced to shreds. Ren was riding on the metal rim.

At the top of the hill the truck turned one way and Ren steered the bicycle into the hospital driveway. He hopped off, rested the bike against a light pole, spat in the palms of his hands and ran them through his wild head of hair. A hospital cleaner, leaning on a mop and smoking a cigarette, looked across at him and laughed.

'You want me to call for the stretcher?'

'Fuck off,' Ren muttered under his breath. He looked up at the *EMERGENCY* sign above his head, lit in blue neon. 'Is this where I go for sick people?'

The cleaner took a last puff on his cigarette, flicked it onto the road and opened the door for him. 'After you.'

The waiting room was lined with wooden benches crowded with elderly people coughing, kids running around in their socks and mothers walking newborns across the room, trying to stop them from crying. A man resting his back against a bench had a bloodied nose, a cut above one eye and a swollen hand. He winked at Ren as he walked by and feigned a left-right combination.

An older man in the back corner was laid out on one of the benches, resting beneath a thick woollen coat. His face was caked with dirt and he wore long grey hair twisted into knots. Ren thought he looked familiar. When the old man saw Ren looking at him he buried himself in his coat and turned his head away. Ren realised who it was.

'Tallboy,' he called out across the room. 'What are you doing here?'

Tallboy ignored him. Ren walked over and sat on the bench opposite. Tallboy pulled the coat collar over his head.

'Tallboy. It's me. Ren.'

A hand came out of the sleeve of the coat and weakly waved. The hand was black and crippled.

'Hey, Tallboy,' he repeated, quietly. 'It's me. Ren. You okay?'

Slowly Tallboy revealed his face, like a tortoise coming out of its shell. 'Hey ya, young boy.' Tallboy's voice had been reduced to a rasp and his breath reeked of metho, which wasn't unusual, except that the last time Ren had seen him Tallboy had sworn off the grog for all time. Ren could hardly believe how poorly his old friend looked, worse than he had during his time on the river.

'Tallboy, you were going to stay with your family. Did you find them?'

Tallboy reached for Ren's hand. His eyes were swollen and weeping. 'You promise me,' he whispered.

'Promise you what, Tallboy?'

'You never seen this old boy, somebody asks you. This is no story to be telling. *Tallboy Garrett? Don't know where that fella's been.* You promise me that one, young bird.'

It would not be an easy promise for Ren to keep. Tex had been close to Tallboy and was sad to see him leave the camp, even though he was angry with him and called him a *fucken deserter.* He'd want to know if Tallboy was unwell in the hospital. Except that he was now in such a poor state himself it would be unlikely he'd know what Ren was talking about.

'If you don't want me to, I won't say anything. I promise.'

Tallboy reached out and squeezed his hand in gratitude. 'How's them old fellas?'

'Tex and Cold Can are doing well,' Ren lied. 'I been at the camp today visiting.'

'And Big Tiny? What's he doing?' Tallboy asked.

'He's gone missing. Maybe he's up in the Myer store sleeping on one of them mattresses you told us about,' Ren joked, trying to cheer him up. 'Remember that story, Tallboy?'

'I remember that one. But it was only a story. All of them stories was bullshit. Tex is no better. Bullshit is all he knows. You know he told me one time, before I ever put that white lady down my throat, *You gonna love her, boy, you gonna love her.* I took that drink and now she's killed me.' He reached out, grabbed Ren by the jumper and pulled him closer until their eyes met. 'Anyone asks, you never seen the Tallboy. He's no place. *He's dead.*'

Tallboy released his grip on the boy and rolled over to face the wall. Ren tapped him on the shoulder. 'Hey, you're not dead, Tallboy.'

'Leave me be,' the old man growled.

Ren realised there was nothing he could do to help and walked over to the admissions counter. A nurse sat behind a sliding glass window, writing on a yellow card. A sign on the wall above the window read *No Visitors – Family Members Excepted.* Ren coughed to get the nurse's attention. She finally put the pen down and slid the glass across.

'Can I help you?'

'I'm here to see my uncle. He's sick.'

'And his name?'

'Rory.'

'I will need his full name.'

'It's just Rory.'

'I'm sorry, but it cannot be *just* Rory. If you are here to see a relative I will need his full name. You are related?'

'It's Brewer!' Ren shouted, pleased with himself. 'Mr Rory Brewer.'

She flicked through the cards on the desk, picked one up and read it. 'Yes. Mr Rory Francis Brewer. He has been in here since late last night. Another boy has been with him throughout the day.'

'That would be my brother. Sonny. Rory's our uncle.'

'Wait here a moment.' She left the desk and pressed a red button on the wall. It opened an automatic door. She was back within couple of minutes – with Sonny in tow. 'Your brother,' she announced.

Sonny winked at Ren and smiled. 'Can I take him inside?' he asked. 'My uncle's been calling his name in his sleep.'

'You may, for a few minutes only. The pair of you will need to leave soon, as Mr Brewer is being moved upstairs.'

Ren followed Sonny along a corridor that had lines of different colours painted into the lino floor. The lines headed off in different directions, like the tracks in the railyards. Sonny led Ren into a room divided by beds on either side, most of them with a blue curtain around the bed, shutting the patients off from the world. Sonny opened a curtain at the end of the room and stepped inside. Rory was laying back with his head rested to one side. He was wearing a white hospital gown, had a plastic tube stuck up his nose and wires running from under the gown. The light on a machine was beeping away at the side of the bed. Another tube ran into a clear bag clipped to the other side of the bed. It was half full of piss.

Rory looked about a hundred years old.

'What happened to him?' Ren asked.

'Last night we were watching the late movie together when he went out the backyard to the toilet. He never come

241

back and I went looking for him. The toilet light was out and I found him laying on the floor in a pool of piss. He couldn't speak and his body was shaking. I got him to his feet and helped him back into the house and put him on the couch. He couldn't stop shaking. I left him and come out in the street. I was gonna knock on your door. Then I saw Mr Portelli coming home from an afternoon shift. He was parking his car in the street. I told him what happened and he come in the house and carried Rory to the car and drove him here.'

'Did the doctors tell you what's wrong with him?'

'Nup. But he can't move or talk properly. They're gonna shift him to a ward tonight and do these other tests on him in the morning.'

Rory coughed and spit dribbled from his mouth. Sonny wiped his uncle's chin with a corner of the bed sheet.

'What've you been doing all day, without me to look after you?' Sonny asked.

Ren told him about being at the river, seeing Cold Can and Tex with the fuel cart, and that Big Tiny had gone missing. 'I couldn't make sense of what Cold Can was saying, except that Tiny had *gone*.' He didn't tell Sonny he'd walked along the riverbank to the convent with Della. He wanted to steer Sonny away from any talk about how he'd spent his day. 'What about you, Sonny? What have you been doing in here?'

'Nothing. Have sat here the whole time, except for going home to pick up some stuff for Rory. They been good to me. Give me some sandwiches to eat and juice made out of real oranges instead of cordial.'

'You been bored waiting round?'

'Not really. It give me time to do some thinking.'

'About what?'

'About my old man borrowing that money from Vincent. He done me no favour doing that.'

'That doesn't take a lot of thinking. You already knew that. Anyway, the loan did you some good. Paid the rent and kept you in the house.'

'Might have, but my old man would have known he wouldn't be round to pay the money back. Planned it that way. And you don't need to be a genius to know Vincent would find some way to get his money back and that he'd come after me, or maybe poor old Rory. Shows my dad has never given a fuck about what happens to me.'

Rory's arm fell from the bed. Sonny lifted it, rested it under the blanket and tucked the blanket into the mattress.

'It's just like Rory warned me. People like Vincent, once you start paying them you never stop. The only way out for me now is to shoot through. As soon as Rory is better, I'm outta here. And I won't be coming back. The newspaper money is up to nearly a hundred and fifty dollars. It's plenty enough for me to get away.'

The curtain around the bed opened. It was the nurse from the front desk. 'You boys need to leave your uncle to rest now.' She stood and waited for them to say goodbye to Rory, tapping her foot impatiently on the floor.

Sonny kissed Rory on his whiskered cheek. Seeing as the nurse presumed he was also a nephew, Ren thought it best to kiss Rory as well. She marched the two of them back to the waiting room. Ren looked over to the corner bench. Tallboy was gone.

'Excuse me?' the nurse called to Sonny as the boys were about to leave. 'When I was taking information from you this morning you said you were the only relative your uncle has.'

'Yep. Me and my brother here,' Sonny said. 'I didn't mention him. Didn't think he'd count, seeing as I'm the oldest.'

'Is there nobody else to care for you?'

'It's just the two of us,' Sonny answered, before realising where the conversation was heading.

'And where are you two going now?'

'Home.'

'With nobody to care for you? Your uncle is your primary provider and is likely to be in hospital for some time. As minors you cannot be living alone without proper care. I will arrange for a social worker to visit the home and make the necessary arrangements for you.'

She picked up Rory's admission card and read over it. 'There is no telephone number listed here.'

'We don't have one.'

'Then please be sure you are home waiting for the social worker. Tomorrow morning.'

'We'll be there.' Sonny smiled.

The cleaner was standing outside smoking another cigarette. He waved at Ren like they were old friends.

'Sonny, you know what she means when she says she'll send a social worker round, don't you? They'll take you into *care*.'

'Yeah.' He laughed. 'I know exactly what she means.'

'What's so funny? They won't let you stay in the house on your own. They'll put you in a foster home.'

'No they won't.'

'What makes you so sure?'

'Because last night when we got here they went through Rory's wallet and wrote down his address. Of his old place. The social worker can call by anytime she wants. She won't find me there.'

'Maybe not tomorrow. Doesn't mean they won't grab hold of you next time you visit.'

Sonny hadn't thought through his next step. His face dropped. So did Ren's. Sonny's bike was gone.

'Fuck!'

'Fuck what?'

'Your bike. I was in a hurry to get up here so I rode it. I left it here against the pole before I went inside.

Shit!' Sonny kicked the light pole with the heel of his shoe. 'How'd you get it here, Ren? I was gonna ride it myself but saw it had a flat tyre.'

'I didn't know it was flat until I was on my way, and I just kept going. I can't believe someone would knock it off. It's a piece of junk.'

'My fucken junk. What sort of arsehole would steal someone's bike?'

There couldn't have been a worse moment for Ren to remind Sonny he'd stolen the bike in the first place.

Walking home, Ren told Sonny about Detective Foy, that Spike had seen him early that morning across the road from the paper shop. 'You'd better be careful. He must have been looking for you. Out that early in the morning.'

'Maybe. And maybe not. Foy does a lot of business along

the street. Probably out heavying the fishmonger or some other poor bastard. He and Vincent, both of them can get fucked. Once I've taken off they'll never find me.'

While Sonny was acting brave, Ren could see he looked worried. He didn't blame him. Just hearing Foy's name spoken aloud was enough to scare Ren. When they got to Sonny's house, Ren waited with him until he'd opened the front door and turned the light on. A pile of mail was sitting on the floor in the hallway. Sonny picked it up and quickly shuffled through it until he found something that interested him.

'Look at this, Ren. A letter addressed to me. Nobody's written to me before, except that time I got the letter for my court date.' He held the envelope up to the hallway lightbulb, as if searching for clues about who might have sent it. 'Wonder who it's from?'

'Why don't you open it up and see?'

Ren was as curious as Sonny to know who had sent the letter. He followed Sonny into the kitchen and watched as his friend tore the envelope open and slowly read the letter under his breath. Ren picked up the envelope from the floor. Sonny's name and address was written on the front in pencil and the address of a religious charity was stamped on the back.

'Jesus,' Sonny whispered to himself.

'What?'

'This don't make any sense.'

He read the letter over again to be sure he had understood it. When he finished he handed it to Ren.

'You want me to read it?'

'Yep.'

Dear Sonny

*I have been wrong to wait until this time to write you. Please
forgive me that. I left you alone sure that I was going to finish
my life. And I just about did that. Knowing I was a coward
and thinking about you and the wrong I have done by you has
gone some way to saving me. I don't have time to go into details
at this time but I am being helped by good people who got me
away from the alcohol and into regular work. I expect that your
uncle Rory has been taking good care of you and that you are in
better hands without me there to be a nuisance. I do not blame
you at all if that is what you are thinking. You are a good boy at
heart. You will know I had the rent paid up to save Rory any
grief with money. You are smart enough to know that I didn't
have as much as a red cent to my name. I have been in work
for some time now and with a weekly pay packet I have slowly
managed to pay off a loan I took out for the rent. It has been
paid in full. I will return home someday. It will be soon I hope.
I expect to be a better man and a better father to you. I am
praying that you will be able to forgive me for my wrongs I have
done to you. And to your mother who I drove from your life.*

*May God bless you
Your father*

'What's he mean with that? *God bless you.* The arsehole,'
Sonny said.

Ren slowly folded the letter, put it back in the envelope and
handed it to Sonny. He couldn't understand why Sonny was
so angry. 'This is good news. Your old man is off the drink

and he's working and making some money. With Rory being sick it will be good to have him back home.'

Sonny slammed the table so hard with his fist a glass sitting on the top bounced off and smashed on the floor. 'If you think that's all it means, Ren, you don't know anything. I'm supposed to be the dumb one, not you.'

'I don't get it, Sonny.'

'That cunt. Vincent.'

'What's this got to do with him?'

'It has everything to do with him. *Think*. My old man took a loan from him and since then I've been Vincent's boy because he told me he hadn't been paid. All along he's been getting his money. Fuck this, I'm not running another message for him.'

'You sure?'

'Course I'm sure.'

'Then you'll need to stay away from him until your dad gets home and can prove the money was paid back.'

'You reckon Vincent's going to give a shit about what my old man has to say? And just because he says he's off the drink in a letter he's written it doesn't mean I can believe a word of it. Or that he'll turn up here sober. He promised me plenty of times before and fucked up the same day. No reason to believe him now.'

'You don't have to. Wait and see. It don't hurt to give him a chance.'

Sonny picked up the letter and tapped the envelope on the table. 'And what am I supposed to do about Vincent while I'm waiting? I don't wanna do one more run for that bastard.'

'For now, maybe you have to. Pretend nothing's happened. Run the messages until your father's back.'

'No! I'm not doing it.'

'Then you'll have to stay away from the pub.'

'Can't do that if I want to keep my job.'

'Then quit your job. Doesn't make any difference if you're planning to take off anyway.'

Sonny swept the mess of broken glass into a pan and emptied it in a bin under the sink. 'Fuck Vincent. And fuck Foy too. You know what should happen?'

'Not exactly.'

'Somebody should fix the cunts. Both of them.'

'Somebody should. And someday it will probably happen. Between the two of them they'd have an army of enemies, and with a bit of luck their turn will come. But it won't be you or me getting revenge, Sonny.'

CHAPTER 16

Sonny felt terrible about having to quit the job at the paper shop. He enjoyed the work, had saved some money and felt he would be letting Brixey down, who had given him a go when no one else would. It didn't stop raining at all that week. Sonny spent his days delivering the papers of a morning through streets awash with storms, visiting Rory at the hospital, where he was able to convince a social worker that he and his *brother*, Ren, were staying with an aunty in Collingwood. He also avoided the pub and kept an eye out for Foy, in case Vincent set the copper on him. By the end of the week he knew he couldn't wait any longer to break the bad news to Brixey.

'This is it for me,' he told Ren as they packed up the newsstand for the night. 'I'm gonna let Brixey know when we get back to the shop. Tomorrow I'll go see Rory, and then I'm taking off.'

'Why don't you wait until your father gets back and you can sort something out?'

'Number one, because I already told you, it won't matter what he has to say. Vincent will use me for as long as it suits him. If my old man tries standing up to him he'll end up with a belting. Or something worse. And number two, waiting for my father to come home could take forever.'

'It would have taken a lot for him to sit down and write the letter. Maybe he's changed?'

'I don't have time to wait round and find out. Come on, let's get back to the shop.'

Brixey was seated at his usual spot, perched on the stool behind the counter, pencilling returns into a dog-eared exercise book. He alternated between a red and black pencil, sticking whichever one he wasn't using behind his ear. When the boys entered the shop, Brixey looked over the top of the reading glasses that hung around his neck from a chain when he wasn't wearing them. Sonny had been on edge all week and Brixey knew there was something wrong without needing to be told. He licked the end of his red pencil and continued his arithmetic. The paperboys knew better than to interrupt him when he was working on the nightly figures. But Sonny had no choice.

'Wait here,' he said to Ren. 'I have to get something from the back room before I talk to him.'

Sonny walked through the shop to the room where the lockers and prams were kept. Brixey's eyes followed him. Ren heard the locker door slam loudly a couple of times. He thought that maybe someone had stolen Sonny's money. He was relieved when he spotted a cloth money bag bulging from Sonny's front pocket when he came back into the shop. Brixey put the ledger book away in a drawer beneath the counter and brushed pencil shavings from his dustcoat.

'Sonny, you've been jittery on me all week, coming in late, forgetting your orders. I've been patient with you, but it's time for an explanation.'

'I know,' Sonny said. 'There's something important that I need to talk to you about.'

Brixey looked over at Ren. 'Don't tell me.' He smiled. 'You two are getting married.'

'My uncle, Rory. He's in the hospital, real sick. The doctors say he could be in there a long time before he's good enough to come home. I been real worried about him.'

'Oh, that's no good,' Brixey let his glasses drop to his chest. 'He's a top bloke, old Rory. You wanna take some time off to look after him? Your job will be here for you. I might even promote Spike while you're away.'

Spike smiled and puffed his chest out.

'Thanks, Rory, but this has to be my last day,' Sonny said. 'I can't come back to work.'

'*Can't?* Why not?'

'It's not only Rory. I've got myself in trouble.'

'Jesus. What sort of trouble?'

Sonny looked over at Ren for support. 'It don't matter. I can't tell you.'

'Of course you can. I might be able to help you out.'

'No one can help me.'

Although Sonny was clearly upset Brixey couldn't help himself but laugh. 'Bullshit. Even an accused murderer is entitled to a defence. Why don't you try me?'

'Tell him, Sonny,' Ren said.

'Do you know who Vincent is?' Sonny whispered, as if the man was standing over his shoulder.

'Who don't?' Brixey growled, not bothering to lower his own voice.

Sonny's eyes searched the shop before going on. 'I've been doing jobs for him.'

'For Vincent? How'd you get involved with a menace like him? I give you plenty of work here, don't I?'

'I never wanted to work for him. He forced me into it. Told me that my father owed him money and had shot through on him without paying up. Now I found out it's not true. My old man paid the money he owed. Every cent of it. But Vincent never let on. He's had me running round for him and won't let me quit. Once a week I do a delivery for him, from the pub. With Ren. I missed last week and the next morning Foy was out the front here. I reckon he was looking for me.'

Brixey was losing track of the story. 'What's Foy got to do with it?'

'Him and Vincent, they do business together. After that night Foy tried to grab me out front of the shop, when you come and helped me and Ren out, he never come near me. Vincent called him off.'

'Of course they'd work together. Arseholes like them two are made for each other.' Brixey shook his head in disgust.

Sonny took the handwritten letter out of his pocket and handed it to Brixey. 'My father wrote me this. Vincent's been lying to me all along.'

Brixey whispered *the no good prick* to himself as he read the letter. 'And what's this job you've been doing for him? Sonny, please don't tell me you've been out thieving for him.'

'It's nothing like that. I run messages on the street. Envelopes with money in them. He said it was a one-off, because the police were watching him from a van in the street. But the van hasn't been there since the first night. He conned me.'

Brixey stuck a finger in the air like he'd had a brainwave. 'Let me take a guess here. You making deliveries to Chris the Greek by any chance?'

'How'd you know that?' Ren butted in.

'Because Vincent is mad on the punt and has always bet more than he can afford. And Chris the Greek happens to run the only SP book along the strip. He covers the lot. Horses. Dogs. The fucken cockroach derby. And a brick on the card game out of the shop itself. That's a wog-only show, of course. I'll guarantee you now, either Vincent laid a big losing bet he's had trouble covering. Or he took a loan from Chris and he's scratching to pay him back. The Greek can't tolerate bad debts. It's a terrible look for business.'

'Why would he send us over there,' Ren said, 'if the cops aren't even watching?'

'Just because the van's gone from the street, it don't mean the two of them are not being tracked. There could be some truth in the story. Even if there's not, Vincent could have sent himself crazy with fear. Or if he's madder than even I know, it could be his way of showing disrespect without having the balls to front up himself. Sending a couple of kids over there with a fold of money is as good as telling Chris to go fuck himself.'

'Chris doesn't look so tough,' Sonny said.

'You don't think so? Don't be fooled by the friendly old Greek. He gets round in his woollen cardigan, not saying much, smiling when he has to, playing the harmless wog. Just the way he likes it. And all the while he has the street in his hand.'

Brixey leaned back in his chair. 'I shouldn't be telling you this, but you're in so much trouble anyway it's time you heard a story for once that might actually teach you something. You remember the bloke they found dead in the waiting room on the railway platform last year?'

'Yeah,' Sonny said. 'He was a debt collector and they say he got on the wrong side of Vincent and he was killed. Every kid in the shop knows that story.'

'Well, they know nothing. Vincent had nothing to do with the murder.'

'Who killed him then?' Ren asked.

'No one can say, for certain. Me in particular. And I wouldn't be careless enough to make an accusation. But what I do know is the same fella had been dodging the Greek over a gambling debt for months. Big money. More than ten thousand dollars. I also know that a couple of nights before he was killed he'd been in the pub mouthing off that *the wog can fuck himself.* Then he showed up dead. There weren't a lot of questions asked over that one. Even by the police. A debt collector paying for his own greed, having his throat cut. You could even call it an act of God.'

Ren put his hand to his throat and thought about the old man who'd been slicing cake for him each week.

'Don't worry, the Greek wouldn't have done it himself,' Brixey added, to Ren's relief. 'It could have been one of the others in the shop. Or maybe they pay a merchant seaman, in town on a Greek liner. Does the job for them, gets his pay and leaves port on the quiet. That's how they like to work. No showboat stuff, the Greeks. Clean up any mess with a minimum of attention.'

The bell over the shop door rang. Rodney, Vincent's offsider, was standing in the doorway.

'Here you are, boys.' He smiled, although it wasn't much of a smile. 'The boss has been looking for you. Sent me to collect. This is a work night for you, Sonny.'

Neither Sonny nor Ren moved. Brixey got down from his chair and walked around to the front counter.

'I'm sorry, mate, but I can't let them leave the shop just yet. The buggers haven't cleaned up.'

Rodney clicked his fingers together. 'Move your arse, Sonny. And you shut the fuck up, old man. Unless you want the heel of a boot shaving your chin.'

Brixey wasn't prepared to back away. 'Come on, mate. They're only kids. Too young for this sort of business.'

'What business?' Rodney asked, like he didn't have a clue what Brixey was talking about. 'They don't have anything to be worried about. I've been as good as an uncle to them. Haven't I boys?'

Brixey put himself between the boys, Rodney and the front door. Rodney hit him so quickly in the stomach nobody saw it. Brixey fell to his knees.

'Arsehole,' he groaned.

Rodney leaned over him, stood on Brixey's hand with a heel and drove it into the floor. Spike, who'd been watching the action from the back of the shop picked up a long wooden pole with a hook on the end. Brixey used it to pull the metal grill down over the front door of a night. Spike charged at Rodney, waving the pole like a long-blade.

'Leave Brixey alone! Fucken leave him!'

Spike swung the pole at Rodney's head, who snatched it in

his hand, tore it away from Spike and almost speared him in the side of the head with it. Spike had enough commonsense in him to keep on running, out of the shop. Rodney snapped the pole over his knee and threw it to the ground. He dug the heel of his boot into Brixey's hand one more time and looked down at him. 'Do yourself a favour, old man, and don't get up. Don't follow us. And talk to nobody. Unless you're ready for a Jewish stocktake in here. I'll put a match to the joint with you tied to a fucken chair.'

Rodney grabbed hold of the boys, one under each arm, and dragged them across the street and into the pub.

'Upstairs,' he ordered.

Every drinker at the hotel looked away as Rodney marched the boys through the bar and pushed them up the stairs into the back room. Vincent was sitting at the desk, the telephone in one hand and a glass of whisky in the other.

'I know,' he spoke urgently into the receiver. 'It was supposed to be last week. Of course you're right, but that's a whack and a half in one hit.' Vincent looked across at Rodney and raised his eyebrows. Although the room was ice cold, Ren noticed that Vincent's face was flushed and he was sweating heavily. 'Let me sort something and get back to you.' He slammed the phone down. 'The fucken wog wants the lot tonight.'

'You got it, Vince?'

'You know I don't have it. Now he's talking extras for late payment. Thinks he's running a fucken bank over there.'

'He is. Sort of.'

'Shut up!'

Vincent stood up, picked up the chair and threw it against

the wall. It smashed into pieces. He yanked the refrigerator door open. Bottles of beer fell from a shelf and rolled across the floor. Rodney ran around picking them up while Vincent took a tin box out of the fridge. He sat on the couch, took a small key from his pocket, opened the box and took out a bundle of notes along with the pocketbook the boys saw him writing in each week. He offered Sonny a seat next to him.

'You been avoiding me, Sonny. I haven't seen you in the pub all week. Just when I have an important job for you to do. I shouldn't need to send Rodney out looking for you. You're on my payroll now, Sonny. And don't you forget that you still owe me.'

Ren began shaking. He shut his eyes and concentrated hard, willing himself to calm down. He could hear Vincent counting the notes.

'How much is there?' Rodney asked.

'Just on three thousand.'

'You owe him almost twelve. You're not even close.'

'It's worse than that. This is supposed to go to Foy. Only reason I've been holding on to it.'

'Foy? How much is he into you for?'

Vincent looked over at Sonny and nodded towards the street. 'That landlord, the one who did us the favour, out of the fucken blue he decided he wanted his money. I got Foy to have a talk to him. I still owe him the fee.'

Rodney looked a little insulted. 'You should have asked me, Vince. I'd have done it for nothing.'

'I needed a guarantee there'd be no comeback. There is none, once Foy knocks at the door.' Vincent picked up the pile of notes and counted them again. 'But he'll have to wait.

The old wolf across the road is howling louder.'

Vincent walked to the corner window and looked across the intersection and down to the Greek club. 'I'll pay what I've got in hand. It'll be enough to keep him off my back for a few days. Then me and you will have to come up with a way to sort this out. I'm not paying any more. The old man will have to go away.'

'We can't do that. He does business all over town. We'd be fucked.'

'We're fucked anyway.'

Vincent opened the desk drawer and bound the money with a rubber band. He rifled through the drawer in agitation. 'Where's my fucken pen?' He tore the drawer from the desk and threw it at the wall as well. 'Go grab us some paper and a pen from downstairs,' he barked at Rodney.

Once Rodney had left the room Vincent turned his attention to Sonny and Ren. 'Let me give you some advice. Never get yourself in debt, not to anyone. It done your old man no good, Sonny. It has done you no good either. And look at me. I'm getting fucked harder than both of you.'

'I'm still in debt,' Sonny answered. 'I owe you.'

Ren was silently praying that Sonny wouldn't be stupid enough to start talking about the letter he'd received from his father and how Vincent had lied to him.

'Right. You are in debt,' Vincent agreed. 'But you can't blame me for that. Your old man stuck you on the bottom rung, not me. And it's up to you to find a way back up, for yourself.'

'I am trying to find a way out,' Sonny said, looking directly at Vincent.

Vincent emptied his glass, stood up and poured himself another. Rodney came back to the room with the pen and paper. He lit a smoke and stood by the window as Vincent sat at the table and began writing. He checked his words after every sentence. When he finished he folded the sheet of paper, tucked it inside the rubber band and ordered Sonny to stand up. He pulled the front of the boy's jeans open, tucked the money inside and patted it.

'Can you feel that wad against your balls?'

When Sonny didn't answer, Vincent leaned closer to him and whispered in his ear, 'You fuck this job up and I'll have them off you.'

As he felt for the money again Vincent noticed the corner of the cloth money bag poking out of Sonny's pocket. He pulled it out, opened it and emptied the contents onto the couch. Notes and loose coins fell from the bag. 'Look here, Rodney, a fucken bonus. Count that. Could be a couple of hundred there.' Vincent stroked the side of Sonny's face. 'Good work, son. Now, it's up to you to do this delivery for me. On top of the cash payment you've just made, I'd calculate that you're close to walking away. What do you think, Rodney? We owed any more?'

'Can't be sure, Vince. I leave the sums to you.'

Sonny was shaking with rage. 'You said that the first time I did a job for you. And that's my money you just took. I've been saving it.'

'Good boy. Be proud of yourself. Shows that you have initiative. I won't forget that when I'm putting the money on a horse. Tell you what. If it gets up I'll give you a sling for your trouble. Now get your arse downstairs and across the street.'

Vincent turned to Ren. 'The warning goes for you too, pretty boy. If young Sonny here fucks this up, or thinks of doing something stupid, don't forget you're accountable for him.'

The minute they were out in the street Sonny headed for the laneway behind the pub. He pulled out the roll of money and unwrapped the note.

'What are you doing, Sonny? He'll be watching for us from the window. If he doesn't see us he'll send Rodney after us.'

'Fuck Rodney. And fuck Vincent. He stole my money.'

Sonny stuck the roll in his front pocket and tore the written note to pieces without bothering to read it.

'What are you doing?' Ren shouted. 'Now we're really fucked.'

'Vincent's gonna be fucked this time, not us.'

'How?'

'Follow me.'

'Where?'

'To the club.'

'Sonny, we can't go in there without the money.'

It was raining again. Sonny pulled his jumper over his head. Ren grabbed him by the arm. 'We can't do this, Sonny. We won't get out of the club alive.'

Sonny pushed him in the chest, almost knocking him over. 'Well, fuck off then and leave me to do this on my own. I'm finished with Vincent.' Sonny was out of control on account of the money he'd carefully saved being snatched by Vincent.

'I'm not gonna fuck off on you,' Ren said, hurrying to catch up with him.

Sonny lectured Ren as they crossed the street, the rain belting down on them. 'You might be smarter than I'll ever be. Up here.' He tapped Ren on the side of the head. 'But not out here,' he gestured to the street. 'I've got it all over you. You're always telling me *we gotta have a plan, Sonny.* Well, I got one now.'

'And when did you think of it?'

'Just this minute.'

'That's great, Sonny. If Chris pulls that knife out and offers us a slice of cake, I'm running.'

Sonny stopped outside the door to the club and took a deep breath, working up his courage before knocking. Nikos opened the door and they followed him into the club. Chris was standing behind the counter, wearing his old blue cardigan over the top of a white shirt, and drinking a coffee. Ren looked at him more closely than he had before, trying to figure out if what Brixey had said about Chris being responsible for the dead body on the railway station could be true. But the old man looked no different. Ren couldn't imagine him as a killer.

Chris waved at the boys to join him at the counter. 'You have something for me?'

Sonny shuffled towards the counter. 'We have nothing for you,' he said, calmer than Ren would have thought possible.

'Nothing?'

'Vincent sent me and told me to give you a message.'

Chris looked puzzled. 'But no package?'

'Nah. Just the message.'

Chris took a step back from the counter. He didn't look

so friendly all of a sudden. He gritted his teeth and his eyes narrowed and darkened. 'And the message? Tell me now.'

Sonny spoke as slowly and deliberately as possible. 'He told me to let you know there is no more money coming.'

Chris stuck a hand behind his ear as if he hadn't heard properly. 'What do you say? Come closer.'

Sonny didn't move. 'He says there is no more money coming.' He hesitated before adding, 'He also said to tell you that if you're not happy to let him know yourself. He said you'd know what that means.'

One of Chris's eyes began twitching. He walked around the counter and rested a hand on each of Sonny's damp shoulders and gently shook him. 'Are you sure of the message? You must be sure.'

Ren felt that he was about to piss his pants again, just as he had done in the back of the police car.

'I'm sure about all of it. He was talking with one of the others, the one who is always with him. Rodney, the one with the lucky card tattooed on his hand. They were counting some money together. A lot of money, and Vincent was telling Rodney he was going to put the money on a racehorse.'

Chris walked over to the door, parted the curtain and looked out into the rain. He called Nikos over and talked to him in Greek. While Chris spoke quietly into his ear, Nikos swore in a violent mix of English and Greek. *Fuck! Dirty malaka!*

Nikos walked to the back of the room, leaned into one of the old men at the card table and whispered something in his ear, before returning to Chris and relaying a message from the man at the table, again in Greek.

'Wait. I will call,' Chris said. He picked up the telephone and began dialling. Ren stared at the phone, realising that as soon as Vincent told Chris he'd sent Sonny across the street with more than three thousand dollars wrapped around his dick, and a note most likely explaining how the next payment would be made, Chris, or maybe Nikos, would take them into the back room and slice them open. Or maybe he'd deliver them back to Vincent and let him do it. Nikos grabbed the phone from Chris's hand, slammed it down and hissed at him through his teeth. Chris listened closely and nodded his head in agreement.

Chris put an arm over the shoulder of each of the boys. 'It is time for you to go. Home. I am busy now. Off.'

Sonny was about to say something. Ren wondered if he was crazy enough to ask for a piece of cake. 'If you ever have work, any jobs done, I could do them for you,' he offered.

Chris smiled at him. 'You are good worker. One day, maybe I will see.'

As the boys were being led out the door by Nikos, Chris picked up the telephone again and dialled a number. Out in the street the boys stood under the shop awning. Sonny lifted one foot onto a bench and retied a shoelace, all the while looking up at the window of Vincent's office.

'So, where's the plan go from here, Sonny? We're dead. You know that, don't you?'

If Sonny was as worried as Ren it didn't show. He took a lot of time tying the shoelace. When he finished he started on the other one.

'What the fuck are you doing? We have to split before Vincent catches up with us.'

'Not yet. We'll wait a bit.'

'Wait? Are you crazy?'

'Let's cross the street. You'll see, something will happen'

They ran across the road and ducked in the doorway of the butcher shop. Ren crammed into the doorway beside Sonny. 'And what's gonna happen?'

'Not sure yet.'

It was cold and wet standing in the doorway. Ren was desperate to go home. Each time he opened his mouth to tell Sonny he was leaving he was told to shut it. 'We'll give it a couple more minutes. I promise, if nothing happens by then we'll take off.'

They waited more than fifteen minutes before anything did happen. A car drove slowly along the street and parked in front of the club. The driver sat in the car and lit a cigarette. After a few minutes Nikos opened the cafe door, poked his head out and waved to the driver. The driver got out of the car and walked towards the cafe.

'Fuck! *It's Foy,*' Sonny said.

'Foy? Why would he be going to the club?'

'No idea. But I don't want him catching us here. Let's take off before he comes back out.'

They didn't stop running until they were almost home. 'It might not be a good idea to sleep at home tonight,' Sonny said.

'Why's that?'

'That Foy. I can't work out what he's got to do with Chris, but I bet he'll come after us.'

'You should have thought about that before you stole Vincent's money. You forgot to put Foy in your plan.'

'It was never Vincent's money in the first place.'

'Not yours either.'

'Some of it should be, for the work I did. And you. I'll give you half the money. You gonna sleep out?'

'I don't want any of the money and I'm not sleeping out. Where you gonna hide?'

'In the signal box. No one's gonna look for me there. In the morning, with the money I got, less your cut, I can get to any place I like.'

'I just told you, I don't want a cut. And what are you going to do about Rory? You forgotten about him?'

'I haven't forgotten,' Sonny protested. 'I'll make sure to see him before I go.'

'You can't desert Rory, when he come and looked after you.'

'I'm not deserting him. If he was here now, he'd tell me to do the same, shoot through.'

'I bet he wouldn't. He'd say running would get you nowhere, I reckon.'

'It'll get me away from here. You have a torch I can borrow?'

Ren went into the house. Archie wasn't home and he could hear Loretta moving around upstairs. When he returned with the torch Sonny offered him his hand, the same as he had done the day he walked home with Ren after stepping in against Milton.

'After I'm gone you will need to spread a story about me. Say it was my idea alone. That I took Vincent's money.'

'I couldn't do that. Never.'

'Sure, you could. Rory and me, we sometimes read crime

stories in the magazines about gangsters in America. True
stories. He read one story to me about a big time criminal
who was old and had lost all his soldiers. They'd been killed
in gun battles or were in prison. He was the only one of his
gang who'd never gone to gaol or been shot. I said to Rory,
he must be the smart one, the leader. Rory laughed and told me I
had a lot to learn. *Smarter than you think,* he said. He reckons
that the biggest crims, the ones who stay out of prison, they
might be the smartest, but they're also the biggest laggers. *In
bed with the police,* is exactly what he said.'

'Do you believe him?'

'Everything Rory has said to me, any advice he's given,
has turned out to be a good lesson. Yeah, I believe him. So,
what you have to do is lag me. Crims do it to each other all
the time.'

'I can't.'

'You can if I'm asking you.'

'If I did that you'd have to write it down, so people knew it
was your idea. I don't wanna be called a lagger. No one round
here would talk to me again.'

'Whatever you want me to do, I will.'

'I better go inside,' Ren said. 'Try and get these wet clothes
off before my mum sees me.'

'Okay. I'm gonna grab a blanket and stuff and go out by
the back gate.'

CHAPTER 17

The next morning Ren got out of bed. The house was cold and it was raining out. He thought about Sonny holed up for the night in the signal box. He put his dressing gown on and went downstairs. Archie was in the kitchen, flipping eggs at the stove and waiting for his favourite radio show to begin, *News Beat*. Its reporters trawled the streets of the city chasing the drunken fights, car smashes, accidents and robberies.

'Morning,' Archie said. 'I thought the smell of bacon might get you moving. Do us a favour and put some toast on.'

Archie looked up at the clock sitting on the fridge. It was five to nine. Ren cut the bread and put it in the toaster, boiled the kettle, put the tea in the pot and placed the butter and milk on the table. Archie liked to be seated with his breakfast in front of him when the show started. He was ready with a raised knife and fork when the pips from the radio signalled nine o'clock.

Archie had a habit of providing a running commentary on each story. The show kicked off with the breaking news of a double shooting in the inner city.

Archie looked up from his plate and smiled. 'Terrific. Last week was awful. All they had was a cat stuck down a drain and a fire in a mattress factory.'

Ren's stomach turned over as he listened to the broadcast.

'... the two male victims were shot at close range in a laneway behind the Railway Hotel in Collingwood as they were about to drive away in a motor vehicle. One male was found slumped in the driver's seat with a bullet to the side of the head, while a second man was located nearby. He had been shot in the back, most likely as he attempted to escape the gunman. The first officer on the scene, Senior Detective Foy, stated that each of the deceased men, Vincent Anthony Lombardi and Rodney James Lowe, was well known to police. *The crime appears to be gang related*, said Detective Foy. He spoke exclusively with our reporter at the scene and urged anybody with information about the crime to please come forward.'

'Outside the Railway,' Archie whistled. 'Don't surprise me. Always been a blood house. No one'll be *coming forward* on this one. You can be sure of it.'

Ren abruptly stood up from the table. While he couldn't be sure what Foy knew of Sonny taking the money, he was sure Sonny would be in danger if Foy got hold of him, unless he had already done so.

'What are you doing?' Archie asked. 'You've hardly touched your breakfast. And the show's not half over.'

'Sorry, Arch, but I don't feel too good. I've been sick most of the night. I think I should have a shower to wake myself up.

I can help you with the dirty dishes after that.'

'Don't worry about the dishes. I'll clean up. Maybe go back to the cot?'

Ren raced upstairs and dressed as quickly as he could. Archie was busy in the kitchen finishing his breakfast and listening to the radio as he snuck out of the house. He headed along the street, climbed the fence into the railyard and sprinted for the signal box. He stood at the bottom of the ladder and called Sonny's name. His friend unlatched the trapdoor and he climbed the ladder. Sonny was wrapped in a blanket and shivering with cold.

'You hear the news?' Ren blurted.

'Not yet. But the carrier pigeon's due any fucken minute.'

'They're dead, Sonny. Shot dead.'

'Who?'

'Vincent and Rodney. I heard it on the radio, just then. They were shot outside the pub last night. Foy's been talking on the radio. He was the first copper there. You know what that means, don't you?'

Sonny jumped up and hugged the blanket to his body. 'You tell me,' he asked, already sure of the answer.

'I bet he killed them after that meeting with Chris. You have to get out of here. Take off, like you said last night. Where's the money?'

Sonny opened a cupboard door, pushed an old signal lamp to one side and pulled out the roll of money. He counted out two hundred dollars and put it in his pocket, followed by a second two hundred, which he handed to Ren. 'I've changed my mind about the money. I'm taking my own back, that Vincent took from me. You should have the same amount,

Ren, for all the trouble I caused you.'

'And what happens to the rest?'

'I want it to go to Rory. He'll have no work when he comes out of hospital. He'll need it.'

Sonny counted the rest of the money and laid it on the ground. Two thousand six hundred dollars. He handed it to Ren.

'I want you to make sure Rory gets it.'

Ren added his two hundred to the pile. 'He can have the lot. I don't want anything to do with it.'

'It's your money. I'm giving it to you.'

'I don't want it.'

'Think about that camera you want to buy, Ren. You take two hundred dollars into one of them shops in the city and you could buy any camera you like.'

'I don't care. It comes from them two being killed.'

'Fuck em. They deserved it.'

'You really don't care that they're dead?'

'Do you? You'd rather have them taking from us and treating us like shit, running round for them? Would you?'

Sonny was right and Ren knew it. Although he didn't like the feeling, he was as relieved as Sonny that Vincent and Rodney had been killed.

'Now, take the money and keep it for Rory. Hide it some place safe until he gets home.'

They heard a car driving slowly along the street. Ren lifted his head to the window. It was Foy driving by, in the same unmarked car he'd been in the night before. The car turned into their street, drove to the other end and parked across from Sonny's house.

'Why would he be driving his own car, Sonny, and not a police car?'

'Because this is all about last night. He's not on police business. You can't leave here until he's gone.'

The boys sat and waited for half an hour or more, sharing a cigarette but saying little. At one point Foy got out of the car and stood in the middle of the road in the rain before getting back into the car and driving away. Ren watched through the window as the car cruised slowly by the railway line, Foy turning his head and searching both sides of the street.

'He's gone.'

Sonny threw the blanket to one side. 'I'm gonna stay here until dark and then take off. I need you to do me one last favour.'

'Like what?'

'I don't want to go back to the house. I need you to get a bag ready for me tonight, with some food in it, maybe a jumper and a raincoat if you can find one. I'll meet you in the lane on dark. I'll flash the torch over the fence. Can you do that?'

'If that's what you want. I hope you've thought this through, Sonny. Maybe you should go now.'

'I give it as much thought as it needs. And don't forget the money. Hide it good. And Ren,' he stopped and barked a miserable cough, 'if Rory never comes home from the hospital, if he dies, you use the money to pay for his funeral. It's important he's buried, not cremated. He told me once he couldn't think of nothing worse than being fried.'

Sonny pushed the money into Ren's hands. 'Be sure to go home by the lane and keep an eye out for Foy.'

★

272

Ren spent most of the day in his room. It would be dangerous to leave the house in case Foy was on the street. He packed a woollen jumper and raincoat into his schoolbag and hid it in his wardrobe. He went down to the kitchen, took a packet of biscuits out of the cupboard and two apples from the fruit bowl. Armed with a screwdriver from the laundry he went back upstairs and picked the carpet tacks away from a corner of the room and peeled the rug back. Ren laid Rory's money, folded into a sheet of newspaper, on the bare floorboards and replaced the carpet. He banged the tacks down and moved the chair from next to his bed over to the corner.

The clouds were so low in the sky it was almost dark by five in the afternoon. He sat by the window watching the pounding rain and looking towards the back fence, waiting for Sonny's signal. He could just hear the sounds of the piano coming from the stable. It sounded as if the keys were being battered with a hammer rather than played. The music stopped and the Reverend Beck appeared at the open stable door. A few minutes later his wife walked across the yard holding the hand of a girl. Ren quietly opened his window to get a better look at what was going on. Even though she was wearing a head scarf Ren could see that it was the red-headed girl he'd spied in the stable with the Reverend. Mrs Beck handed the girl to her husband and walked back into the house. He ushered the girl into the stable and closed the door.

Ren kept one eye on the back fence and the other on the stable door, convinced that something terrible was happening behind it. A little while later a dark figure appeared in the yard. It was Della, acting peculiar, creeping across the yard in the rain like a mangy cat, towards the stable. She put her ear to the door for a moment, then disappeared into the laundry. She came out carrying a wooden chair, which she placed under a small window directly above the door. She stood on the chair and looked into the stable. She watched with intensity before jumping off the chair. She stepped back and covered her mouth as if she was trying to stop herself from vomiting. Ren watched as she wedged the back of the chair under the door knob and ran back across the yard and into the house.

Ren had been so fixated on Della he almost missed the flashing light of the torch winking at him from over the back fence. He grabbed his schoolbag and a duffle-coat out of his wardrobe and quickly climbed out of the window. He crossed over to Sonny's roof, slid down the drainpipe into the yard and opened the back gate. Sonny was huddled in the lane, shivering to the bone.

Ren pulled the spare jumper and raincoat out of the bag. 'Get into the back toilet, strip your wet stuff off and put these on.' He handed Sonny the jumper and spoke to him through the toilet door. 'It's pissing down. You'd be better off at my place. You can hide out in my room for the night.'

Sonny pulled the wet jumper over his head, threw it out into the yard, put the dry jumper on and the raincoat over the top. 'Nup. I'm gonna head to the river and camp with Tex for the night. I'll move on early in the morning.'

'Might not be anything left of the camp with this rain.'

Sonny had made up his mind that he was leaving and there'd be no stopping him.

They walked to the end of the darkened lane. Della was standing beside the telegraph pole, as if she'd been waiting for them.

'What are you doing here?' Ren asked.

She looked at the bag over Sonny's shoulder. 'Are you going away?'

'Nothing to do with you,' Sonny said.

They could hear a banging noise, coming from the stable.

'I need you to take me with you,' Della said.

'You got no hope,' Sonny told her.

She turned to Ren. 'Please?'

'I don't want you with me,' Sonny said. 'This is crazy, Ren.'

The pounding on the stable door got louder and they could hear the sound of a girl's voice calling for help. Sonny wouldn't look at Della. 'Fucken tell her, Ren. She's not coming with me.'

Della knew better than to waste her time on Sonny. She stepped forward and looked into Ren's face. 'Please help me. Or my father will hurt me.'

The streetlights suddenly came on, exposing the three of them huddled together in the lane. Sonny walked to the middle of the road. 'I got to take off, Ren.'

'Sonny, wait,' Ren said. 'I'm coming ... we're coming with you.'

'No, Ren. I'm not looking after her.'

'You don't have to. We'll camp with you tonight and go our separate ways from there.'

'I have enough shit to deal with, Ren. You want to help her out, she's your problem. She's fucken conning you,' he added, as if Della wasn't there at all.

Ren took Della's hand and they followed the beam of light from Sonny's torch until they reached the hole in the fence. Ren climbed through ahead of Della and turned to help her.

They slid down the greasy bank together and scrambled to catch up to Sonny. He was standing on a tree stump, the beam of his torch pointed back up to the shadow of the mill.

'What are you doing?' Ren asked.

'I heard something. The fence rattled, and I saw something move.'

'It's just the wind.'

'I don't think it was. Something else.'

'Like what?'

'I dunno.'

It was difficult to see much through the gloom. The relentless rain of recent days had swallowed the banks on both sides of the river. The water continued to rise and the roar of water spilling over the falls was ferocious. The boys looked downriver, realising the camp beneath the iron bridge would be gone.

Ren sniffed the air. 'Can't see a fire, but I can smell smoke.'

Sonny sniffed also. 'It's coming from the wheelhouse. They'll be in there trying to keep dry. We'll need to shelter there too.'

'I'd rather drown than go in.'

Sonny looked down at the rising water. 'If we stay here we'll drown anyway. You can please yourself.'

Ren turned to Della. 'I saw what you did back there,' he said, 'locking your father in the stable. Why'd you do that?'

'Because of what I saw.'

'What did you see?' Ren asked, suspecting he already knew the answer.

'Betrayal,' she spat. 'My father's betrayal.'

Della had a peculiar look on her face, one as disturbing as

her father's, Ren thought. Sonny had opened the wheelhouse door. Smoke poured out. He shone his torch inside, coughing and waving a hand in front of his face. 'Tex!' he called. 'You in there?'

There was no answer.

'Maybe they're not here?' Ren said. 'It could be an old fire smouldering.'

'Don't matter. We can stay here the night and in the morning I go my way, you and her the other.' Sonny looked back at Della, standing by the rising bank 'Don't be trusting her, Ren. Come on.'

Ren had avoided the wheelhouse from the first day he visited the river. He reluctantly stepped through the door. Della skidded along the bank and followed him. The smell was terrible, like a rotting animal, so powerful it couldn't be disguised by the smoke. As they moved through the first room they found that the rain appeared to be as heavy inside the wheelhouse as it was outside. Water streamed down the brick walls and ran across the floor. Sonny shone the torch up at a tangle of rusted metal pipes. Curtains of cobwebs caught the light and glittered in the dark.

Sonny called out to Tex. A deep moan came back.

'Hear that? They must be down below.'

Sonny shone the torch down the staircase and followed the beam of light. Near the bottom of the stairs something shot out of the darkness, ran across his feet and was gone. Ren's throat burned when he breathed in and his eyes were watering. Sonny made his way along a passageway, its walls covered in moss. He stopped at an open doorway and peered inside. 'I found them.'

Tex and Cold Can were camped on a long wooden tabletop in the storeroom, sitting around a kero lamp, damp blankets hanging from their shoulders. They resembled a pair of old sailors adrift in a lifeboat. The men were caked in so much dirt the colour of their skin had become unrecognisable. The room was thick with smoke from a wood stove burning in the corner. The legs of the stove were submerged in water. Della looked from Tex to Cold Can and back again as if they were ghosts. Ren waded across to the table and shook Tex to get his attention. 'You can't stay here Tex. The water is coming up real fast. You and Cold Can will get trapped.'

Tex lifted the kero lamp from the table, passed it over Ren's face and smiled at him.

'The bird,' he said, turning to Cold Can. 'Is the bird.'

He moved the lamp across Sonny's face and then onto Della's. He paused and examined her closely, then grimaced, as if he didn't like the face he was looking at. He leaned forward and whispered in Ren's ear. 'One question, bird.' He grinned.

Ren tugged at his rotting blanket. 'We don't have time for this, Tex. You got to get out of here. We all do. Tell him, Cold Can. Please.'

Cold Can said nothing. He'd go along with whatever Tex wanted, until the end, if that was the way it had to be.

Tex turned to Sonny. 'Big Tiny fella? Never come up?' he asked.

Neither of the boys knew what had become of Tiny. 'Don't know where he is, Tex,' Sonny answered, shaking his head.

Tex's eyes lit up. A little of his old self was in those eyes. 'Saw a picture when I was sleeping,' he said. 'Old Tiny down in the water. Ghost river caring for him.' He shook a gnarled finger at the boys. 'True story. He went in the water. And he never come up.' Tex nudged Cold Can. 'Never come up. Told you.'

Sonny shone the torch around the room. The water was rising quickly. 'We got to go now. And we need you to come with us.' He had to raise his voice above the torrent of running water. 'I can carry you out, Tex. Give you a piggyback.'

The blanket dropped from Tex's shoulders as he reached for Sonny with both hands. 'Go and leave old Tex be.' He pushed Sonny gently on the chest with an open hand. 'You no river boy any more. I have my business. Can't be seeing you no more. Leave me be.'

'You're wrong about that, Tex.' Ren was almost crying. 'We want to help. Or you're gonna die in here.'

Tex took a long slow breath and raised his voice. 'You were the best boys. Now be men. Let me be with the river.'

Tex looked at Della again. Her face glowed in the low light of the lamp. He raised a hand towards her and she stepped back into the darkness.

There was nothing left the boys could say to persuade Tex to move. The water rose further, extinguishing what was left of the smoking fire. Sonny spotted a stack of old blankets on a shelf. Tex watched on as Sonny placed a dry blanket over his shoulders. He moved across to Cold Can and did the same, then dampened a corner with water and slowly cleaned the grime from Cold Can's face. He then wiped a corner of the blanket over Tex's face. The old man smiled up at him and whispered, 'You is a good boy, a good boy.'

Ren stepped forward and wiped his own face before saying, 'I love you, Tex.'

Tex reached forward, wrapped the boy in the blanket and held Ren's body to his own. The river was held in that body. Tex rubbed a gritty hand across the back of Ren's neck and let him go. 'I know. Loved me.'

Sonny said a few quiet words to Cold Can that Ren couldn't hear on account of the noise, which was increasingly louder. Sonny turned to Ren. 'We have to go now or we'll be trapped.'

Ren, and then Della, followed Sonny, wading through water up to their waists. Ren stopped and looked back into the room and saw nothing but darkness. Climbing the stairs, he felt a sense of fear and betrayal in equal measure. He was sure he'd never see Tex again, and that there was nothing he or Sonny could do to avoid what was about to happen. It didn't stop him feeling like a coward. As he reached the top landing, water gushed over his shoes and down the stairs to the floor below. It would only be minutes before the storeroom went under.

Escaping the wheelhouse Ren saw that the rain had almost stopped and the wind had picked up. The fresh air filling his lungs tasted sweet. He sat on the bank of the swollen river, exhausted. If the river had taken his body at that moment, he would have been too weak to fight against it. He glanced up at Sonny, seated in the hollow of a tree, looking just as beaten. Della had lifted her soaking dress above her knees, exposing her thighs. She didn't seem to care that Ren was staring at them.

The moon broke through the clouds and the light bounced

off the foaming caps of rapids that had formed below the falls. The river was about to encircle the wheelhouse. A rifle-cracking sound whistled through the air as an upturned tree, bigger than a house, careered over the falls, snapping branches off as it cartwheeled over the rocks.

Neither of the boys noticed the shadow cast against the wall of the wheelhouse. Della saw it at the last moment and screamed as her father tore through a hedge of blackberry and charged at her, grabbing her by the throat and slamming her into the dirt.

It would have been wrong to mistake her cries for fear. Della was consumed with rage. She struggled with her father as he dragged her closer to the broken bank. Instead of fighting him, she gripped hold of his heavy coat with all her strength and refused to release him. Ren stood rooted to the spot and watched as Della crashed into the water, taking her father with her. They went under.

'You see them, Sonny?' Ren called.

Sonny jumped from the stump and ran along the bank, shining the torch in the water and following the raging current towards the iron bridge. Ren saw Reverend Beck surface near the middle of the river, his mouth wide open, snapping at the air. The uprooted tree closed in on him and scooped him up in its branches as if catching a fish in a net.

Sonny turned and headed back along the bank. 'You see her?' he asked.

'No, I don't. But did you see what just happened to the Reverend?' Ren asked, in disbelief.

They heard a sound coming from the bank. Somehow Della had managed to drag herself out of the water. She slid up the bank like a giant eel and slowly got to her feet, coughing and spitting out river water. She wiped a hand across her mouth. Her clothes hung from her body like a second skin, her long wet hair hiding her face from view.

'My father?' she asked.

Ren pointed downriver. 'He went that way.'

If she was upset it didn't show on her face. She turned to the river and spread her arms. 'The Lord preserves all who love Him, but each of the wicked He will destroy.'

'Amen,' Sonny added.

'Where we gonna go now?' Ren asked Sonny, as the rain started to spit again.

'Only place left is the car graveyard. We can shelter in one of the wrecks.'

'I'm leaving the river,' Della said.

'For where?' Ren asked.

'Home.' She looked across the river. 'My mother will need me to take care of her. She doesn't cope alone.'

'What about your father?' Ren asked. 'You'll have to report him missing. They'll send a boat downriver and try to find him. He'd have a chance of making it to one of the islands.'

'Chance plays no part in our life or death,' she said, somewhat mysteriously. 'My father's fate will be decided by Him.'

Sonny wasn't interested in Ren's questions. All he wanted was to see the back of Della.

'Come on, Ren, we have to move.'

Della turned, hitched up her long dress and began hiking up the bank to the mill.

'Crazy bitch,' Sonny mutttered to himself.

★

The boys dragged themselves to the wreck of the Holden. Ren got into the front seat and Sonny in the back. Each of them shivered with cold. As the inside of the car warmed a little the windows misted over and the outside world vanished.

'You know I never thought I'd seen anyone as loonie as that Reverend,' Sonny said, 'the way he preached in that church. Until I saw the look on her face just now. Della killed her own father, pulling him under with that coat and boots on.'

'Maybe he's survived. Freed himself from the tree.'

'Be a real miracle if he has.'

'I don't blame her, for what she's done.' Ren told Sonny about seeing the red-headed girl being taken across the yard to the stable by Della's mother. 'She's in on it, her mother.'

'Why would she go home to her then?' Sonny wondered aloud.

'Dunno. Maybe she'll kill her too.' He laughed nervously and rested his head against the car window. Every bone in his body had frozen solid. He'd have no explanation for his mother and Archie in the morning and knew there wasn't a story he could invent that would get him out of the trouble he would be in. He didn't want to begin thinking about the punishment he was facing. He could hear Sonny breathing quietly and looked across at his friend in the back seat. Despite what he'd gone through in recent weeks Ren had never seen Sonny looking so peaceful.

CHAPTER 18

Sonny shook Ren awake in the morning. He sat up, rubbed his hands over his face and turned to the back seat. Sonny patted a bulge in the shirt pocket under his damp jumper. 'I bet you'll wanna see what I got here.'

He pulled out a pouch of tobacco, wrapped in a plastic bag. He opened it and showed Ren the cigarette papers and box of matches inside. He rolled two cigarettes and passed one to Ren. 'This will help warm us up.'

The car soon filled with smoke.

'So where's the plan at now?' Ren asked. 'You look like a drowned rat and you've only just got started running away.'

Sonny took the deepest drag possible on his cigarette. He held the smoke in his lungs and slowly released it before answering. 'I'm going home.'

'Home. You not shooting through? Make up your mind.'

'I can't leave Rory.'

'What's changed?'

'I was thinking about poor old Tex in the wheelhouse last night and about how if I'm not around, Rory could end up like the river men. With nobody to look out for him.'

'What about your old man?'

'If he turns up and he's sober I'll give him a chance. And if he comes back and he gets on the piss, I'll tell him to move on and leave me and Rory to ourselves.'

'You forgotten about the money owed to Chris? And there's Foy.'

'Chris only knows what I told him, that Vincent wasn't going to pay him back the money. He wouldn't have called for Foy to go after them unless he believed there was something to the story.'

'Except that you told him you saw Vincent counting out a bundle of money to put on a horse.'

'Chris might be thinking Foy got hold of the money. Or that Vincent laid the bet with some other bookie before Foy got to him. I mean, look at me, Ren. I'm near as spastic as Spike is, with my bung eye. They wouldn't think I was smart enough to try something like this.'

'That Chris, he likes you, Sonny, cause he knows you got some go in you. I reckon he'd be onto you. Like Brixey said, he's a smart old fella. And Foy, he might not think you're smart enough, but he knows you're brave enough. You won't get away from him so easy. Me either.'

Sonny thought about what Ren said before answering.

'You remember that time, Ren, when you said to me *It's no free country for us*. I was so angry with you because I knew it was the truth. I reckon I could go any place and I'd find trouble. I'm good at it. Might just as well stay round here as be anywhere else.' He looked over the seat at Ren and smiled through the haze of smoke. 'Anyway, you'd be fucken lost without me.'

'Wouldn't get in so much trouble.'

'And you'd never have as much fun.'

When they got out of the car the sun was shining. Their river was gone. It had been replaced by a vast lake. The lower section of the pylons holding up the iron bridge had all but disappeared and the old ghost gums lining the banks were reduced to treetops.

The boys made their way along the ridge, skirting the expanse of water below. All that was left of the wheelhouse above the waterline was the pitched open roof. Ren thought about Tex and Cold Can trapped inside. 'There's no way they could have got out of there,' Sonny said, reading his friend's mind.

'Tex didn't want to get out. He knew his time was up. I hope they stay down there with the ghost river and are never found. The way Tex wanted it to be.'

'You really believe that story?' Sonny asked.

'I believe in Tex. Everything he told me about the river, I believe it all. Some people believe in religion. Well, I believe in stories. You believe in God, Sonny?'

Sonny screwed his face up, as if the question made him feel uncomfortable.

'Dunno. I never thought about God. Only thing I ever believed in is that I got to look after myself. You believe?'

'Nah. I went to Catholic school when I was younger. But only because my mother had a job cleaning the church and they let me in for free. Best thing about Catholic school was a hot lunch every day. I prayed like crazy at that school. No God ever spoke back to me.'

'But you believe in the ghost river story?'

'Sure. The Doc never came back up. Or Big Tiny. You see the Reverend Beck last night? He come straight back to the top. The river was spitting him out cause he was no good. They'll find his body for sure. I bet they don't find Tex and Cold Can.'

'Della was spat out. I reckon she's no good either.'

Ren looked up and followed the flight of a bird gliding high in the sky, surveying the water below. 'Look at that one, Sonny. It's a black kite. Read about it at the library. Don't see a lot of them round here.' He shielded his eyes from the sun with his open hand and watched the bird. 'You know how you changed your mind about leaving. Well, I've changed my mind too, about the money. The two hundred dollars. I'll have it, Sonny, if it's still okay with you.'

'I bet you're gonna buy that camera with it.'

'I am.'

'I might let you take my picture. Mug shot.'

Before climbing through the fence into the back of the mill they turned and looked across to the cliff-top.

'Hey, Sonny, do you reckon you'll ever be brave enough to jump from there?'

'Nah. Never thought I was. I was stringing you, Ren. What about you?'

'I was stringing too.' He smiled.

They climbed through the fence and walked to the gates of the mill. Ren couldn't believe what lay in front of him. The compound was gone. It had been swallowed by the earth, leaving a massive crater in its wake, as wide and deep as a football oval. The boys stood at the edge and looked down at the heavy machines that had been working to destroy the river. The machines lay on their sides, drowning in a muddied pond at the bottom. They looked like the remains of prehistoric creatures revealed to the world.

Sonny scratched at his grubby cheek. 'Maybe Tex was right. The ghost river swallowed the earth. Took it down with her.'

'Gonna take them a lot of time before they can do any more work here.'

'Yeah. Maybe not before next summer. I'm gonna swim at Deep Rock and at the swimming hole by the falls every day.'

'Yeah. Every day,' Ren agreed.

They turned the corner at the top of their street, each of them caught up in their own thoughts, but before Ren could step up onto his verandah he was roughly jerked backwards and wrapped in a bear hug. It was Foy.

Sonny was about to run off, but stopped when he saw that Ren was trapped. 'Fucken leave him alone!' he yelled.

Foy squeezed Ren by the neck. 'I'll be happy to, as soon as you pricks hand over the fucken money Vincent owed me.'

'We don't have no money,' Sonny said. 'Vincent was putting it all on a horse.'

Foy squeezed a little harder on Ren's neck. His face began to turn blue. 'I went through that room and turned it upside down. You forgot to take this with you.' Foy reached into his back pocket with his free hand and pulled out Vincent's pocketbook. 'It's listed here. The last entry. *$3000 – C.* I don't think that stands for Cunt. Now tell me where the money is or this one has his neck snapped in half.'

The front door of the house flew open and Loretta tore into the street. 'Let go of him!' she screamed. 'You let my son be.'

Foy held up an open hand. 'Stay away, woman. Get back in the house, where you belong.'

Loretta swung a punch at Foy, hitting him in the side of the face. He released Ren and as he tried to push Loretta away, he slipped on the wet bitumen and fell to the ground, hitting his head against the gutter. The commotion in the street brought the neighbours out — Mr and Mrs Portelli and a couple of their kids, an old pensioner from further along the street, and Della and her mother.

Foy got to his feet and snarled at the small crowd closing in on him. Loretta put an arm around Ren. 'You leave these boys alone,' she spat. 'You don't need to be coming around here. Leave us in peace. Good people live on this street.'

Foy looked at Loretta with a viciousness few were capable of. He turned to Sonny and whispered in his ear. 'I'm going to catch up with you another time, son. You were born for trouble. Wild and too fucken stupid, you are. I'll be waiting for you next time you fuck up.' He walked through the small crowd, got into his car and drove off.

Sonny looked down at the ground and saw that Foy had dropped Vincent's notebook. As Loretta examined Ren's neck for any bruising, Sonny flicked through the pages of the book noting the regular payments to *C*, but also to *Foy* – no initial. He stuck the book in his back pocket.

'Come on, Charlie,' Loretta said. 'Inside. You too, Sonny. You'll be staying with us until your uncle is out of hospital.' She turned to her son. 'And Charlie, you've got a lot of explaining to do.'

Before Ren followed his mother into the house he looked along the street to Della, standing out near her front gate. She looked back at him, with an odd look on her face. It was as if Ren was a stranger.

It was many months later, on an early summer night, when the northerly breeze picked up and a familiar scent filled Ren's bedroom. It was forecast to be warm again the following day and Ren thought about a swim in the river, but with none of the enthusiasm of the summer before, as there was no one around to share it with. After Rory had come out of hospital he decided it would be better for Sonny if they moved away and avoided Foy altogether. They shifted across to the other side of the city. Before they left, Sonny handed Foy's pocketbook to Ren.

'I want you to keep this for insurance. If that prick Foy gives you a hard time you go to Brixey and show him this. He'll know what to do. And another thing. If my father shows up back here you give him the full inspection before you let him know where we've moved to.'

Rory had organised a van to move the few bits of furniture worth keeping. Ren stood on the street watching as the van was loaded. Sonny helped with the move and was about to get into the passenger seat when he saw Ren standing on his verandah.

'I'll be seeing you, Ren.'

'Yeah. When?'

'When the weather picks up. They don't look like filling that hole in the ground. I'll be back for a swim.'

'You will?'

'Course I will,' Sonny answered. He turned away without saying goodbye and got into the van.

Ren walked to the middle of the street and watched until the van had turned the corner and driven away. He walked over to Della's house and stood at the front gate. Some days after the flood the Reverend Beck's body had turned up downriver, shackled to the skeleton tree, his body whipped and beaten. The police had arrived at the house to notify Della and her mother of the news. How the Reverend had ended up in the river during the storm was a mystery and when his death was reported in the papers it was treated as *misadventure*.

Within a matter of weeks Della and her mother moved out of the street. Seeing the stable door ajar, Ren and Sonny had climbed the fence and taken a look inside. The chairs and most of the holy pictures had been left behind. The piano was gone, along with the framed image of Father Jealous Divine and his Virgin White Bride.

Ren bought himself a new camera with a telephoto lens and taught himself to take photographs. Some weren't so good, but as he slowly came to understand the camera he took some that were almost as beautiful as the picture of the bird he'd once stuck on the back of his bedroom door. Every chance he got he headed for the water with his camera, making pictures and remembering the stories of the river, some that he'd first heard from Tex and others he'd made up himself. It soon became difficult for him to distinguish the truth from the wild imaginings of both a young boy and an old man.

It surprised Ren that the story he remembered most clearly was not one of his own, or a tale told by Tex. It was a story Tallboy Garrett had entertained him and Sonny with on one of the first nights they sat around their campfire with the river men. They were all there that night, Tex, Big Tiny Watkins, Cold Can and the Doc.

'I got a beauty for ya,' Tallboy announced, before standing to his feet and clearing his throat. 'There was this one time, way back, and I was working with this trapper fella along the river. Not here.' He waved. 'Further up there is another place with the ferrets, giving them fucken rabbits a hell of a time. The ferret, he's boss of the bunny, but he has his own enemy. He's got to defend himself from them old cats along here. Them cats, once they got the blood in the nostrils they would take out a team of ferrets in a morning's work.'

'You sure of that?' Big Tiny interrupted.

'Yeah, I *is* fucken sure.' Tallboy scowled.

'They bring down a hunting dog if they was in the mood, a pair of cats working together, of course. I'm working with this old boy that day, Hector, and we catched a cat in one of them traps we set up round the rabbit holes. A big old Tom that come bolting out the burrow into the cage. That boy had fangs like a sabre-tooth and nuts big as bowling balls.

293

'Hector, he hooks a snare round the Tom's neck. The Tom growled and spat. He was angry and would have went us if he got himself free. Hector is hanging the cat by his neck and drops him in a sack with a decent old stone. He ties it up with wire and throws the sack into the water. A splash and the sack went down.

'I says to him, *What are we doing, Hec?*

'*Waiting.*

'*For what?*

'*See in good time.*

'So we waited. Then we waited some more. I spot some bubbles in the water and the old Tom bobs up. He swims to the bank, sneaks into the scrub, giving us the *fuck you boys* with a snarl and a spit as he goes.'

After Tallboy had finished the story he sat down by the fire next to Ren.

'That story,' Ren asked, 'does it mean something? Or is it just a good story?'

'It means plenty. You find yourself down at the bottom of the river, for some it's time to give in to her. But other times, young fellas like you two, you got to fight your way back. Show the river you got courage and is ready to live. She needs to see that. Or she'll take you. That's the most important story of all.'